KAY'S LUCKY COIN VARIETY

- A Novel -

Ann Y. K. Choi

Phyllis Bruce Editions
Simon & Schuster Canada
New York   London   Toronto   Sydney   New Delhi

SIMON &
SCHUSTER
CANADA

Simon & Schuster Canada
A Division of Simon & Schuster, Inc.
166 King Street East, Suite 300
Toronto, Ontario M5A 1J3

Phyllis Bruce Editions, published by Simon & Schuster Canada

This Simon & Schuster Canada edition May 2016

SIMON & SCHUSTER CANADA and colophon are registered trademarks of Simon & Schuster, Inc.

For information about special discounts for bulk purchases, please contact Simon & Schuster Special Sales at 1-800-268-3216 or CustomerService@simonandschuster.ca.

Library and Archives Canada Cataloguing in Publication

Choi, Ann Y. K., author
Kay's lucky coin variety / Ann Y.K. Choi.
Issued in print and electronic formats.
ISBN 978-1-4767-4805-4 (bound).—ISBN
978-1-4767-4806-1 (ebook)
I. Title.
PS8605.H62K39 2016   C813'.6
C2015-905072-3
            C2015-905073-1

Manufactured in the United States of America

10 9 8 7 6 5 4 3 2

ISBN 978-1-4767-4805-4
ISBN 978-1-4767-4806-1 (ebook)

For my mother,

who taught me that we create our own luck,

my daughter Claire,

who inspires me to learn and live in the moment,

and in loving memory of Cathy,

who showed me the value of friendship

PART I

A Flight of Stairs

Chapter 1

$\mathcal{I}$ was behind the counter of our convenience store, Kay's Lucky Coin Variety, reading the *Toronto Star* when I heard tires screech and someone screaming obscenities. A horn blasted. I looked out the window.

"Are you freaking crazy?" the driver was yelling. Tico merely kept honking the bicycle horn he wore around his neck as he finished crossing the street.

"Hey, Mare," he said. "Got anything for me?"

"You okay?"

He nodded. He wasn't much of a talker, which was a good thing; he smelled awful. I handed him the loaf of day-old Wonder Bread my mother kept aside for him. He came in for it every Tuesday at 8 p.m. My mother had a soft spot for him because his eyes reminded her of Gregory Peck's. She was convinced Tico's current hardship was a result of bad deeds in a previous life and took pity on him. Tico smiled at me. His teeth were grossly decayed, some were missing. He nodded a quick thank-you and left. I heard his horn again as he crossed to the other side of the street.

I got back to the newspaper. Often a real-life story would trigger ideas I could later weave into a story or a poem. The *Titanic* had recently been discovered on the bottom of the North Atlantic. While my brother, Josh, was fascinated with the mathematical improbability of its collision with an iceberg, I was intrigued by the idea of hundreds of people trapped in a sinking ship. I imagined mass hysteria, floating bodies draped in wet evening clothes, white faces stargazing through frozen eyes. A dark-haired prostitute I hadn't seen before walked in and interrupted my daydream. She looked around and strolled over to the gum rack. Her red fishnet tights had a tear just below the hemline of her red miniskirt. *So much red*, I thought, and wondered if she knew about the rip.

I didn't recognize her until she handed me a ten-dollar bill to pay for a box of condoms and a pack of Wrigley's Big Red chewing gum. In an instant I was transported back seven years to Mr. Mills's fourth-grade class.

It had been an unusually warm October day when I transferred into a new elementary school in Toronto. After years of working in other people's variety stores and at miscellaneous jobs since emigrating from Korea in 1975, my parents had saved enough money to buy their own store in the centre of the city. I stood shyly in the doorway of the new classroom as the principal informed Mr. Mills of my arrival. Then came the awkward introduction. "Class, this is . . ." I finished Mr. Mills's sentence for him. His eyes scanned the room. So did mine—there were no Asian students in the class and no empty desks. Mr. Mills rolled his chair by the windows and offered it to me. My cheeks burned as I crossed the room, knowing every eye was summing up my faded hand-me-down purple hooded sweater and jeans, my self-inflicted, uneven bangs, my chopstick-thin body. I sat down, convinced I was unworthy of friendship. The lesson proceeded. A handout was distributed and we were instructed to take out a pencil. I had nothing to write with.

"Delia," Mr. Mills said, "lend the new girl a pencil." Remembering names was clearly not his forte.

A pale girl with Goldilocks-blonde hair fumbled through her pencil case and passed me a brand-new pencil that smelled oddly of cinnamon. I was about to thank her when a rough scar on the back of her hand caught my eye. It ran from above the wrist to below the middle finger, a startling blemish on such a delicate hand. When we returned after our recess, I was deeply disappointed that Mr. Mills had arranged a desk and chair for me and that I was now seated towards the back of the class, three desks directly behind Delia.

When I finally got the nerve to ask about the scar a few weeks later, it was too late. Delia had stopped coming to school. I asked Mr. Mills about her, but the only thing he volunteered was that she had moved away. No one seemed to know where. Or care. And I forgot about her.

Almost seven years later, the scar was still a jagged island surrounded by calm waters. I examined Delia's face as she studied the Jamaican patties at the end of the counter. She looked older than sixteen, but she was biting long fake nails the same shade of red as her outfit. Her once-beautiful blonde hair was now solid black, like mine. I could almost smell the mousse and hairspray that kept it puffed up.

I struggled to stay composed. She didn't bother to check her change before dropping it into her purse. My heart pounding, I watched her leave the store, then dashed to the door to see where she was headed. She didn't go far. She was still standing at our corner four hours later when I crept into my brother's room to peek out his window.

I was thankful Josh was a deep sleeper. Had he been awake, I might casually have asked him if he'd noticed the new girl working the corner. Then I had the idea to check his log, kept hidden behind his bookcase. I'd found the spiral notebook last year when I was snooping. It recorded how long it took a prostitute to return to the corner after being picked up. Josh had turned his observations into a science. Because he spent so much time tending the cash register, he noted what brand of condoms each prostitute preferred and what cigarettes she smoked. He'd even assigned the girls names: *Trixie, Babe, Suzie X.*

I took the notebook to the bathroom, the only place I could get away with having a light on at that late hour. There she was: *"Scarlet: white, 5'5", black hair, grey eyes, scar on hand, ears pierced five times left, three times right . . . fave gum, Wrigley's Big Red."*

Where had she been for the past seven years? How had she ended up working this corner?

It rained all the next day and evening. I was so busy mopping up a trail of footprints left by customers that I almost missed Delia when she came into the store. A big, round security mirror hung from the back corner, and I was able to watch her talk to my brother at the cash. Her back was to the mirror, but I could see my brother's face was lit up.

"Yeah, I don't get out much," Delia said, her voice warm and full. "But I loved that movie! I loved Ally Sheedy's character."

I felt my entire weight shift, with the mop becoming my crutch. I'd seen *The Breakfast Club* and knew exactly what they were talking about.

Prepared to make my way to the front, I dropped the mop into the pail. The wooden handle clanged as it hit the metal. Both Josh and Delia turned to look at me. I fled into the back storage room.

"You okay?" I heard my brother yell.

"Need the bathroom!" I replied, trying to catch my breath. I was surprised I'd found my voice that quickly. Through the crack of the storage-room door I watched Delia finish her conversation with my brother. She waved to him as she left.

The next morning at 6 a.m., I sat drained at the kitchen table, watching my mother as she made breakfast. Despite living in Canada all these years, she still insisted on preparing a typical Korean breakfast—steamed rice, soup, kimchi, and several vegetable and meat dishes. I was desperate to mention Delia, but didn't know how to begin.

"You don't have to make so much food," I finally said in irritation.

"Something smells good," said my dad, walking in.

My mother handed him a cup of green tea she had set aside to cool. "Breakfast is the most important meal of the day," she lectured, "not dinner. What do you need such a big meal for when you're going to bed? It just makes you fat." She stopped cutting vegetables and added in Korean, "There's so much flawed thinking with some of these white people. Can you imagine what it would do for the health care system if everyone ate rice, kimchi, and soup three times a day? We'd be paying less taxes for one thing."

"Listen to your *omma*," my dad said. "She's always right." He winked, took a sip of tea, and left.

In that instant I knew my parents would never agree to help a white under-aged hooker. Instead, I envisioned my mother smacking the side of my head and telling me to go study. "Become a lawyer first," she would yell at me in Korean. "Then think about saving the world!"

I left the kitchen and went into my room. I was at a loss, convinced my mother couldn't offer me any advice. However, I was determined to initiate a conversation with Delia the next time she came to the store. Maybe I could ask her if there was anything I could do to help her get off the street.

I was behind the store counter, looking up the movies playing at the Eaton Centre. Unlike some white girls I knew who planned elaborate Sweet Sixteen parties, I was content treating my closest friends to lunch at Mr. Greenjeans and a movie afterwards. I'd even allowed myself to indulge in fantasies of asking Delia to join us, a joke really because it was nearly the end of the month and I still hadn't found the courage to say a word to her. Rubina, my oldest friend, could finally meet her.

The door opened and Delia walked in. I was shocked to see the broken Valentine that was her face. A small cut near her eye ran in the direction of her natural expression lines and the surrounding area was patchy with bruising. A cut on the edge of her lips made one side of her unpainted mouth look inflated. Her neck had strange red marks on it. I was so stunned, I almost cried out her name.

As always, Delia avoided eye contact with me as she laid her usual purchases on the counter. She made a peace sign with her fingers, and I removed two cigarettes from an open box of Export "A" and placed them on the counter between the condoms and the Wrigley's Big Red. She dropped her change in her purse and left without a word, the scent of cigarettes and cinnamon trailing her out the door.

Delia's battered face haunted me that night. I saw her white body lying still, her grey eyes wide open, staring at the ceiling as raw hands, white and black, pawed and probed her naked flesh. I squeezed my eyes shut, trying to shake the image. When I realized I couldn't sleep, I got up and wrote in my diary. I saw myself back in Mr. Mills's classroom. I saw Delia's pencil sitting in her pencil case, surrounded by sticks of Wrigley's Big Red gum, waiting for my arrival, ready to connect our two lives. But now she was in a dangerous place. My parents would say it was an immoral world. How could I help her?

But our history would repeat itself. Delia disappeared.

I waited for her every night as weeks passed. I became so desperate for answers, I turned to my brother. We were in the store.

"Do you know what happened to the girl with the scar on her hand?" I asked. "I haven't seen her in a while."

"She's gone." He looked up from a *Sports Illustrated* magazine. "I don't know where, but she said she needed a fresh scene after what happened to her. Can't blame her." He turned back to his magazine but my silence prompted him to look up again. "Sorry she didn't say goodbye."

"What do you mean?"

Josh closed the magazine. "She mentioned she recognized you from Mr. Mills's class," he said, avoiding my eyes.

My thoughts went blank for a moment. "But she never said anything," I said finally.

"She was really embarrassed. Try to understand—"

"But she told you—" I felt myself getting hot. Why had she turned to him instead of me?

"She was pretty messed up. She probably didn't want to burden you with her problems." He rolled the magazine and tapped it against the counter. "She was a really nice girl. She told me she wanted to be a party planner. Throw confetti in the air and make people happy. I really felt bad for her—she didn't have a whole lot." His eyes finally met mine. There was a sadness there that washed over my anger. I wondered if perhaps he too had hoped to help her—that we'd both spent all this time wrapped in the same concerns.

Our convenience store sat on Queen Street in downtown Toronto. It was west of Bathurst Street at a corner popular with prostitutes, the homeless, and the occasional patient from the nearby mental health hospital. The CN Tower, the world's tallest free-standing structure, was less than a ten-minute drive south, but much to the disappointment of any out-of-town guests, we had no view of it. Not that we had time for sightseeing. At seven every morning, Christmas being the only exception, we opened for business. Of all the staple items we sold—milk, bread, and newspapers—cigarettes and condoms were our best sellers.

My parents owned the two-storey building and we lived in a small apartment above our store. The entrance to our home was on the side of the building, facing a narrow one-way street off Queen. The windows shook each time the streetcars rumbled by, and we got used to the scream of sirens, even learning to distinguish the differences among fire, police, and EMS. But the apartment was comfortable though small for the four of us. Josh, who was a year younger than me, had the bigger corner bedroom with windows facing in two directions. His friends used to sleep over all the time until my mother discovered why. The boys would turn off the light and peek out at the prostitutes on the street corner.

By the mid-eighties, most of the variety stores in Toronto were owned by Korean immigrant families. At least, that's what the KBA—the Korean Businessmen's Association—reported in the *Korea Times* newspaper. Established in 1973, the organization had become big enough to have paid employees and offer membership services and benefits.

I disliked working in the store and hated working the cash. I preferred to line up rows and rows of canned tuna and boxes of instant soup. On hot summer days, I welcomed the job of refilling the coolers with cans and bottles of soft drinks. This wasn't as easy as it sounded because I had to reach behind the cold drinks to place the new ones that needed time to chill. My favourite job was restocking the magazines. I was fascinated by the porn, although I didn't have the opportunity to examine it in any great detail, as my parents were vigilant. Because we were robbed frequently, I was never left alone for long. Nothing that would ever make the six o'clock news, although we once had a patient from the mental health hospital come tearing in with a butter knife held dramatically in the air. "I need a goat to sacrifice!" he screamed at my mother. "Sell me a goddamn goat!" When my startled mother stared wide-eyed at him, he turned to me. "You—you!" he stammered. He waved his free hand, a finger pointed at me like a street sign rattling in the wind. "What's your name?" When I mumbled Mary, he yelled, "Ming, tell her—tell her in Chinese or whatever you people speak!" We captured the entire incident on security videotape, minus the sound, but the police took it away before we could show anyone.

Another time, two skinny white guys came in claiming they had a gun. They were both freakishly tall but their baby faces made them seem less intimidating. They obviously had no idea we made three cents for every newspaper we sold and that we had to sell milk at cost just to bring customers into the store in the first place. "You should be robbing a bank," my dad told them, his advice sincere but difficult to understand because of his thick accent. The two of them took off with less than fifty dollars in cash, a bag full of cigarettes, and the latest edition of *Penthouse*, which I'd placed on the shelf minutes earlier.

Because most stores closed between 10 and 11 p.m., my parents, whenever they had company, had visitors drop by very late. At least once every few months, I'd be awakened by my dad and his friends in the living room singing, drunk out of their minds on *soju*. Although I'd never tried it, I was told it tasted like vodka. The women drank *boricha*, a barley tea, and talked quietly in the kitchen. Josh and I stayed in our rooms. Although it was a nuisance to be kept awake so late, we were secretly happy to hear our parents laugh and be part of a circle in which they spoke their language and felt a sense of belonging. I sometimes felt sad my parents and their friends had to meet like fireflies in the night, sacrificing sleep for laughter, food, and gossip.

The men liked to sing and each of them had a favourite song. Mr. Young, who owned a tiny store north of us on Dundas Street, always sang "Arirang," a traditional folk song considered Korea's unofficial anthem. Even I was moved by his rich and powerful voice each time he sang.

My dad's favourite song was about a famous general. Dad's family had kept official record books that showed he was a direct ancestor. Born in 1316, the general became a national hero when he led his men to victory during a number of battles against Japanese pirates who began raiding the Korean coast in the 1350s. He went on to win increasingly more important battles against the Mongols, reclaiming northern territories lost to them during the Yuan dynasty, as well as the Jeju Islands to the south. This gained him tremendous favour and influence with the king. However, as the song goes, his great popularity also made him great enemies, who in turn conspired against him, and on one cold November day in 1388, the general was branded a traitor and beheaded.

My dad, who never sang unless he was drunk, always sounded sad whenever he belted out the song about the general and the glory days when a man could be a real hero. When one of his friends teased him and wanted to know why he couldn't be a hero himself, he laughed and said, "In this country, I'd have to learn English first!"

It was true that my dad, despite living in Canada for ten years, hadn't really learned to speak or write English. It never seemed to bother him, unlike my mother, who kept piles of instructional English-language cassette tapes—ranging from beginner to advanced levels—by the cash register, and played them in between customers.

"Why don't you make him learn like you do?" I once asked my mother. "Aren't you at all embarrassed by him?"

"Your father's accepted his fate here," she said.

Although for once I don't think she intended to make me feel bad, I felt guilty that my dad saw himself as limited in the same country that my mother was sure would lead me to a great and brilliant life. Unlike my dad, I was never going to accept *my* fate.

Chapter 2

My mother was forever complaining about some physical ailment. "I'm a sick woman," she would remind me any time I forgot to practise the piano or, even worse, brought home the forbidden B on a test or an assignment. "Stomach ulcers and a bad knee, the doctors say, from working too hard and climbing so many stairs on my poor leg." Her right leg, which she'd broken falling into a well in Korea when she was sixteen years old, had never healed properly. So it was a huge mistake to tell her I was planning to become a writer—worse, a poet. It wasn't even my idea. It was Mr. Allen's. He'd been my grade-nine English teacher, and I got him again in grade eleven. "You should study creative writing. You have a flair for it," he said. It was easy for me to agree; I had the biggest crush on him. My friends and I thought the photos of him in the school yearbook were good enough to grace the cover of *Tiger Beat* magazine alongside other guys we had a crush on like Shaun Cassidy and Mark Harmon. I'd even begun to keep a separate notebook of all the words Mr. Allen used in class that I didn't know, although I wondered when I'd ever use words like *visceral*, *superfluous*, or *enthrall*.

"If you only knew just how many packs of cigarettes, bags of milk, and thousands of newspapers we had to sell," my mother said, shaking her head. I could see she was lost in her usual world of regrets. "Look around." She gestured at the shelves crowded with supplies. "We sacrificed everything to come here. Do you think I enjoy working sixteen hours a day, people thinking I'm stupid because I can't speak English? No, you're going to make something of yourself here." She stood up from her stool behind the counter. As she pressed her palm into her lower back, she straightened it slowly as if it were a struggle.

My mother saw any small act of defiance, any questioning of her authority, as a betrayal, a deliberate attempt to shatter the dream. My parents had never taken a vacation, not even to visit relatives back home, though they faithfully sent money to support their parents. None of her family members or friends in Korea would believe working in a variety store could be so demanding and even dangerous. My family cringed each time the newspapers wrote about store robberies or deadly shootings, all too aware we were easy targets, especially at night.

"Sometimes I feel like a sitting duck," Mrs. Cha told my mother. Her family owned a store in Regent Park, considered one of the most dangerous neighbourhoods in Toronto. "It's only a matter of time before someone blows my head off or my heart explodes waiting for it to happen."

"*Ai-goo-cham-neh!*" my mother had said. "That's silly talk. We'll both grow old and have our sons take care of us. They'll give us many grandsons and make every sacrifice worth it."

"At least you'll be free of that expectation," Josh joked to me. "You'll go on and marry some white guy whose parents won't care."

Knowing he was burdened with such an obligation, I wanted to hug him as I'd seen so many families on television do whenever they were overcome with emotion. But our family didn't hug.

Josh had calculated my parents would have to sell roughly 32,102 packs of cigarettes, 4,570 boxes of condoms, and 266,678 copies of the *Toronto Star* to put a degree in my hands. He'd even determined we had to sell 889 Elvis Presley ceramic-bust piggy banks. Prominently displayed in our store window, they were hugely popular with the drive-by traffic. We were always amazed people would take the time to stop, find parking, and pay for something so tacky, and so incredibly overpriced.

Unlike me, Josh had lots of Korean friends as well as Canadian ones, and moved in and out of both circles with ease. He took tae-kwon-do lessons and watched dated Korean soap operas on VHS video. At the same time, he spent what little free time he had at the arcades with his non-Korean friends and a blonde girl named Tillie everyone thought was his girlfriend.

The only time Josh ever raised his voice at me was when he walked into our apartment and heard me plucking away on his guitar. The fact that my parents had paid close to five hundred dollars for his prized possession meant it was officially hands-off. It rested on a stand by his bed like a giant trophy. Josh took pride in telling everyone the Simon & Patrick guitar was "Canadian," because it had been made by hand in a small village in Quebec. Like the artisan who had given life to his beloved instrument, Josh handled it with the greatest care. The more he played it, the fuller and richer it resonated. There was something about the guitar's sound and cedar-gloss finish that made me want to touch it and play it too. On the days he knew I'd have friends over, Josh put it in its case and placed it safely away in the closet.

When I told my mother I wanted guitar lessons, she frowned and said, "But you're a girl. If you practised like you should, you'd think the piano was just as good as the guitar."

Like all Korean girls, I took piano lessons once a week. Even back in Korea, I'd taken lessons. Piano was the choice instrument, followed by the violin. It was considered essential for a girl as young as three or four to study music as a sign of her grace and the family's ability to afford the finer things in life. To get to the Royal Conservatory of Music on Bloor Street, I had to take the Queen streetcar east, and then ride the subway north. Because there was nothing to look out at during the ride, I floated in and out of other people's conversations, hoping to get inspiration for a story. I discreetly wrote down bits of conversations in notebooks. It was the best way to get authentic dialogue.

"I don't get it. Is it a girl's name or a boy's name?" a woman asked. I looked over to see a plain-looking white woman with short hair and big silver hoops in her ears. "Wouldn't you want a name that would show the difference?" she asked. The woman next to her, who I guessed was Chinese, shrugged as she searched for something in her bag. Her long black hair fell over her face and spilled into her belongings, which clearly annoyed her. She tossed the strands aside and said, "You might not be able to tell if it's some ethnic name either, so what's the diff?" She pulled out a pair of oversized designer sunglasses, smiled, and added, "It's just a name." The train stopped, and they got off.

As the train pulled out of the station and into the tunnel, I stared out into the subway dimness and caught a glimpse of my reflection in the glass. My parents used to delight in telling people I was nameless for weeks after being born, as my grandfather consulted with ancestral spirits over the right name. A name, like a picture, was worth a thousand words. It was a single-word poem that defined a person. I was only four years old when I told my mother I hated my name. She scolded me. "You have a beautiful name. Names must be treated as sacred. Your reputation will one day be built on it." When Josh was born a year later, twice as much effort went into finding his name.

But in the end, both of us would lose our carefully chosen Korean names.

"They need new names," the principal said. My mother, my brother, and I were in his office. I was about to turn six years old and registering at a Canadian school for the first time. A timid young woman, whom we didn't know, translated for us. "It'll help them fit in. Their teachers would never be able to say a name like this." The woman pointed to my name, Yu-Rhee, and to my brother's name, Chun-Ha, on our official entry papers. My mother was silent. I was afraid to look at her face, although I could easily picture her jaws locked, her eyes downcast and unmoving, as we were told our names would only invite other children to tease us. It became so quiet all we could hear was the clock ticking. I was relieved when the translator finally started speaking again, although we were unprepared for what she would say. "You have no choice. It's the school board's policy . . . it'll help the children fit in."

We didn't know any Canadian names. The three of us turned helplessly to the principal. Oblivious, he broke into a smile, revealing a set of brilliant white teeth. Their unevenness caught my eye. He made a grand gesture with his hands as he offered the names: Josh on one open palm for my brother, and Mary on the other for me. My mother agreed with a single nod.

The principal then brought both palms together and applauded loudly. The translator told us, "Mr. Darcy says you have great names—they are his children's names." He turned to show us a framed photo of his family that sat on a shelf behind him. His children had blonde hair and thousands of little brown spots sprinkled all over their little pale faces.

I thought about Mr. Darcy and his children as I banged "Für Elise" on the keyboard. "You seem a little distracted," my piano teacher said as I stopped playing. "Are you nervous about the upcoming recital?"

I shrugged. I wasn't distracted any more than usual. I wasn't even thinking about the recital, which I hadn't bothered telling my parents about. They would say no if I asked them to attend, as always. Unlike at Josh's tae-kwon-do tournaments, there were no gold medals to be won at piano recitals.

Later that day, I'd just taken over the register from my mother, who'd gone upstairs to make dinner. As I opened my English notebook, I started thinking about what Mr. Allen had told us earlier in class. "No story writes itself. Look for inspiration." I had to create a sketch of a character I'd later use in a short story.

A customer with spiked red hair walked in. He was wearing a black jacket, jeans, and sunglasses with the mirrored shades I so hated. I didn't recognize him, so I watched carefully as he went to the back cooler, then up one aisle and down another.

"Gimme a pack of du Maurier Kings," he said as he placed a two-litre bottle of Coke, a bag of chips, and three cans of our cheapest cat food on the counter. He walked over to the magazines and took one from the top row. "I owe your husband from before," he said, and pulled out his wallet.

"You mean my dad," I said. I placed the cigarettes on the magazine, covering the bare breasts of two women. Upside down, I could still read the caption: "Shades of Singapore: Subservient and Sexy." I reached for the pile of receipts clipped together by the register. "What's your name again?"

"Didn't say yet," he said. I looked up and saw my own reflection in his glasses. "It's Leon."

I thumbed through the receipts. My dad was terrible at keeping track of customer tabs. He had his own system of scribbling names spelled phonetically in Korean.

"Altogether, you owe twenty-seven dollars and two cents," I told him.

He took three ten-dollar bills from his wallet. "So. What's your name?"

"Mary." I handed him three dollars.

"Nope," he said as he handed me back a dollar. "I don't wanna owe nothin' more." Then he asked, "So, whatcha studying there, Mary?"

I didn't answer. He touched my hand as I dropped change into his outstretched palm, and my flesh crawled. As I bagged his purchases, I noticed the thick silver chain bracelet he wore. I'd already memorized his face: pale and stubbled skin, mouth bitten in, freckles everywhere, even on his neck. I imagined he had a tattoo or two somewhere.

The back door opened and my dad entered.

"Hey!" Leon called out to him, "just paid my money—to your daughter here." He turned back to face me. He took his glasses off. "See you around, Mary," he said with a slight nod.

His lizard eyes had me recalling Mr. Allen's words, "Look for inspiration."

It was the last Saturday afternoon in October and I was at home waiting for my girlfriends to arrive. We were going to try out Erin's new Ouija board. Our previous homeroom teacher had nicknamed the four of us the mini–United Nations. Rubina had emigrated from Pakistan and was a faithful Muslim. Linda was a devoted Italian Catholic and always wore a gold cross around her neck. I told everyone I was a Buddhist, although I rarely went to the temple. As immigrant children, we led parallel lives and were bound by parallel expectations of great achievement, which ultimately led to a lot of conspiring against our respective parents.

Erin was the only one of us who'd escaped the burdens of the dream. She was the last of five children, and her family had been in Canada long enough for her Irish-born grandfather to have fought in the First World War. She was allowed to go out on weeknights, wear short skirts and makeup, and pierce her ears more than twice. We all loved her, and envied her freedom, but each of us kept what our parents said about her to ourselves.

I'd first met Erin at Linda's birthday sleepover two years earlier. Her father had died that May. According to Linda, it was Erin who'd found him hanging naked from his bedroom ceiling. Erin never shared any of that with me, and I never asked, although my mind refused to stop visualizing what she must have seen. To this day I'm haunted by images of a man with paper-white skin, a belt around his thin neck, dangling from a hook in the ceiling. How long had he suffered? Did he cry out for help only to realize it was too late? At least there would have been no blood. Just the thought of blood made me feel faint.

At Linda's sleepover, my friends and I pledged we would be best friends forever. We promised one another we would only surrender our virginities to our true loves, though later that night, Erin confessed she'd already been with her older cousin—something Linda responded to with exaggerated disgust until Rubina told us her parents were first cousins. I had nothing so exciting to reveal.

"Why don't you have any Korean friends?" My mother would always begin the same way on the days my friends were coming to visit. Then her voice would turn accusatory, hostile. "You don't like Korean people. You're ashamed of our culture. But you'll marry a Korean man if you know what's good for you."

Although I was always silent, I hated when she talked this way because part of me knew she was right. I wished I was bold enough to say to her: *You can't force me to be proud of my culture when you've given me nothing to be proud of.* Life, I imagined, would be easier if we were white, ate white food, and took vacations at places like Myrtle

Beach or Cape Cod. I also secretly desired a white last name, a name
I didn't need to spell out for people. It was remarkable how many
people misspelled Hwang. It annoyed me that many people believed
I was Chinese.

"I totally understand," Rubina said when I told her. "It drives me
crazy when people think I'm Indian."

I was relieved to discover that Rubina and Linda were hearing
the same accusations and threats from their mothers about cultural
expectations. The three of us swore we'd never allow our parents
to decide how we'd live our lives and, above all, whom we would
marry. It was Erin, the only one whose mother didn't tell her what
to do, who suggested we silently hum Cyndi Lauper's "Girls Just
Wanna Have Fun" whenever we had to endure our mothers' rants.
She wrote out the lyrics for us, and it became our secret song.

My parents, as usual, were downstairs in the store that Saturday. Josh
was away at a tae-kwon-do tournament in Hamilton. My friends
and I sat around the Ouija board on the carpeted floor in his room.
According to the board, Rubina would be the first of us to marry.
She beamed, proud in the revelation. Although dressed in jeans and
a sweater, she was by far the most traditional, donning a scarf to
hide her lovely black hair from the world. Because her parents were
as strict as mine and had similar expectations, I felt she understood
me in ways the others couldn't. It made me appreciate her friendship
that much more.

We asked the board who would marry second, and the wedge
began to move under our fingers. Linda, who was clearly alarmed

at Rubina's suggestion that we use Erin's father's spirit to answer our questions, bit deep into her lip and drew blood. I cringed. She whispered something to herself and kissed the cross she wore, leaving faint traces of red on it. Linda could be melodramatic but always went along with us in the end. Her parents wanted her to become a nurse and she had to work the hardest of us to maintain her grades. Though she never admitted it, we knew it embarrassed her that her father, who worked as a custodian at our school, could be seen outside smoking in his grey uniform with the teachers during his lunch break.

According to the Ouija board, Erin would marry next, followed by me. We didn't bother spelling out Linda's name as she was the only one left.

We were waiting for the pizza to arrive. Hungry and impatient, I went over to the window to see if the delivery guy was anywhere nearby. Instead, I saw Leon, still wearing his mirrored sunglasses, standing across the one-way street, talking with Suzie X and another girl.

"What're you looking at?" Erin came over and pulled the curtains back.

Leon, who was lighting a cigarette, looked up and saw the two of us. I hid, feeling I'd been caught doing something wrong.

"Get away from there!" I snapped.

"Yeah, he's kinda creepy," Erin said as she continued to stare out the window.

Then everyone was at the window, curious to get a peek. I closed the curtains, but not before catching another glimpse of Leon, still looking up at us.

"Who wears shades like that anymore?" Linda asked. "It's almost dark anyway."

"The guy's obviously a pimp," Erin said, as if she knew everything, adding for dramatic effect, "He's probably armed and dangerous too, ready to beat the hell out of any girl who gets out of line."

The doorbell rang, and we all stared at each other. I panicked at the thought of creepy Leon. The bell rang again, followed by a booming knocking on the wooden door downstairs.

"We should call the police," Linda whispered.

It was Erin, peeking out the window again, who finally said, "It's the pizza guy."

I ran down to find an annoyed delivery man.

"Can I have a slice?" Leon called out from across the street. Suzie X and the other girl giggled. He didn't wait for my response, just flicked his cigarette butt into the sewer and turned back to talk to the girls.

We were almost done eating when the downstairs door slammed. We froze until I recognized my mother's heavy footsteps.

"You girls have played enough," she said to me sharply in Korean. "Tell your friends to go home so I can make dinner."

I rushed my friends out before the pungent smell of pickled garlic and cabbage could swallow our small apartment, complete with the Ouija board and all its crazy predictions.

The Sunday after my friends had visited, my dad's friends stayed late again. With so little sleep, Monday was a bad day. I was supposed to be writing the sketch of Leon, but since my dad had kept me up half the night with his singing, I ended up writing a long poem about life trapped working in a variety store. I thought I might dedicate it to Erin, who'd once told me she thought having a store was the coolest thing in the world because it meant free pop, free smokes, free anything I wanted. I showed the poem to Mr. Allen instead.

"It's very good," he said. My heart skipped at his praise, but then he asked, "Did you show it to your parents?"

"My parents can't read English," I said, which wasn't entirely a lie. They'd kill me, I thought, if they knew I was exposing our secrets to the world. It wasn't the Korean way.

Chapter 3

$\mathcal{F}$or the last three days, someone had been stealing our *Toronto Star* newspapers. Bundled and tied together by string, fifty copies arrived early each morning and were left outside our store. Losing the papers was a big problem. People who came to buy them usually bought other items too—a pack of cigarettes, a jar of peanut butter, a couple of rolls of toilet paper.

"They're still charging us for the papers," my mother said, reporting what the *Toronto Star* had told her. My parents and I were in the store. It was after ten thirty on a Friday night. Because Josh had left earlier in the evening to attend another weekend tae-kwon-do tournament in Hamilton, I was stuck doing his share of the work, as well as my own.

"We should call the police," I said, handing my dad a box of cereal. He was balancing on three stacked milk crates as he neatly arranged the overstocked cereal boxes on the top shelf.

"No, no, no." My mother came out from behind the cash register and walked over to the front door. Looking outside, she said, "They wouldn't care about the papers. They'd think it was a waste of their time." She was always reluctant to call the police. That would mean

bad publicity for the store. No one would buy a business with a reputation for problems, if and when the time came to put it on the market.

"We've got to be more careful now that Minjoo Lee's one of
them." She was referring to another shopkeeper's son. He was a new
police officer and stationed in a nearby precinct. His mother was
known to be a terrible gossip in Little Korea. Also called K-Town,
the area stretched two subway stops along Bloor Street West. The
Lees were one of the first Korean families to set up shop there in 1967
when immigrants from Central and South America dominated the
neighbourhood. "We had a grocery store that had the freshest and
cleanest fruits and vegetables in Toronto," Mrs. Lee said. "I would
polish those apples till I saw my gold tooth reflected on them. That's
what we were known for!" She'd since retired but never tired of
repeating her old stories.

Though I couldn't see my mother's face when she spoke, I could
imagine the tension on it. As far as she was concerned, maintaining
the store's reputation was foremost, and having a Korean cop with
access to private information about our store was bad news.

"He went to university, and for what!" my mother said. "He
should have been a dentist. At least then he'd be someone worth
knowing instead of avoiding."

"We can't afford not to have the Saturday *Star*," my dad said,
accepting the last box of cereal.

"Maybe we should put a camera outside," I said.

He shook his head. After shifting his weight, he jumped off the
crates, landing neatly, knees bent. "I'll spend the night in the store,
stay up all night if I have to, or at least until the delivery man arrives,"
he said. "I'll catch whoever it is stealing our papers." He flashed me

a smile, hidden from my mother. There was the sparkle in his eyes of a man called to action. "I'll snap a photo of him. Canada's most wanted . . ."

My mother walked towards us. "What if there's more than one person? It sounds dangerous."

The thought of my dad spending the night on the floor by the register, armed with only a Polaroid camera, frightened me.

"If only Josh were here," my mother said. "He could spend the night with you."

"I could stay down here," I said. I felt excited and scared at once. I'd never been in the store after closing. What if there were mice? I'd have to stay awake all night. I stole a glance at the pink boxes of wake-up pills we sold. I could sneak a few of them. They'd helped me get through my final exams last year.

My mother shook her head vigorously. "You wouldn't know what to do if anything happened. No, we need Josh. He's a boy—"

My nervousness turned to an indignant defiance. "If anything happens, I'll call 911. I wouldn't do anything stupid . . ." My voice trailed off when I saw my mother bite her lower lip.

My dad looked at the clock: It was 10:50 p.m. The store would close in ten minutes. "You can stay," he said. He headed for the broom closet to grab a mop, avoiding my mother's reaction.

I glimpsed a smile on his face again, and pretended to straighten the magazines. I knew better than to think I had got my way just yet. My mother usually had the last word because my dad didn't like confrontations. "We really are monkey and rat," he once told me, speaking in English. He was referring to their Chinese horoscope signs. "She the big gorilla," he said, beating his chest with two fists, "and I Mickey the mouse." He raised his fists above his head to make rodent ears. Although my mother rarely laughed at his goofy jokes in front of us, I would sometimes hear her laughter through their bedroom wall at night.

A long minute passed. Finally my mother said, "Go up and brush your teeth. Grab some blankets."

I left the store smiling, my arms wrapped around myself. It was cold, even with my coat on. Trixie, Babe, Suzie X, and Leon were standing on the opposite corner. I heard Suzie X say she needed something from the store before it closed. She ran across the street in my direction, her red scarf almost slipping from her neck. Our eyes met briefly and we exchanged a polite smile. I avoided looking at the rest of her gang, especially Leon, who'd stopped spiking his red hair and had begun to look like a creepy Howdy Doody.

The floor behind the counter was raised a foot off the ground. As I lay there next to my dad, I realized the width of the area was similar to that of my twin-size bed. Within seconds, he'd fallen asleep. I'd never slept so close to him before. It was awkward and I was soon annoyed by his snoring and the stale smell of dust and grime that surrounded us. When I elbowed him, he turned on his side and fell silent.

But I still couldn't relax. I got up and sat on a chair by the cash register. The street lights cast menacing shadows throughout the store. Grabbing my blanket off the floor and wrapping it around me, I walked over to the window facing the corner. I saw Suzie X leaning into a black car talking to a man, her red scarf draped over her head.

She must be cold, I thought. In some twisted way, I felt glad for her when she finally got into the car and drove away, even if it meant I was left alone.

It was only half past eleven. I felt hungry. The chocolate bars were in the aisle closest to me, but I hesitated to walk over. I thought of the wake-up pills, but I felt so alert, I pushed the impulse out of my mind. Besides, I'd need to take the pills with water, and the idea of having to go downstairs to use the dank, poorly lit washroom filled me with dread.

For the next half hour I sat still, my knees pulled up to my chin, my blanket—my only source of protection—pulled over me. Each time a car or a streetcar passed, the shape and size of the shadows changed. I envisioned mice, the size of wild beasts, roaming our basement, waiting for me to fall asleep so they could make their way upstairs. In spite of my fear, I started imagining their every detail and wished I had my notebook and pen to disappear into. When the minute hand marked half past twelve, I mustered up all my courage and headed for the chocolate bars. As I boldly reached for an Oh Henry!, I heard something scamper across the floor—something big. Terrified, I ran and shook my dad awake.

"It couldn't have been a mouse," I said. "It was too loud and too fast!" Using my hands, I tried showing him how big the creature was.

He shrugged, yawned, and said, *"Jah. Bali bali jah."* Sleep. Quickly, quickly sleep. Apparently, the thought of his daughter being devoured by monster-size mice didn't worry him. I shook him again and told him I wanted to go upstairs. Half asleep, he unlocked the door to let me out, and told me not to wake my mother. A gust of wind whipped me as I turned the corner. I reached into my coat and pulled out the key. I'd just entered the building and turned on the dim overhead lights at the bottom of the stairs when something shoved me from behind. Before I could turn around, I was pushed into the wall. Then I was whirled about, my back hitting the same wall. A mess of red hair and cold flesh pressed into my face. Leon stepped back and flattened his hand over my mouth. I couldn't move or scream. He shoved into me, his free hand unbuttoning my coat before reaching under my shirt. I struggled to see if the door was still open so I could scream to anyone outside, but Leon had shut it.

"I can feel your heart, Mary," he said. His breath reeked of alcohol. He leaned closer and whispered into my ear. "I've been wantin' you something bad since I first saw you."

I held my breath and squeezed my eyes shut, desperately trying to think what to do. Then, with all my strength, I pounded on him. He was strong enough to grab both my wrists with one hand and still keep a hand over my mouth. His fingers gouged into my cheek. The stench of cigarettes on his hand and alcohol on his breath overwhelmed me and I felt my stomach tighten and turn. I tried to scream again.

"Don't. Don't, Mary," he said. "Don't make me hurt you."

I felt my body lift as he peeled me off the wall. He was trying to get me to the stairs. I fought back and my head slammed into the end of the handrail. Everything went black. I felt the stairs, hard and cold, under me.

When my eyes opened again, he was over me.

"You still with me, Mary?" he asked. He grabbed a fistful of hair and yanked my head back. He slapped the side of my face. "This won't be any fun 'less you're with me."

I remembered a story my mother once read to me. A child, lost in the woods, pretended to be dead to escape a bear attack. I closed my eyes and let my body, already limp, dissolve into the stairs.

"Stupid Chinese bitch!" he said.

His fingers dug deep into me as he tried to turn me around. Something hit my stomach, the pain hard and sharp. My breath caught in my throat, yet I remained still.

"Wake the fuck up!" He hit me, kicked me—I couldn't tell which—again and again.

Just when I thought I couldn't bear it anymore, he stopped. His heavy, ragged breathing filled the hollow of the stairwell.

Maybe he thought he'd killed me. Or he was too exhausted to continue. The door opened. I felt a rush of air against my skin and the cut on my head. I opened my eyes slowly. He was gone.

Chapter 4

On the Monday after the attack, my parents didn't make me go to school. Instead, I spent the day on the sofa, propped up by pillows, watching game shows and soap operas. The painkillers I was taking every four hours left me feeling drowsy, and I floated in and out of sleep. My mother brought up magazines for me. "No eating around them," she told me. That way she could still sell them.

"Mrs. O'Doherty asked about you," Josh said as he came upstairs. "You okay?" His eyes were soft.

I nodded. Each time the outside door opened and I heard the sound of footsteps, I winced. Josh placed take-out lasagna on the coffee table. I turned off the TV and tried to sit up, but I ached all over.

"I'm not hungry," I said.

Mrs. O'Doherty was an eighty-seven-year-old woman who lived alone above a store a couple of blocks east of us. She stopped to chat whenever she came in. If the weather was bad, we'd carry her groceries. She always invited us in and tipped us with the cookies she'd bought at our store. I always threw mine away—they looked like flattened rocks—but Josh ate his.

"She wondered why she hadn't seen you in a couple of days."

Josh helped himself to a bowl of chips on the coffee table. "The police came by her place asking questions. They told her there'd been an assault in the neighbourhood."

"Did you tell her that I fell?"

"No, *Omma* did."

My mother had told everybody I'd fallen down a flight of stairs—everybody but the police. As usual, she wanted to avoid bad publicity for the store. Just like with the newspapers. She never even talked to me about the attack.

The smell of lasagna filled the room. I wished Josh had bought himself dinner as well. We both considered take-out a treat. When I offered him some, he hesitated, as if he wanted to say something but couldn't find the words. He offered a weak smile and got up.

"I'll eat something later," he said. The door to his room scraped against the frame as he shut it.

That was one drawback about having our store. We didn't eat meals as a family, because one of us always had to be in the store. I turned the TV back on. The laugh track to *Three's Company* filled the silence.

"How is it?"

I turned my head, startled to see my mother standing in the doorway.

"I told you, no eating around the magazines," she said.

"Wow, you care more about your damn magazines than about me!" I flung my arm out, knocking the lasagna off the coffee table. Pain shot through my ribs as I reached down to scoop the food back into the container. Tomato sauce smeared the pages of the magazines sprawled around me.

Without looking at me, she grabbed the magazines off the floor and sofa, stacking the clean ones on her left arm. Josh, who'd heard me yelling, came out of his room.

"Let him know if you need anything else," she said. Her footsteps were heavy on the stairs and the outside door slammed behind her.

"You know what she's like," Josh said. "The way she deals with things is to bury them inside—make like nothing's ever happened."

But it did, I wanted to scream. To me. Something terrible. Why couldn't she talk to me? Still, I knew better than to confront Josh, who was more accepting. We were Korean. We'd been taught from birth not to ask why or why not.

Two officers, a male and a female, had found me. We didn't know who had called them. They'd asked me a thousand questions at the hospital. My parents and I felt foolish that we didn't know Leon's last name or phone number, although we'd let him run a tab with us. I don't know if the officers believed us. Then, as the male officer took my parents aside to ask more questions, the female officer stayed with me. She had gentle blue eyes and blonde hair pulled back into a tight bun. She asked me, did my parents have bad tempers; how was I doing in school; did I have a boyfriend? Both officers came to our home a few days later, asking the same questions. They even asked Josh about our parents, who were downstairs in the store at the time.

Maybe it was because the police were seen combing the neighbourhood and asking questions, but after that, no one stole our newspapers anymore.

*   *   *

I began to have strange dreams. In one of them, I was a little girl back in Korea. Dressed in blue flip-flops and a yellow dress, I was walking down a street when a large cart pulled by an old man selling knick-knacks—toothbrushes, slippers, long johns, and notebooks—lost its balance and fell into an open ditch parallel to the road. Knee deep in filth, the old man cursed at me viciously, blaming me for not getting out of his way.

I remembered class discussions about the prophetic value of dreams in the books we'd studied. I thought of Calpurnia, Caesar's wife, pleading with Caesar not to ignore her dreams of disaster. Was I losing my mind, or overreacting to my attack? I refused to let myself sink into that dark space, tempting as it was.

That first Friday after the attack, Rubina dropped by with my homework. She was my oldest friend. We'd met in grade four, the same time I met Delia.

"How're you feeling?" she asked.

I lifted my shirt and showed her my stomach, my back, and then rolled up my PJ bottoms to show her the back of my legs. Rubina's eyes teared up and her mouth opened as if to say something but instead she looked away. I hadn't washed my hair since the attack. It was plastered down. I gently touched the scab where I'd hit my head.

"God, you look awful," she said finally, still avoiding eye contact. Then, realizing what she'd said, she forced the same smile—

compassion mixed with pity—that the female officer had as she took photos of my injuries.

The first time I'd seen my wounded face was in a hospital bathroom. I thought of Delia when she came into our store all cut up. *But I did nothing wrong*, I thought. Then I silently apologized to Delia: *No one deserves to be beaten up.*

"Linda thinks it was Erin's father's ghost that pushed you down the stairs," Rubina said. "For making it answer our stupid Ouija board questions."

I giggled and felt a sharp pain in my chest and stomach. "Don't make me laugh," I said. "It hurts."

"Sorry. Oh, I almost forgot—this is for you," Rubina said. She pulled a gift wrapped in floral paper out of her bag.

I pulled out a beautiful sky blue scarf. "I love it. My favourite colour." It felt soft and light around my neck.

"It's dumb, but I saw it at Cotton Ginny and thought of you." She smiled. "No, seriously. Linda's pretty scared something bad's gonna happen to the rest of us."

So I told her the truth and swore her to absolute secrecy. Rubina took in every word, her dark eyes on me, and I found I enjoyed telling my sad story to such a captivated audience.

"So, what do you know about this guy?" she asked.

"Not much. He buys a lot of cat food and porn. He's into Asians," I said, thinking back to the magazines he chose.

"Do you think that's why he went after you?"

I didn't know how to respond; I hadn't made that connection.

"Do you think he did what he did because he thought he'd get away with it because you're—" Rubina stopped.

"What?"

"I don't know. My mother thinks white men believe they can do pretty much whatever they want with us and get away with it cuz they're white. At least that's what happened to her sister at work."

I was skeptical, but then I remembered Mr. Darcy, my old principal—the one who had told my mother that my brother and I needed new names if we wanted to go to school in Canada. My head began to throb and I wanted to lie down.

"Is there anything I can do for you?" Rubina asked. "I'm already praying for you."

"I don't pray."

"That's okay—I have to do it five times a day—I more than make up for you and Erin."

I thought of Linda, and wondered how often she prayed to her Catholic God.

"Don't Buddhists pray?" Rubina asked. She was looking up at a pink paper lotus lantern hanging from my ceiling, a miniature version of the real thing.

"Yeah, my mother goes to the temple with her friends, but I've only gone once or twice on Buddha's birthday." I had to admit it was a magnificent spectacle—paper lanterns, designed to look like lotus flowers, hung from every corner of the temple ceiling. My mother would help prepare months in advance, cutting out delicate, translucent pink, green, and white paper petals and gluing them to a wire lantern frame she'd shaped herself.

"The light in the lantern symbolizes wisdom," I said. "The lotus flower is supposed to be special because it grows in murky pond water. The flower represents enlightened Buddhists, and the pond, the world we live in." I looked back up at the pink lotus lantern. There was one hanging in every room of the apartment. None of them lit up.

"Tell everyone I'm fine," I told Rubina, although it still hurt even to breathe.

My mother wouldn't let anyone else visit me. Unable to read or write for long without getting a headache, I found my mind swinging like an out-of-control pendulum. Should I tell anyone else the truth? I felt sure I was on the brink of a breakdown.

Instead, I had a break*through*. I decided I would tell Mr. Allen the truth. I trusted him and believed he'd never hurt me. Eyes closed, I imagined his reactions, allowing myself to indulge in his looks of shock, then concern. I let him hug me; hold me. Yes, *the truth would set me free*. I giggled at the cliché, and when I sat up I felt light-headed, dreamy. This must be what it felt like to be drunk. Curiosity overcame me. I forgot Mr. Allen. I picked up a bottle of *soju* my dad had left out on an end table. *It's only made of sweet potato. It won't hurt me.*

My dad rarely drank alone, and if he did it was never *soju*, which was considered a social drink to be served with food called *anju*— dried squid or anchovies. I searched the kitchen but since there wasn't any, I dumped a bag of trail mix into a bowl and sat back down on the sofa.

"Here's to the general," I mimicked my dad, and lifted my shot glass. "And here's to my goddamn virginity still being intact!" I'd seen the relief on my mother's face when she found out at the hospital. They could still marry me off, without shame, to some Korean guy. The *soju* burned as it went down my throat. After that initial sensation, it felt warm and wild in my belly. I poured myself a couple more shots and drank to my uncertain future. I'd stay at home forever and ruin whatever chances I had at getting into university. *Hell*, I thought, *I'll take over the family business, or worse, move back to Korea and marry a black American soldier stationed in the army base near Itaewon.* I heard the door knob downstairs rattling, panicked, then everything went dark.

Josh found me. I woke up as he wordlessly carried me to my bed.

"When did you get so strong?" I asked as I lay there, my head hazy. "I guess all those martial arts lessons are paying off." I closed my eyes and heard the vacuum cleaner turn on. He was cleaning up the mess of trail mix that had spilled on the floor.

My mother eventually came upstairs, and I heard Josh tell her I wasn't feeling well and had gone back to bed.

"Anything else I could get for you?" he asked, as he handed me a glass of water.

I wanted to tell him I loved him, that he was the only person who understood me. I also wanted to thank him for not lecturing me and for covering for me with our parents. Of course, I didn't. Instead, I told him I wished we were from a white family.

"Don't you think it's weird," I asked him, "that there's no way for parents to tell their kids they love them in Korean?" It was true; *sa-rah-ng*, which meant "love," was used only to express romantic love. Rice, on the other hand, could be *sahr*, which was uncooked, or *bap*, which was cooked.

Josh said, "You should go back to school. You need to get on with things. What about going back on Monday?"

But that's in two days, I thought. He was right, though. After two weeks, the sheer boredom of being upstairs in our tiny apartment all the time was getting to me. What had once felt protective now felt confining. I wished my parents would order me to go back, but they said nothing. Maybe they had the same fears I had: Leon was out there somewhere waiting for me. Or maybe this was their way of saying, *Sorry this happened to you and sorry we lied and the whole world thinks you're a klutz for falling down a flight of stairs.*

I couldn't sleep, so I grabbed my diary from under my bed. It had been a while since I'd written anything. I flipped to a blank page and stared at it. Finding I couldn't write, I got up and peeked out the window, desperate for a hint of life. The streets were deserted. It was 3 a.m., Monday. In six hours, I'd be back in my homeroom class. A shiver ran down my spine. I'd be standing for the national anthem, followed by *Our Father, who art in heaven, hallowed be thy name* . . . I grabbed my pillow and hugged it as I sat on my bed, rocking myself back and forth. Half an hour later, just as I'd lost all hope and was finally drifting off, the phone rang.

My grandmother, my *harmony*, had passed away. By the time our store opened at 7:00 a.m., it had been decided that my mother would go back to Korea and I would accompany her.

Chapter 5

$\mathcal{I}$ shadowed my mother as she prepared for our trip. We would be gone for seven days. In a day and a half, she made and froze a dozen Korean meals for Josh and my dad, and arranged for the eldest son of a family friend to help out at the store. She raided our apartment, looking for gifts she could give to family and friends: shampoo, hand cream, mouthwash; and for the children: colouring books, crayons, and pencils with Barbie on them. She even counted out the number of prescription painkillers I'd need during the trip and stored the remaining pills in a Ziploc bag to leave behind.

I wondered if my *harmony*'s death had been expected, because for a woman who constantly complained about aches and pains, my mother moved now with incredible speed and purpose. I'd been surprised she had valid passports for us. I wondered if she was feeling guilty she hadn't visited in so many years. But I wasn't comfortable asking her, so I asked my dad instead.

He spoke to me in Korean, as he always did for serious talks. "Your *harmony* had breast cancer." His voice was a whisper. "But your mother had no idea. No one bothered to tell her."

"Is she going to be okay?" I asked. "She hasn't even cried."

"When she puts on a stone's face," he said, "you too must be a rock for her." He took his left hand and cupped the right one balled in a fist so the "stone" became a "rock."

I understood his message, although I refused to believe I could ever be as strong as my mother, let alone protect her from the forces of life.

"Yeah, no one bothered to tell her." I repeated the same words to each of my friends, who listened intently when I called them one after another on Monday evening.

"You've already been away from school so long," Rubina said. "People will wonder if you'll ever come back."

Her laughter left me feeling oddly sad, and to my surprise, my mind filled with images of Delia. How many beatings had she endured? Attempted rapes? Actual rapes?

"Hey, are you there?" Rubina asked, and repeated the question.

"Yeah. Don't worry. I'll be back before you know it." Unlike Delia, I'd never abandon my friends. Anyway, Delia and I were never really friends.

We flew KAL. Almost everyone in economy class was Korean. The woman beside me began talking immediately. My mother looked down on people who spoke her dialect. As soon as I saw the woman, I knew what my mother would think of her: She was a *muh-chang-hee*. A "show-off."

"You have the smallest hands," she observed.

I was relieved she'd not mentioned the fading bruises on my face. I didn't say anything. She wore a Gucci watch, an elegant tennis bracelet, and an enormous diamond ring above her wedding band.

"This trip is our last hope," she said. She removed her glasses, which also sported the Gucci logo. "You wouldn't believe how much the geomancer charged us for his work."

I asked my mother in English, "What's a geomancer?"

She responded in Korean, "You know how a palm reader reads your palm to tell you how long you'll live, or what hardships will come to you and when? A geomancer does the same thing with the land."

"Yes," the woman said. She leaned forward to talk with my mother. "A geomancer told us the reason my husband's business failed in Korea was that his ancestor's grave was located in the wrong place, so we moved to Canada for a fresh start, and for a while things were going well, but then our business began to fail again, and now my husband is very, very ill."

My eyes fell on the diamond ring and the countless smaller diamonds on her bracelet, and I wondered how she defined a failed business.

"I'm on my way back," she told us, gently rubbing the diamond on her ring, "to try and relocate the grave of my husband's ancestor in order to appease our ancestral spirits and let them finally rest."

The woman looked at me and said in English, "You have the same look as my children. You think we're *me-chah-saw*." Then, as if I might not understand the Korean word for "crazy," she lifted her finger and made little circles by her head.

"That's the problem with this generation," a male voice joined in from across the aisle. "They don't believe in our ways." The man explained how he and his wife were on their way to testify in a hundred-year-long legal battle with another clan over their ancestral burial grounds.

I'd always known Koreans were superstitious, but I was stunned at how freely they shared such personal stories with complete strangers.

"So," the woman next to me asked, "why are you going back?"

"My grandmother just passed away," I said.

She said to my mother, "I'm sorry for your loss."

My mother nodded. "It's not just the Koreans. Many cultures believe in geomancy and practise ancestor worship."

I thought of a Korean version of Hamlet's father's spirit roaming the streets of downtown Seoul, demanding Hamlet relocate his grave so he could rest in peace.

It wasn't until we were above the Pacific Ocean that everyone began to fall asleep. My ribs were aching and I couldn't get comfortable. I closed my eyes and tried to think of my grandmother. I focused on a photo I had of her, a black-and-white shot of her dressed in the traditional *hanbok*, a loose-fitting blouse with a long and puffy skirt that made her look shapeless. I found myself wishing we had more photos of her and the rest of my extended family. We barely had enough to fill one album. In fact, we didn't even have many photos of *us*—we didn't own a real camera, just an old Polaroid someone had given us.

I felt sad that I didn't really know my grandmother enough to miss her, and tried to think of anything else that might trigger a memory. Not just of her, but of Korea in general. What had I been thinking as I left there?

Fragments of memory, like glitter, reflected light and captured our final few moments in Korea. I took out my spiral notebook and wrote: *Memories Outside Kimpo Airport, April 18, 1975.* I remembered being mean to Chun-Ha because we were dressed in matching outfits, white shirts with blue-and-black checkered overalls; watching my dad standing among the men, smoking cigarettes, looking up at the sky and commenting on the good flying weather; thinking that my mother and aunts looked like clowns, with their mascara smeared by tears and lipstick smeared by goodbye kisses; smelling the faint scent of cinnamon on my grandmother's breath as she slipped a coin into my hand and told me it had magical powers to keep me safe, no matter where I was.

I remembered the chaos as we tried to organize ourselves for a final photo and dropping my magic coin in the confusion; my uncle telling me to look at the camera and smile; my mother telling me to smile, or else; my grandmother telling everyone to leave me alone.

I remembered the silence that fell like a giant white parachute over my mother, my dad, and my brother as we walked into the airport, and seeing my grandmother waving goodbye, looking down, my eyes desperately searching the ground for my magic coin. And just as I was about to lose all hope, I remembered the relief I felt when Chun-Ha slipped it back into my hand.

My mother and I joined a long line to get through Customs. We didn't realize we were in the wrong line until an airport worker, seeing the Canadian passports in our hands, redirected us to a much shorter line. I was pleased until I saw my mother's face, her eyes locked on the FOREIGNERS sign in front of us. I could see how anxious she was.

As we made our way out of baggage claims, more English signs greeted us, welcoming us to the "Land of the Morning Calm," and wishing us a happy stay. Colourful banners announcing the upcoming 1988 Olympic Games hung from the ceiling. I stuffed several glossy tourist brochures into my bag.

My mother's two younger sisters, my *kun emoh* (big aunt) and my *jag-eun emoh* (little aunt), met us. Everyone started crying, and I was both happy and relieved to hear my mother say it felt good to be back home.

"Oh, your pretty face," my *jag-eun emoh* said in Korean, touching my chin. "We were so sorry to hear about your accident."

I looked at my mother, but she distracted herself with her luggage.

The sisters talked non-stop, laughing occasionally, during our drive to my *kun emoh*'s home. Seoul had changed. I grew dizzy watching the colour-coded taxicabs speed in and out of the ten-lane city streets.

"The grey and white ones are basic, for cheap people," my younger aunt said from the front passenger seat. "The black ones are for the rich. Luxurious inside." She pointed to several in front of us.

"Almost as good as this car," my other aunt said, referring to her own vehicle.

I looked out at the endless rows of high-rise apartment buildings set against a dreary November sky. It made me claustrophobic. Were there any houses left in Seoul? This was not the Korea I remembered. I closed my eyes and tried to see the little house I had grown up in, a worn-down mountain in the background. I pressed my head against the seat and fell asleep.

*   *   *

"Why don't you rest?" my *kun emoh* said as soon as we walked into her apartment. "I saw you sleeping in the car."

She took the bag from my hand and led me to a room at the end of the hall. It smelled familiar, and I realized it was the same scent of the walnut oil that had been used to clean the wooden furniture in our rooms when we lived in Korea.

"You and your mother will be staying in here," my aunt said, and left me alone there.

The room looked like a den, with a wooden reading table, matching display cabinet, and an elegant four-pane folding panel with Korean calligraphy and brush paintings on them. The reading table was designed to be low to the ground so that one had to sit on the floor to read or study.

"*Ondol* floors! I've missed them," I heard my mother laugh in the other room. Korean homes used a network of underground flues to transport heat from room to room, which warmed the floors. Even my great-grandfather's rice-thatched house, made of clumsy earthen walls, had under-floor heating that made its rooms cozy and inviting.

My aunt had laid out two mats on the floor for us to sleep on, a pillow and neatly folded blanket at the end of each. I wished the room had a chair to sit on. I examined the pair of wooden ducks, traditional wedding presents that symbolized faithfulness, on the top shelf of the display cabinet and several celadon pottery vases next to them. The lower shelf had a few books, all hardcover and in Korean, except for an oversized copy of *Webster's New World Dictionary*, which seemed out of place.

I opened the cabinet drawers to find them perfectly organized, silk handkerchiefs in one, and documents, arranged in coloured folders, in another. It was the plain shoebox in the last drawer, however, that excited me.

Black-and-white photos spilled out of the box as soon as I took the lid off. A photo of my mother, my two *emoh*s, and a third woman I didn't know. A photo of my great-grandfather bent forward at almost ninety degrees, a mountain of straw tied to his back. Another photo showed him tying rice stalks for thatching. I wished that just once he had looked up for the camera, so I could get a better look at his face.

A head shot of my *harmony* made me pause. I realized just how much my mother resembled her mother. *Harmony* had her hair tied back as my mother often did. I'd forgotten about my grandmother's scar, high above her left eyebrow. Her eyes were big and beautiful, yet haunting, as if they held a million secrets.

To my surprise, in an envelope at the bottom of the box was a photo of a white soldier. I flipped the photo over. Someone had written in English: *Craig Dawson, Second Infantry Division, 1952*. Unlike my great-grandfather in his photos, Craig stared right into the camera and smiled, his teeth white against his military uniform and the backdrop of dark earth and a mountain distant in the background. Who was he?

I heard a male voice and quickly put the box back in the drawer. The door to the room was pushed wide open, and my aunt introduced a boy, who bowed formally to me. I bowed in return, and then wondered if I should have. I didn't know if he was younger or older than me. It turned out he was a neighbour's son, whom my aunt had invited over to entertain me.

My aunt brought us green tea, and we sat on the floor sipping it.

"If my English is good enough, I can get a job as a translator for the Olympics," he explained, seeming eager to talk with me.

"You have a British accent," I said. It sounded so strange—a Korean boy with such a foreign accent.

"I've spent the past three years studying in London," he said, and blushed.

I wanted to apologize. I'd forgotten the basic Korean courtesy of *kibun*—a strict code of etiquette meant to avoid upsetting anyone's feelings or injuring their dignity. This was likely keeping him from asking about my bruises.

"Have you been to the United States?" he said.

"No."

He seemed disappointed.

"I would like very much to visit the United States of America," he said. "But I'm afraid my chances are slim; my father hates the Americans."

"My father hates the Japanese."

The boy's eyes grew narrow. He sounded suspicious as he asked, "Can you blame him?"

"It's been more than thirty years."

The boy frowned, then, as if he had memorized his history textbooks, drilled off facts about how the Japanese had, during their colonization of Korea, exploited Korea's natural resources and tried to destroy the Korean culture and language. As he spoke, fragments of what my mother had told me years ago came to me: The Korean language was prohibited from being taught to or even spoken by Korean students in school. To attend school, my *harmony* had taken a Japanese name.

"Don't they teach you any of this in your schools?" the boy asked.

"No, we learn Canadian history."

"Which is just over a hundred years old," he said, and added, "Confederation, 1867."

I was surprised by his knowledge but tried not to show it. "We also study European history." I was beginning to feel defensive.

"Do you know anything about the Korean War?"

"Only that five hundred Canadian soldiers died in it."

"*Three million* Koreans died."

Well, obviously, I thought but didn't say. It was *their* war.

The boy seemed exasperated. "Did you even know that your *harmony* got the big scar on her head when her teacher beat her for writing a poem in Korean? That he hit her so hard with his baton he split her head open?"

My first thought was: My *harmony* wrote poetry? I felt a new bond with her. But the idea of someone—especially a teacher—hurting her made my stomach churn. I touched my bruised forehead. "I fell," I said, catching his eyes looking at my head. Then, before he could ask any questions, I asked, "What was her Japanese name?"

The boy looked back down. "I don't know," he said. "The only reason I know anything about your *harmony* is that she used to visit regularly along with your *emoh*, who is best friends with my mother." He paused. "I can't believe your ignorance. The Imperial Japanese Army kidnapped more than two hundred thousand Korean women to serve in their military brothels. They were routinely raped and tortured. Most of them died. How could you not hate the Japanese for what they've done?"

I was taken aback by his bluntness, but had to admit he was

right—I *was* ignorant. I wasn't even sure if what he was saying was true. It sounded too farfetched. An awkward silence followed. We were both relieved when my aunt called out for us to come and eat.

As we sat on the floor around the dinner table, my aunts talking over each other, I couldn't stop thinking about my grandmother.

"Are you okay?" the boy finally asked.

"I'm sure she misses her grandmother," my *kun emoh* answered for me. "So does my In-Suk. I wish she could be here with us tonight but she's busy preparing for her university exams. And her father, well, he's always very busy with his company. I hardly see him anymore."

Their conversation turned to complaining about their husbands. I was just relieved they were leaving me alone.

I couldn't fall asleep on the floor. My ribs still ached, even though I'd taken a pill. I turned and turned until finally my mother, annoyed, told me to stay still.

"How come you never told me how *Harmony* got her scar?" I asked. I felt stupid that the neighbour's boy, with his British accent and knowledge of Canadian history, knew such an important detail of my grandmother's life when I didn't. "Did you know she wrote poetry?"

"Your *harmony* also painted and sang. She was a happy woman even though she carried the heavy burden of producing no sons. She was an incredibly strong woman until . . ." Her voice trailed off. I sat up in the dark. "My *kun oni* disappeared and everything changed."

I was confused and asked her which sister she was referring to. Then, as if being in a foreign place gave her permission to speak freely, my mother told me about her *oni*, her sister Mi-Ra, a third aunt I hadn't known existed.

"Mi-Ra *oni*, being the oldest, had been sent north to care for an elderly aunt and uncle who lived in a tiny village. This was before war broke out in 1950. One day, as she was searching for food, she wandered into an area civilians weren't allowed to be in. She was taken and interrogated by UN soldiers assigned to guard the area. They were convinced she was a spy, but one American soldier took pity on her and, through the use of an interpreter, she was found innocent of any crime. She ended up falling in love with that soldier."

I got up, turned on the light, and found the photo of the soldier I'd seen earlier.

"Yes, she sent us that photo," my mother said, sitting up, her face white and emotionless. "He was only twenty-two years old. A college graduate. He'd just finished basic training before being assigned to the Main Line of Resistance." She stopped and took a deep breath before lying back down. She explained that the Main Line was where the UN forces once faced Chinese and North Korean troops across "no man's land." "We received two letters from her telling us how happy he made her," my mother said. "My cousin, who was like a brother to us, wanted to go up north and find her, but it was too dangerous. The war had begun. Our father didn't want to risk his nephew's life—even to get back *Harmony*'s beloved Mi-Ra." My mother paused. "When the war ended, we tried searching for her. I didn't know my sister very well; I was only eight or nine years old when all this happened. There were rumours that she'd gotten separated from her American soldier. My cousin spoke with his commanding officer, who told him he'd been sent back to America. What became of my sister, no one knew. Eventually we were forbidden to talk about her because it made your *harmony* so sad."

Tears fell down my mother's face as she stared at the ceiling. I wanted desperately to comfort her but didn't know what to do. I remembered the silk handkerchiefs in the drawers and offered her one. Then I put the photo box away, turned off the light, and lay back down. I couldn't stop thinking about my lost aunt. Why had no one searched for her since? I started to ask my mother but stopped when I realized what mattered in the moment.

I whispered, "I'm so sorry about *Harmony*."

I wanted to put my hand on her shoulder or arm, but she rolled away from me and told me to go to sleep. It didn't take long for her to roll back, and her gentle snoring finally helped ease me into a troubled sleep of my own.

My grandmother's funeral took place the next morning, the fifth day after her death. This was the first funeral I'd ever attended. Family and friends climbed an old mountain, covered with a light dusting of snow, to reach the family's temple. Clouds stood motionless above the city off in the distance, barely visible through the early winter mist. An old lady sang mournfully, while others in the funeral procession rang little bells or held burning incense. Everything, from the narrow pathways we meandered along to the ancient temple decorated with painted flowers, mythical beasts, and intricate patterns, felt magical to me. I looked at my mother. Her face relaxed, her steps light, there was a calmness to her I hadn't seen since she'd received the news of my *harmony*'s passing. Her peacefulness left me feeling at ease for the first time since we'd arrived in Korea.

Once we were inside the temple, a monk performed a series of prayers and rituals to keep evil from my grandmother's spirit, and to lead it towards the "pure land" or towards a good family for reincarnation. We bowed several times and made our way back outside. My uncle, who was really my mother's cousin, had already attended to the task of cremating my grandmother's body, and was now carrying her ashes. My grandmother had requested that they be scattered in the temple yard.

Another funeral ritual was taking place at the other side of the temple. The people there were observing the official end of the mourning period. Gathered around an old wagon, mourners placed blankets, clothes, shoes, towels, and other items into a pile. To my surprise, the women took off their coats, exposing themselves to the winter wind. They all wore traditional white *hanbok*, which they removed to reveal black western-style suits. They carefully placed the *hanbok* on top of the blankets and clothes before putting their coats back on. The men removed black armbands from their coat sleeves and placed them on top of the women's *hanbok*. A fire was lit and the pile was soon aflame, sending smoke in our direction.

My mother pointed to the wagon. "That's symbolic of the journey into the afterlife. The family has gathered all the things someone who has died needs to make such a trip." She looked back at where her mother's ashes were scattered. "After forty-nine days, the spirit needs to make the journey to the 'good land,' heaven"—she paused—"or back here with us." Looking up at the sky, she said, "We need to pray so your *harmony*'s spirit can be guided to a good place."

I knew she wanted to educate me in her Buddhist ways, but my mind began to wander. I thought about Erin and the Ouija board, and her dead father's spirit. I felt relieved I'd never have to see my friends' reactions to any of this. I visualized Linda, rubbing the cross she always wore, scared and suspicious of everything from the monk dressed in his colourful burial garb to the scent of incense and fire that filled the sombre mountain air.

The other family dispersed, and a little girl, no more than seven or eight, walked past me. Her top coat button was undone, revealing a black string at the end of which was an old bronze coin the size of a quarter with a square hole in the middle. My heart leaped. It reminded me of my magic coin, the last thing my grandmother had ever given me. It suddenly felt precious; more valuable and more important than anything else in the world. But where was my coin now? I'd forgotten about it over the years. The girl continued towards the outhouse at the far end of the temple yard and disappeared inside.

I wanted that coin.

I thought of following the little girl, tackling her if I had to inside the outhouse. No one would see us. Anything to make sure that I had a magic coin again. I heard my mother's voice calling from inside the temple, but, rather than answering, I stared at the little footsteps in the snow. I'd taken a step towards them when a woman—the little girl's mother?—walked by me. The opportunity lost, I turned and ran into the temple.

As everyone wailed and prayed on cue, I was consumed by thoughts of the magic coin. My eyes closed. I imagined my *harmony*'s eyes and the lost stories they held. I thought of the poems she'd dared to write as a child and the injuries she suffered for them. I thought of the pain she must have felt at the loss of her daughter Mi-Ra, and of my mother, who one day had left for the other side of the world, and hadn't come back. I wondered how my *harmony*'s spirit would ever find peace.

My thoughts returned to the little girl, who was probably long gone. Darkness seized me. I thought of my grandmother in pain, Delia in pain, my own pain. It was as if being on Korean soil had somehow freed me from the chains that had kept me silent. I didn't hold back the tears. As my mother and aunts rocked themselves in an uncontrollable sobbing, I lost myself in that chaos. I wept, out of sadness that I'd never know the woman who was my grandmother, but also out of sheer helplessness that someone had hurt me.

Finally, the darkness lifted, the tears stopped. I suddenly remembered where I'd last seen my magic coin—in the pocket of an old coat hanging in the back of my closet. A bell chimed in the distance. The smell of incense filled the room. Then, silence. I felt exhausted, yet strangely at peace. I took it as an invitation, a signal that it was time to let go, time to move on and try to find peace like my *harmony*.

"Why does your mother call you 'Mary'?" he asked, catching me off guard.

He was Joon-Ho, the boy who lived next door. He'd been given the task of keeping me entertained for the two days my mother was spending catching up with friends. We were at an eatery in the lower level of a mall after souvenir shopping. Because he was a few years older, his name was off-limits to me. Instead, I was expected to call him *opah*, which meant "older brother." Because I was younger, he was allowed to call me by my name.

It wasn't fair, but the Koreans had strict rules about names and how they could be used. Just as my friends would never think of calling their mothers and fathers by their first names, Koreans never called *anyone* older by name, regardless of who they were. Instead titles were assigned to show relationships. That was why I called my aunts *kun emoh*, "big maternal aunt," and *jag-eun emoh*, "little maternal aunt," without any names attached. Even husbands and wives avoided names, using terms of endearment instead.

My initial thought was that my name was none of his business, but then I found myself explaining, in detail, what had happened to Josh and me when we first enrolled in a Canadian school.

"That's no different from what the Japanese did to Koreans here," he said. He stared at the large bowl of noodles in front of him. "I didn't think they did things like that in Canada."

I nodded, pleased that I was changing his squeaky-clean image of Canada. "When my family first arrived in Toronto," I said, "we lived in government-subsidized housing. I used to wake up in the middle of the night because there were mice scratching in the walls. Once, I woke up and found five baby mice in my hair. I was so horrified I squeezed them to death trying to get them out."

"What about now? I thought everyone lived in big houses with front *and* back lawns. It's such a big country."

"We live above our store," I said, biting into my pizza.

"That must be dangerous," he said. My puzzled look forced him to explain. "Well, there's been a lot of tension between Korean shopkeepers and black customers reported in the news. You must know—L.A., New York . . . Do you get a lot of black customers?"

I thought back to what Josh had told me about an incident in L.A. involving a black customer who felt he'd been treated with disrespect by a Korean store owner. It upset some black people that the majority of small shops in some predominantly black neighbourhoods were Korean-owned. "But who else would do such work and allow themselves to be treated like sub-humans?" my mother had responded. "Only madmen would work such crazy hours and give up their entire lives!"

"No, it's not a problem." I took a big gulp of Coke. "We get along with everyone." The truth was we didn't have many black customers, and the vast majority of those who robbed us were white. The only other people who harassed us were the homeless who came into the store looking for a place to pee.

A group of teenagers sat at the table in front of us. One of them, a girl about my age with black-rimmed glasses and very short hair, made eye contact with me as she sat down. Then suddenly everyone at the table looked my way.

I whispered, "They're looking at me." I drew my hair onto my face, a feeble attempt to hide my bruises.

He turned around, but they were no longer looking.

"It's obvious to them that you're a foreigner," he said, going back to stirring his noodles.

"How?"

"Your hair? Your earrings? It's like a sixth sense for us. We just know. Besides," he said, between bites, "we're speaking in English."

My left hand touched the gold hoop dangling from my right ear. I glanced down at my grey Roots sweater and Levi's blue jeans. "I feel weird. It's strange with only Koreans everywhere. I don't have any close Korean friends back in Canada. I think there's fewer than a dozen of us in my whole school."

The boy tilted his head as if trying to envision me in a school setting. "You don't feel out of place . . . ?"

"I guess you get used to living in a multicultural city. Skin colour isn't a big deal once you get to know people."

"I don't see how," he said matter-of-factly. "It's the first thing you see—the first thing that separates everyone."

"Well, come visit Canada and see," I said. "Who knows, you might like it so much you'll want to live there. You wouldn't have to serve in the military or anything." I knew that he would have to enlist for his mandatory service in the spring.

"Why wouldn't I want to serve? It's my civic duty." He put his chopsticks down. "I would proudly lay down my life for my country."

"My father's oldest brother was killed during the war. War's stupid. Why do you think so many families move to Canada?"

"Life there doesn't sound all that great based on what you've told me."

I tossed my pizza crust on the tray, annoyed he had used what I'd told him against me.

Outside, the crisp winter air felt fresh and cleansing. I hoped it would clear some of the smells of kimchi and other Korean food from my coat and hair. But then, remembering I was in Korea, I relaxed and stopped feeling self-conscious the way I did back in Canada. The boy extended a hand to offer to carry some of my shopping bags, a gesture I appreciated, but he ruined it immediately when he said, "I bet you can't wait to get back home."

It wasn't what he said, but how he said it, implying I was merely a visitor in the country. The word *home* hung in the air, and I remembered Erin and her remark about going back home, *to* Korea. It hadn't annoyed me at the time, but it bothered me now in the same way the boy's comment had bothered me. He looked at me for a response, but I started walking. I was tired and bored with all his questions, his little insults, and his stupid accent, which irritated me more with each word.

"This has been the longest week of my life!" my mother said. She gently eased onto the mats on the floor.

It was true. She'd been keeping busy, every minute of her time occupied with seeing childhood friends or visiting temples. I'd only seen her in the past few days at breakfast and at night. She'd also never mentioned her sister Mi-Ra again.

"They think we live like kings," she said.

There was a bitterness in her voice as she talked about her old friends, and it made me strangely happy. I'd been feeling neglected by her constant need to be out and doing something, but never with me. In spite of our fatigue, neither of us was able to sleep well on the floor, even though my aunt had doubled the mats for us.

I watched as my mother's eyes scanned the small room, with its fancy reading table and cabinet, both probably fashioned by some master craftsman, unlike our furniture from the Brick back home. She never bought anything—clothes, furniture, even presents—unless it was on sale.

"Ah-goo, ah-goo!" my mother muttered. She wasn't used to sitting on the floor now and had taken to uttering the strangest sounds

as her legs bent clumsily under her. "Ji-Young and I started teaching together," she said as she peeled off her socks. "She had no idea what she was doing—had no sense of how to properly discipline children. I remember the first time she whipped a child, she ran to the bathroom and cried, because she felt sorry for the child! And now she's a principal. A principal! With her own office, and a secretary." My mother sighed deeply and told me to turn off the light. I hesitated, wondering if I should ask her if she was okay, or if she wanted to keep talking. I looked at her lying on the mat, eyes closed, one arm resting on her forehead. I switched the light off. Without a window in the room, we were thrown into darkness, which I think we both welcomed.

My dad's parents lived with their oldest son, his wife, and children in Busan, a three-hour train ride south of Seoul. We'd left this visit to the end, since my mother was not fond of her in-laws. Reluctantly, she'd packed a bag of gifts: whisky, cigarettes, shampoo and conditioner, and body lotions.

I sat by the window on the train. My spiral notebook and pen poked out of my handbag, reminding me I could use the time to write. As a child, I used to visit Busan with my dad. We always took the bus because it was cheaper. Some of my fondest childhood memories were of the ride itself. During each trip, my dad bought one hard-boiled egg and several small bags of steamed snails from the little old ladies who sold them outside the station. For the next several hours I'd sit on the bus, using a safety pin to dig out the snails, their empty shells falling all over the floor beneath me, no matter how hard I tried to keep them on my lap.

"That's the Han River." My mother nudged me.

Annoyed by her interruption, I looked out the window to see bluish grey water, and then Seoul, with its tall grey skyscrapers in the background, and beyond that, more endless grey sky. For a moment, I felt lost and disoriented. I ached for Toronto.

I had little memory of my paternal grandparents but I did remember my cousin Eun-Jin, now twenty-four years old, who'd spent some time studying in Seoul and had visited us regularly. She greeted me with a big hug and took me to her bedroom to catch up.

When she was fifteen, Eun-Jin's parents had sent her and her twin brother to study English in London. He was currently completing his master's degree in engineering at Cornell. Eun-Jin was completing her master's in international languages at Seoul National University. She spoke English, French, Spanish, Mandarin, Japanese, and, of course, Korean. "Have you had a chance to see much of Seoul?" she asked, her English, like Joon-Ho's, spoken with a British accent. She took my hand and sat me on the floor. "It must have changed so much since your family left, yes?" Her room was cluttered with paperback novels: *The Great Gatsby*, *Wuthering Heights*, *Jane Eyre*.

"So what do you plan to do after you graduate?" I asked, avoiding her question. I didn't feel like elaborating on my feelings and dreaded explaining yet again why my face looked the way it did. Instead, I stacked some of the novels that littered the floor into small piles. They stood like little pagodas around us.

My cousin shrugged and said, "Get married. Start a family."

"What kind of job can you get speaking so many languages here in Korea?"

"I think many North American women work by choice. The

competition for jobs in Korea is so fierce it isn't considered right for
women to take jobs away from the men."

"But you speak six languages," I said, waving a copy of *Crime and
Punishment* in the air. "You're so smart and talented. You could work
for the UN—"

Eun-Jin laughed. "You've always had such an imagination.
I don't know if you remember, but when you were six, when you
found out you were moving to Canada, you told me you were scared
because you thought your hair would turn yellow and your brown
eyes would turn either blue or green . . . Do you remember? You'd
confide all your secrets in me. And you didn't want to go. Now you
want me to go abroad too . . ."

I smiled, although I couldn't remember the incident she was talking about.

"Actually, I wanted to study law," she said, "but my mother
thought languages—literature, the arts—would attract a better
husband." Her eyes lit up, and she leaned over, knocking down my
paperback buildings.

"You must swear to secrecy," she said, and wrapped her hands
over mine.

I nodded. She confessed she was corresponding with a professor
she'd met and had an affair with during one of her exchange trips to
France.

"He writes to me in French. This way, my parents have no idea
what he's writing. In fact, they think he's a girl. He was clever
enough to send me a family photo with him and his sister in it."

The idea, however romantic, seemed hopeless to me.

"I have no idea what we'll do," she said. "I've been lucky recently.

My parents wanted me to marry someone they heard about through a marriage hunter, but when they did the clan background check, it turned out we were cousins, seven times removed! Can you believe my luck?"

I was sad for my cousin, but, at the same time, surrounded by her English novels, a warm and familiar energy between us, I felt relaxed. I'd just started to tell her this when we heard loud, accusatory voices coming from the living room. Eun-Jin and I jumped up and ran to see what was happening.

"But we've been sending money every month for the past ten years! You haven't seen any of it?" My mother's voice was so high-pitched it started cracking.

My grandparents looked like wilted flowers. Both nearly deaf, they shook their heads, and my grandfather looked up at my uncle, then at my aunt, who sat rigidly on recliners across from my grandparents.

"Go back to your room," my uncle ordered my cousin. She complied, and I followed.

Fifteen silent minutes later, my mother and I were back on the street, heading for the train station, her face as white as a ghost's.

"All this time, all this time your father and I've laboured in that store to send money back to our parents—your grandfather never knew. Your aunt and uncle have been using it. They've been to Hawaii, twice! When was the last time your father and I took a vacation?"

Outside the train station, my mother was breathless and wanted to sit down. We found a bench. I looked for the bag that had held the gifts, because I'd put a water bottle in it, but I realized it had been left behind at my grandparents'.

"They had the nerve to ask for more money! Can you believe that? Your aunt who has never worked a day in her life. So few women here have. Even when I lived here, I worked! My sisters—my friends—they stay home, take golf lessons, expensive vacations, and complain about how hard life is because their children won't listen to them, or because their husbands' mistresses are stupid enough to leave lipstick stains on their husbands' pants. Ha! Meanwhile, we work like animals sixteen hours a day, seven days a week, with people who complain we overcharge them and then steal from us, even attack our children—" My mother began sobbing.

I'd never seen her unravel so quickly and so completely. It was almost six o'clock and people, mostly men wearing dark coats over their suits, were rushing in and out of the train station, oblivious to us. Across the street was a row of vendors. I watched a group of men buy food from the carts before crossing the street. As they passed us to enter the station, they left behind a nauseating smell of dried squid and fish. Seeing my mother so helpless, I almost burst into tears myself.

For as long as I'd known her, though life had repeatedly tried to hurt her, my mother had worn her dignity like an invisible coat and refused to show her wounds to anyone. Now she sat, lost and vulnerable. I stood over her, trying to shield her from people. How could I help her, protect her, comfort her? I remembered the stone my dad had made using his fist. But I had no idea how to be that rock for her.

"Ai-goo-cham-neh!" a woman exclaimed.

I looked up. It was the Gucci lady from the airplane, the woman with the fancy jewelry.

"What are you two doing here?" she asked. "And what in

heaven is the matter?" She sat down next to my mother and, unlike me, seemed to know just what to do as she placed one hand on my mother's back and the other on her lap. They sat silently this way for some time, my mother's sobs gradually subsiding. A woman wearing a purple beret, her dog on a leash, caught my attention. There was a light energy in her walk. Even her dog seemed happy, its tail wagging enthusiastically.

"Times have changed since I last visited," the Gucci lady said. "I've never been so lost in this country."

I couldn't believe she was feeling out of place too. And although my mother said nothing, I knew that was exactly what she was feeling as well.

"You know," the lady said slowly. "I'm staying with my husband's sister's family. Vultures, they're all vultures. I told them how sick my husband was, but all his sister cared about were my rings, my watch. 'Take them!' I told them. 'Everything.'" She took off her leather gloves to show us her bare hands. "I've been sad too." My mother and I gasped in surprise.

"Come," the woman said and locked arms with my mother. "It's far too cold to be out here today. Let's go get a bite to eat. My treat. I know a place around the corner. It's not nearly as good as my restaurant, but it'll do." She smiled. "Yes, my husband and I own Little Seoul House on Bloor. You and your daughter must come visit it sometime." She paused, then added, "I have a daughter, probably around the same age as yours. I have a son too. Very bright. First year at the University of Toronto. Wants to be a doctor."

That got my mother's attention, and I knew a seed had been planted in her head for a future marriage match. She ran a hand over the lady's left wrist, where the watch and bracelet had been. "I'm very sorry you had to give them away . . ."

"Don't be!" the lady said and smiled. "They were all fakes!"

They laughed, and just like that, my mother was all right again. Relieved, I followed the two women, who looked like long-lost friends exchanging stories as they walked.

On the last day of our visit, I took the shoebox back out and removed a photo of my grandmother, one of my lost *emoh*, and one of my mother with her other two sisters. I stuck them in the back pages of my notebook, hoping no one would miss them.

Joon-Ho came to say goodbye. "I have a present for you," he said, and handed me a small gift bag.

Feeling bad that I had nothing for him, I scribbled my address on a piece of paper and invited him to write to me, or look me up should he ever visit Canada.

"Well, goodbye, then," he said, half bowing his head. He turned and left.

I looked in the bag. It was a beautiful origami swan of textured white paper, silky and soft to the touch. The bird's neck was long and elegant, and tied with a thin red ribbon. Joon-Ho had even glued on two black dots for eyes. I was touched by the unexpected gesture. I packed it with care.

Chapter 6

My parents completed a major renovation project as I began my final year of high school. The store next to ours, a flower shop, had gone out of business and my mother had bought the property. They combined the two spaces into a larger convenience store. When I saw my mother hanging a new paper lantern over the register, I got the idea to attach my magic coin to it. It dangled off a piece of string. "We finally have a lucky coin to match the store's name," I said.

A group of my parents' friends came to our home to celebrate. The Gucci lady who owned the Korean restaurant had a daughter my age, Kate, and the two of us had become friends. Unlike me, Kate had friends who were Korean and attended the same Christian church. Her brother, whom my mother had hoped would express an interest in me, ignored me whenever I visited.

"My mother wants me to have more white friends and bring them home," Kate had told me, "but I can't because our house smells Korean. What do you expect living above a restaurant? And besides, my father would probably scare them. Even when he's only talking, he sounds like he's screaming."

It felt good for once in my life to have a Korean friend.

Kate's parents brought several platters of food from their restaurant, which my mother accepted with thanks, though I knew it
annoyed her because she'd spent the day cooking for her guests.
Kate came along, and the two of us hung out in my bedroom.

"Your brother's kinda cute, eh?" she said.

"Josh?" I said, surprised. "He's younger than you."

"I know, I know," Kate said. She flopped onto my bed. "I'm not
into him or anything. I'm just saying . . ."

I told her that for the past few weeks I'd seen him holding hands
with a tall white girl named Andonia, who was new at school.

"My parents would kill me," Kate said. "If they even suspected I
liked someone, I'd be dead." Then she mimicked her father by dropping her voice. " 'I'll kill you if you don't listen to me. Go ahead, call
the police. I'll die in jail and rot in hell if I have to.' "

Unlike my dad, who, when he got drunk, started singing about
his glorious ancestors and passed out, Kate's father was violent. She
shared family stories that scared me. He had even pushed her mother
down a flight of stairs years ago, leaving her with a broken leg and
sprained wrist. But, Kate pointed out, what goes around comes around,
and her father had been diagnosed with liver complications the day her
mother's cast came off. He was forced to stop drinking. I was intrigued
by his twist in fate and the notion of karma, which my mother believed
was the heart of Buddhism. *What goes around really did come around.*

"That's pretty," Kate said, pointing to the origami swan hanging
on my dresser. "Did you make it? I've always wanted to learn how
to fold paper cranes."

"That's a swan. The guy I met in Korea gave it to me."

"Was he cute?"

I reached under my bed and pulled out a shoebox to show her a photo I had of Joon-Ho and me standing outside Changdeokgung Palace in Seoul.

"He must like you if he made that crane for you. Do you like him?"

Swan, I wanted to correct her, but didn't. Joon-Ho had annoyed me with his silly-sounding accent and smug attitude, but he'd also given me a gift.

"Is that your mom?" Kate asked. She reached into the box and took out a black-and-white photo.

"No, that's my lost *emoh*, but I'm not supposed to talk about her." I'd asked my mother about Aunt Mi-Ra a few times since our trip, but she always pursed her lips and I knew better than to press her.

Laughter drifted from the living room. A male voice, louder than the others, was talking about the awful plight of Korean immigrants in Toronto. Kate's eyes rolled.

"He's sooo embarrassing," she said. "You know why we came to Canada? My father had an affair with his boss's wife. It's one thing to have a mistress, most of them do, but your boss's wife? He lost his job. He used to be a hot-shot executive with Hyundai. Then he tried to start a company of his own, but that got nowhere, and word spread about his boss's wife. My mother couldn't take it anymore."

I thought about the first time I met Kate's mother on the plane. She'd told us their business had failed, but blamed it on the burial location of her husband's ancestor.

The men were singing now, Kate's father's loud voice off-key. "You can't sing!" a woman said laughingly. We didn't hear him again.

It was close to three in the morning when I woke up. Kate and I had fallen asleep on the floor. I poked my head out the bedroom door, which looked right into the living room. Everyone had left except for Kate's parents. Her father was yelling at her mother. His speech was slurred.

"She's right, you shouldn't drive," my dad said. "Give her the keys."

Kate's father started swearing at his wife, who pleaded with him to stop. His face was red, his jaws locked. He was about to strike her but my dad got in his way. As the two men struggled, both women begged them to stop, and Josh came out of his room, his eyes squinting as they adjusted to the light. Grabbing both men, he managed to separate them. Kate's father headed for the front door. Her mother started calling for Kate. I went back to my room, where she was still curled into a ball asleep on the floor.

"What happened?" she asked as I shook her awake. Then we heard her father screaming her name up the stairwell.

"He's drunk."

"But he hasn't had a drink in over a year," she said, rubbing her eyes.

"I'm sorry," I said, scared for her.

As soon as the family had left, I asked my mother how she could just let them go. What would Kate's father do once they were alone?

"It's none of our business." She started collecting plates off the coffee table.

"Don't you care?" I said slowly, then, growing more desperate, "Don't you care that your friend might get beaten up? Her husband's already broken her leg and God knows what else. She was there for you in Korea, remember? Now that she needs you, you're going to do nothing?"

My mother looked as if she was about to hit me. I felt tears running down my face. She took a step back. All the colour seemed to leave her face.

Looking around the living room, she said, "We'll clean up in the morning." Then she walked into the bedroom where my dad was already in bed, and closed the door.

For several weeks, I tried to reach Kate, but she never returned my calls. I even thought of going to her restaurant, but wondered if it might only get her into trouble. I was surprised at how much I missed her. It was nice having a Korean friend who could relate to what I experienced with my family. Although I didn't know why, I felt I owed her an apology. Eventually, I got angry at her for ignoring me, and decided to let the friendship go.

It wasn't until I was with my friends at Mr. Greenjeans months later, in the Eaton Centre, that I saw her again. This time we were celebrating Rubina's birthday.

"I can't wait till next year," Erin said, raising her mug of Coke. "We'll all be legal and can toast our birthdays with the real thing!"

We clinked our respective glasses and wished Rubina "Happy Eighteen."

As my friends and I were leaving, I noticed Kate and a guy in a booth. He was black. They were seated side by side, sharing a plate of pasta. I wondered how Kate's parents would react if they knew she was on a date—especially with a black boy. He laughed as he allowed her to feed him. With makeup on and her hair swept up, gold earrings hanging from her ears, Kate looked prettier than I'd ever seen her. *Her face is glowing,* I thought, *she's so happy.* I walked away before she could see me.

I'd just stepped off the streetcar near home and was standing on the corner waiting for the light to turn green when a young woman about my age approached and asked, "How're you doing?"

I didn't recognize her at first, but then realized it was Suzie X, dressed in a brown coat and jeans. I'd never seen her in pants before, and she was closer to my height without her four-inch heels. She walked with me.

"Sorry 'bout what happened to you," she said.

I stopped and looked at her. Without lipstick, her mouth looked shapeless, as if nothing coherent or intelligent could ever come out of it.

"I saw him coming out of your place. He pretty much ran outta there. He didn't see me being dropped off. Anyway, after he took off, I peeked inside and found you. I called the police, though I didn't give 'em my name or anything."

I felt as if I'd been struck in the chest. After telling almost everyone that what had happened to me was an accident, now I was being reminded of what really took place. The panic I'd left behind in Korea came rushing back. I didn't know if I should feel afraid someone outside my family and Rubina knew the truth.

I looked straight at her, but she stared down at my shoes. Both of us stayed silent, frozen in the middle of the sidewalk. A taxi slowed down and the driver leaned over and waved at me. It was Mato, a customer who came into our store every Saturday afternoon to buy thirteen lottery tickets.

"Need a ride anywhere?"

I shook my head. He waved and drove off.

"Anyway . . ." Suzie X said, looking up again. "I'm really sorry. He was a total creep and I don't know anything about him, so don't ask. I haven't seen him around since. I think he's left town."

I was relieved to hear that. "What's your name?"

"It's Mona Lisa," she said with an embarrassed smile, "like the painting." She rolled her eyes. "Yeah, stupid name, but hey, we don't name ourselves."

I wondered how she'd feel knowing my brother had called her Suzie X.

I smiled back and thanked her. I didn't know what else to do. After all, she'd called the police for me.

"See you around," she said. She did up the top button of her coat and walked ahead, past our store, until I could no longer see her.

I followed slowly behind, allowing this newfound information to sink in. Leon, like Delia, had moved on. I reminded myself I'd chosen to do the same.

Chapter 7

Josh used to work the Sunday-morning shift until he started going to church with his friends—actually, with his girlfriend, Andonia, a detail we kept from our parents. Now I was left to open at 7:00. At that hour, there was a stillness in the city that made being in the store so boring it was almost painful.

It was the last Sunday of May, and pouring. More than an hour had passed since I'd opened, and there hadn't been a single customer. Because my mother had insisted, I'd brought homework with me. I'd even decided to make use of my time and write something I could later share with Mr. Allen. But my mind refused to do anything but yawn. I went over to the magazine rack and flipped through several, hoping to find words or inspiring phrases to steal. Every teen magazine focused on the prom: fashion trends for the prom, makeup trends for the prom. There was even a piece on how to dress your date for the prom. I felt relieved my friends and I had agreed to go dateless.

An article entitled "How Eyebrows Can Make or Break Your Face" got my attention. I'd never plucked mine. Using the small magnetic mirror my mother kept attached to the side of the register, I studied my eyebrows.

"Ohmigod," I heard myself say. They were a mess from every angle.

I took a pair of $1.99 tweezers and started plucking my right brow. It wasn't as easy as the instructions suggested. When the area I'd plucked around my right eye turned red, I got nervous and moved on to my left eye. Getting the two brows to look alike proved impossible. I ran to the bathroom and stared at myself in the larger mirror. My eyelids were red and puffy. I looked at the clock: 8:15. Erin would kill me for calling her at that hour.

The door opened and I ran back inside the store. Mrs. O'Doherty walked in. She shook her umbrella and leaned it by the door.

"Mary, I brought you the record I promised to lend you. Boy, it's wetter out there than—" She stopped. "Good grief! What happened to your eyebrows?" She set the record album—Rachmaninoff's Piano Concerto No. 2—down. Seeing the magazine, she smiled and said, "Getting ready for the prom, are we?" Then, sensing my distress, she said, "Let me help you with that."

Before I could say yes or no, she was behind the counter. "The trick is to pluck one hair at a time," she said. There was a faint scent of peppermint on her breath. "You know, I raised three daughters— Teagan, Rosemary, and Siobhan. I'm surprised that at your age you don't wear any makeup."

"Your daughters have nice names," I said, but what I was really thinking was that I was eighteen and wore no makeup. The only thing I'd ever seen my mother apply to her face was Pond's cold cream, which we sold.

"So, do you have a dress for the prom yet?"

I shook my head.

"You know, you have a lovely face and a little makeup would help highlight your cheekbones."

I was flattered. No one had ever suggested I was pretty. I looked into Mrs. O'Doherty's blue eyes and thought for the first time that she must have been an attractive woman in her younger years. She carried herself with a quiet confidence, her face lightly made up with mascara, a trace of blush, and neutral lip gloss. In spite of the gloomy weather, she wore a pale yellow cotton dress. A slim black belt made her waist look smaller than mine.

"Is there any special boy you'd like to ask you to the prom?"

I didn't want to answer yes or no, so I just nodded as she tweaked my brows.

"There," she said as she finished.

I looked in the mirror. Although the skin around them was still puffy and red, my brows were even.

"Don't worry about the swelling," she said, and took a purple freezie out of the ice-cream cooler. "Put this over your brows for a minute. It'll take away the stinging."

I watched, freezie pressed against my head, as she walked back and forth, adding more items to the milk she had got from the back cooler, and placed her bag on the counter.

"So, tell me about this boy," she said.

"He's older," I said. "We talk about poetry and books. He's quite the reader. And he loves classical music. He even plays a little piano. I'll have to play this Rachmaninoff for him." And remembering the movie posters on his classroom walls, I added, "He's a real film buff. He's seen all the classics." I spoke with confidence although I didn't know much about Mr. Allen, including how old he was. Unfortunately, I couldn't tell white people's ages. I'd asked Erin, who guessed he must be in his late twenties.

"My Stephen—God rest his soul—was sixteen years older than me," she said, putting down a box of oatmeal cookies. She touched the cross she wore around her neck. "We were married thirty-seven years before he passed on. Age has nothing to do with love and happiness." She smiled. "Why, I was eighteen when I married. Stephen was the eldest of three brothers. We came to Canada during our honeymoon. Stephen wanted to start a new life here—didn't see much of a future back home. His father was a dairy farmer who wanted Stephen to take over his farm—which he had no desire to do. He wanted to study, you see. He had a real interest in architecture and designing." She opened her wallet to pay.

"If you like, you could leave your groceries here and I'll bring them over once Josh arrives—which won't be long," I told her. My mind was still focused on the fact that there had been such an age gap between the two and yet they'd made their relationship work.

She nodded. Her hand reached for the freezie.

"See there," she said, winking. "You look lovely. And with a little makeup, you'll be turning heads like I once did." She put the freezie back in the cooler.

"Did your husband ever become an architect?" I asked. I didn't want to be nosy, but I suddenly found myself intrigued by Mrs. O'Doherty.

"Not exactly." She sighed. "We came to Canada in 1916—there was the war. Times were hard. I got pregnant right away. Stephen found a job working for the *Toronto Star*—it may have been called something else back then. He did that until 1921, when the city took

over the TTC. He became a streetcar driver. I'd sometimes envy
him, meeting new people every day. Of course, I was at home with
my babies, and likely pregnant or on the verge of getting pregnant."
She shook her head. "The curse of being Irish Catholic."

I didn't quite understand what she meant, but it dawned on me
Mrs. O'Doherty had had a rich life, full of details I knew nothing
about. It also occurred to me that I didn't even know how my own
parents had met.

"I'd love to hear more about your life sometime," I said sincerely.

Mrs. O'Doherty seemed surprised and let out a soft laugh as she
waved goodbye.

After she left, I slipped the tweezers into my pocket and placed
a few magazines on fashion and makeup advice between my binder
pages. *So much to learn*, I told myself.

When Erin announced that she planned to attend the University of
Western Ontario because it was *the* party school, the rest of us felt
betrayed. Although we'd never said so, I'd always assumed we'd all
go to the University of Toronto.

Now that Erin was abandoning us, I too felt a strong desire
to leave Toronto, to get away from the store and my parents. I'd
planned to tread softly about the idea with my mother, but she saw
some of the different university brochures in my room.

"Why are you even *thinking* about some other school?" As far
as the Koreans were concerned, the University of Toronto was the
only university that existed in Canada. "It doesn't make any sense,"
she said. "Why throw money away when you've already got a place

to live? And what about the store? You want me to pay someone to help do your work while I'm also paying for your tuition? You think I have that kind of money?"

"I hate the store."

"Careful. Even white people have a saying about biting the hand that feeds them. Where do you think we'd be without it? When we first got to Canada your father and I were slaving away in a factory during the day, and catching night crawlers at night. No, no, no . . . At least this store is ours," she said. "When we first bought it, it was a dump. Now it's twice as big because we've all worked three times as hard. Why? So you and your brother can have a good life. A better life than anything your father and I will ever know."

I nodded but I was thinking I would be happier if the store burned down and my parents were forced to get regular nine-to-five jobs like my friends' parents, freeing Josh and me from a life of servitude.

I was even more depressed when, a few days after Erin's announcement, my mother's sister called to announce Joon-Ho's arrival. He'd been released from military service, receiving early discharge after an injury. He was coming to Canada to study at the University of Toronto.

"The last thing I need is a surrogate son to look after," my mother mumbled after she got off the phone.

"Why's he coming so early? It's June. Classes don't start till September."

My mother explained he was coming to study English for the summer at a language school before beginning university. He was enrolled in a Master of Engineering program.

"He has no family here," my mother said, "and we've been asked to help. He's renting a room near the university, so at least I don't have to cook for him."

"How's *kun emoh* doing?" I asked.

"Fine. I'd be fine too if I had nothing to do all day but play golf and take origami classes. Her daughter's off somewhere studying in another country—she never sees her husband, he works all the time."

I was beginning to feel sorry for my *emoh*—hers sounded like a lonely life.

"Then there's my other sister. She spends all day on her back trying to get pregnant." She stopped, shook her head, and told me to go practise the piano.

"And don't play anything too sad," she said. "There's enough of that already in my life."

"Do you miss your family back home?" I asked my dad. We were on our way to pick up Joon-Ho from the airport.

"My family's here, and this is my home."

I thought back to the night my mother and I got home from our trip to Korea. She was still in a rage about all the money they'd sent to his parents over the years. "No more!" she shouted. "I'm not breaking my back to support your stupid brother and his stupid wife."

My dad said nothing, and I never heard of that matter again.

I wondered what injury Joon-Ho could have sustained for the army to let him go early, and was almost disappointed to see him looking his usual self. He bowed, and my dad took one of his bags.

As we drove to his rented room, he explained in Korean for my dad to understand, "During combat training, I shattered my left fibula and tibia. They broke in seven places. The doctors initially told my parents I'd never walk again. But after surgery, two steel plates, sixteen screws to keep them in place, a graft where they took chunks of skin from my upper left thigh, and months of physiotherapy, I was able to walk again. My parents pleaded with my superiors to let me go, since I was their only son—and only child. And they did."

I found his story anti-climactic, but my dad seemed interested. He asked Joon-Ho questions about the army that bored me, and I regretted coming along for the ride.

A couple of days after his arrival, Joon-Ho visited us. I showed him around the store, which took less than two minutes, then took him upstairs. He met Josh, and as they began talking about guitars and music, I went to my room. Eventually, Joon-Ho showed up at my door. His face lit up when he saw the origami swan he'd given me hanging from my dresser mirror.

"It looks like two swans," he said, staring at the swan and its reflection. "Swans mate for life, did you know?"

I felt irritated by what I took to be his assumption.

"What happened to the eyes?" he asked. "I remember gluing two dots on the head."

"They fell off," I said, and wondered how blind swans fended for themselves in real life.

I asked Joon-Ho if he was hungry. My mother had told me to feed him something, so I got cold noodles out of the fridge for him and Josh. Grateful that my brother was around to entertain him, I slipped out. I wanted to look for prom shoes before the shops closed.

*   *   *

As I waited for the last student to leave Mr. Allen's classroom so that I could chat with him, I stared at Audrey Hepburn in a poster for *Breakfast at Tiffany's*. Old posters hung above the blackboards and windows, all four walls decorated with images of actors and actresses from films such as *Casablanca*, *Gone with the Wind*, and *Godzilla vs. The Thing*. Mr. Allen had joked we could escape into them if we got bored with his lectures. Audrey's hourglass figure in a sleeveless black dress was stunning. I wondered if I could find the same dress in a vintage store up at Kensington Market. Maybe wear it for the prom? Surely then Mr. Allen would see I was no longer the immature student he'd taught years ago.

"It's a wonderful movie. Ahead of its time," Mr. Allen said.

He was wearing a cream-coloured shirt and a black tie with red music notes on it. I looked into his eyes trying to determine their exact shade of blue, but lost my nerve and looked away before I could decide.

"My mother threw out the brochures Queen's University sent me," I said, and walked away from Ms. Hepburn and her perfect body towards Mr. Allen's desk. "I found them in the garbage, still in the envelope." I dropped my backpack on a chair.

"It's a great school," he said. "Great English department."

"Well, I'm pretty much stuck going to U of T. My parents need me at the store. My mother thinks it would be a good idea to consider a business degree. Or law. She doesn't see much of a point in getting an English degree."

"It's your life, Mary," he said.

What a typical white comment to make. He had no idea. If it were anybody else, I wouldn't feel the need to explain.

"You have no idea how hard my parents work. I owe them everything. Unless you own a store, you can't imagine what a burden it is." My defensiveness surprised me, yet I was too embarrassed to share what sometimes happened at the store.

Recently, my mother had gotten into an argument with a shoplifter who left empty-handed, screaming obscenities, telling her to take her "chinky self back to China." Two days before that a homeless guy had demanded to use the washroom. When I told him no, he pulled his pants down and relieved himself right there on the floor.

"Maybe I don't understand." Mr. Allen paused. "Where's your store anyway?" When I told him, he smiled. "I know where it is. I used to play ball at Trinity Bellwoods Park. I had an agoraphobic aunt who lived above one of the shops till she passed away." He looked thoughtful. "There's a movie I want you to watch. Do you have a VCR? I'll drop it off this weekend. It's an oldie but there's a message in it I think you need to hear, Mary."

Before I could say anything, he looked at his watch and said he needed to run.

I stood by the lockers watching as Mr. Allen, briefcase in one hand and bag full of student assignments in the other, headed for the stairwell at the end of the hall. My heart was racing. I'd be seeing him outside school for the first time. He cared enough about me to go out of his way on a weekend. I thought back to Audrey Hepburn—what would she wear if she worked in a variety store? Not that she'd ever have to stoop that low. I waited, hoping Mr. Allen would look back and wave goodbye, but he didn't.

*   *   *

The movie was *Guess Who's Coming to Dinner* with Sidney Poitier, an actor I'd never heard of. I sat through most of the movie angry at my mother for making me miss Mr. Allen—he'd come during the thirty minutes I was forced to practise the piano—wondering why he'd wanted me to watch a story about a black and white couple in San Francisco and the discrimination they faced. But then, near the film's end, John, the main character, told his father his life was his own to live—that he didn't owe his father anything. I stopped the movie and rewound it several times, absorbing John's words, casting my mother in the scene so she could hear me say, *I owe you nothing. You labour in the store like a slave because you're supposed to. I never asked to be born, but you brought me into this world, so you owe me the best of everything you can provide for me.* I imagined the expression on my mother's face. I couldn't live here the way she did, thinking like a Korean woman, trapped in her Korean upbringing and values.

But unlike John in the movie, I'd stop short of telling her I loved her. It wasn't the Korean way.

"I want a Canadian name," Joon-Ho said one day when we were working in the store together. "What name do you think is a good one for me?"

It seemed like such a huge responsibility. I immediately thought of Dunstan Ramsay and the impact being renamed had on him in *Fifth Business*, a novel we were studying in English class.

Joon-Ho was flipping through one of the parenting magazines we sold. It listed the top one hundred most popular names for boys.

"How about Michael?" he asked.

I shook my head. "Almost every other Korean is a Michael."

"Kevin? Benjamin? Anthony?"

I shook my head each time. He seemed too Korean for me to see him fitting into any of them.

"Andrew? David?"

"There's already too many Koreans with those names," I said.

"James?"

It was a name I'd always been fond of. I liked it too much to let him have it.

He flipped through several pages. "Patrick?"

"Too Irish."

"Sean?" He paused, said it again, and added, "Connery. Like Double-O-Seven."

I tilted my head. Even said with his British accent, the name didn't fit. Or did it? I thought, for the first time, that his eyes were rather attractive, with a double fold most Koreans weren't born with.

"I used to know a Sean," I told him, thinking about the first crush I'd had on a boy. "He turned out to be an idiot."

Chapter 8

*E*rin betrayed the group again. She had a prom date. We'd all agreed to go dateless but now she had a boyfriend, Jake, from whom she was inseparable.

"The tables sit eight," Erin said. "Let's all bring someone."

There were supposed to be four of us going: Erin, Linda, Rubina, and myself, but in the end Rubina wasn't allowed to go. Her parents didn't believe in the prom.

That's how I ended up asking Joon-Ho.

I introduced him on prom night as Sean. When I told my friends he was in Canada to study engineering at U of T, they seemed impressed, especially Erin, who told him repeatedly that she liked his British accent.

"He's cute, eh?" she said. We were in the washroom reapplying lipstick after dinner. "My God—he's working on his master's degree." She was wearing a neon pink dress with such large puffy sleeves I thought they'd sprout wings and scoop her away.

It wasn't until Erin started making a big deal about Joon-Ho that I began feeling possessive of him. I silently cursed her boyfriend for getting sick and cancelling at the last minute. Linda hadn't bothered asking anyone. Had I known I'd be the only one with a date, I'd have gladly made some excuse to Joon-Ho.

"So, do you really like him?" Erin asked, gazing into the mirror. Her lipstick was Barbie-doll pink, complete with sparkles.

I shrugged. A girl in a blue floral dress rushed into the washroom. Before she could reach a stall, she threw up, her white orchid corsage falling into the mess. Both Erin and I jumped out of the way.

"Gross," Erin whispered, pinching her nose. "*She's* had one too many." She grabbed my hand and we left.

I was wondering if we should have helped the girl or told a teacher about her when I saw Mr. Allen. I hadn't seen him in a suit before and he looked beautiful. My heart started pounding and my cheeks grew warm.

"You go ahead. I need to ask Mr. Allen something," I told Erin.

"You need to make up your mind about which guy you're chasing," she said, and slipped away before I could respond.

When I walked up to him, Mr. Allen smiled. "Mary," he said, "you look lovely. I don't think I've ever seen you in so much black before."

I looked down at my full-length evening gown and willed myself not to sweat. Unlike Audrey Hepburn, I decided I wasn't yet ready to go sleeveless. Still, I was hoping a simple black dress would make me look older and create an illusion of sophistication. A love song began to play and I felt dizzy as I wondered what it would be like to be in Mr. Allen's arms. I even imagined passing out. He'd be forced to catch me.

"You look great too," I said. "I love your tie." I was tempted to reach out and trace the tangerine-coloured paisley designs that looked so sharp against his light blue dress shirt.

"This is about the only dance I don't mind chaperoning," he said, scanning the banquet hall.

It was crowded with boys in dark suits and girls in big bright dresses, many of them with layers of ruffles and thick shoulder pads that reminded me of characters from the TV soap opera *Dynasty*. A handful of girls had chosen to wear ethnic dresses, silk Indian saris and colourful traditional Chinese dresses. One girl wore a red silk kimono with large white cranes on it. She even wore Japanese geta sandals.

"It's wonderful to see everyone celebrating," Mr. Allen said. "But I notice that Rubina isn't with you girls tonight."

"No, her parents wouldn't let her come. They disapprove of dances." Then, seeing Joon-Ho look my way, I added, "Mine only let me come so long as my cousin came along. He's visiting us from Korea. He was in the army until he got hurt. Broke his leg in seven places. He's studying engineering . . ." My voice trailed off when I noticed Mr. Allen's attention turn to Ms. Nakamura, one of the music teachers. She was talking with the DJ. Even I had to admit she looked great in her short cherry red dress, which made me feel like a nun in my head-to-toe black.

"That's exciting, about your cousin I mean . . ." Mr. Allen said, his eyes still on Ms. Nakamura. "Please make sure to introduce me to him before you leave." With that, he excused himself and walked in her direction.

"I just love your accent," Erin was telling Joon-Ho yet again as I got back to the table. "It sounds sooo sophisticated." Then turning to me, she said, "Did you know that Sean spent time studying in London?"

I shot her a look, which she ignored. She took a big gulp of Coke and stared at the lipstick stain on her glass before saying, "Linda, take a picture of us." She picked Joon-Ho's camera off the table and passed it over before posing close to him.

Linda looked down at the camera. "A Kodak Disc 4000. I've seen these on TV. Was it expensive?"

Before he could reply, she asked, "Do you have proms in Korea?"

While I appreciated her clumsy attempt to divert attention away from Erin, I was growing more and more annoyed that Joon-Ho had become the focus of all the conversations at our table.

"Yes," he said. "But we had more of a formal dinner."

Michael Jackson's "Thriller" was playing now, and everyone around us got up and headed for the dance floor. "Dance with me?" Erin asked and burst out laughing, revealing pink lipstick-stained teeth.

"Are you high—?" I asked.

"So you were saying there's no dancing . . ." Linda piped up and forced a smile.

"I like to dance, but I have to be careful," Joon-Ho said, and explained his leg injury. Capitalizing on his enthralled audience, he rolled up his pant leg to reveal his scar.

"I wanna kiss it . . . can I?" Erin giggled.

Disgusted, I got up and headed for the washroom again. Linda followed.

"What the hell is she doing?" I said. Looking in the mirror, I couldn't believe how angry I appeared.

"You shouldn't be surprised. She always gets this way today," Linda reminded me.

Then I remembered. Today was the anniversary of the day Erin's father had hanged himself. I had a flashback to the summer we'd used the Ouija board to invoke his spirit to answer our question "Who among us will get married first?" I sighed. Perhaps what we should have asked was whether our friendship would survive past prom, past graduation, and into the lives that awaited each of us beyond the walls of high school.

I looked around the washroom. Although someone had cleaned up after the girl who had gotten sick, and probably others too, the air was thick with the stink of vomit, alcohol, and cheap fragrances. *I've got to stop coming in here,* I thought. *I've got to stop running away from what I want.* I also had to accept that Erin was who she was and did what she did because she was hurting.

Out in the hall, I scanned the room for Mr. Allen. I spotted him under the balloon drop where the prom king and queen would be announced later, ending the night. He moved from group to group, chatting with everyone. I wanted so badly to ask him to dance.

But the night passed, most of the songs fast with everyone dancing in a crowd. I slow-danced with Joon-Ho three times, although in my imagination I was with Mr. Allen. I was in the washroom yet again when the last dance was announced, a slow song. When I came out, Erin was dancing with Joon-Ho, her body pressed into his, her arms thrown over his shoulders.

"Looks like your 'cousin' has found a new friend," Linda teased.

"What?" I asked, more annoyed than confused.

"Mr. Allen came by and wanted to meet your 'cousin' from Korea," she added, and laughed. "God, you have such a pathetic crush on the man . . ."

I missed him! Suddenly the air in the room was thick, the music too loud, and I was ready to leave.

"You look especially beautiful tonight," Joon-Ho said as we walked outside. He took my hand in his.

I'd never had my hand held before, and it felt nice, especially in the cool night air. The moon was full and glowing. We walked in silence, his blazer over my shoulders keeping me warm. It held a faint scent of cologne I could easily imagine Mr. Allen wearing. We eventually hailed a taxi, which stopped first in front of the store.

"Thank you for inviting me tonight," Joon-Ho said.

"Let me pay for the ride," I offered. The cab had already run over twenty dollars. Joon-Ho shook his head and brushed my hand away from my purse.

"No," I said. "You were my guest. I have money."

Joon-Ho wrapped his right hand around both of mine, crushing my wallet between them.

"Hey! That hurt."

He released his grip, but didn't apologize. *"Mar-joom-duhrah,"* he said, "Listen to me."

He'd switched to Korean deliberately, I was sure, because Korean, unlike English, distinguishes degrees of politeness and authority when one is talking "up" or "down" to someone. I couldn't believe he was giving me an order, as one would a subordinate or a wife!

I saw the driver watching us in his rear-view mirror.

"Everything okay back there?" he asked.

"Fine," I said, and got out, slamming the door.

"You're back sooner than I expected," my mother said.

I was annoyed to see Kate's mother was over again. The two

women were in the living room watching videos of Korean soap operas they'd rented from a nearby Korean grocery store. A plate of shrimp-flavoured chips and cups of tea sat on the coffee table.

My mother stopped the video. "How was it?"

"A nightmare like the rest of my life." I was too tired to pretend otherwise.

"You're always so dramatic," my mother said.

"They all are," said Kate's mother.

"I hope you had *some* fun. Your dress cost enough."

"I'll pay you back," I snapped before mumbling good-night to Kate's mother and walking to my room.

"At least your daughter's in school instead of wasting her life like my useless child," I heard Kate's mother say. "Thank goodness my son's doing well. Top of his class."

"Josh is doing well in school too," my mother said. "We're hoping he'll get a scholarship down the road—"

I closed my door behind me and collapsed on the bed, reaching around for my blue scarf to wipe away my tears.

The idea that I owed my mother nothing continued to haunt me as the fantasy scene based on *Guess Who's Coming to Dinner* played over and over in my head, first in Korean, then in English. There was something about the words being spoken in English that conveyed more power each time I said them. I was a Korean Audrey Hepburn delivering a dramatic monologue that I'd written.

English was beautiful, I thought, because it was free from the honorifics of the Korean language that placed everyone within a strict social hierarchy. I decided I would major in English.

Chapter 9

$\mathcal{J}$ was angry the day Josh left for a summer retreat with his church friends. He'd be gone for a month. "He's not even Christian," I yelled at the TV before turning it off. Now I was stuck doing his share of work.

I went into his room. Though he'd taken his guitar, the stand had been left behind. The two small hooks that kept the instrument upright looked like open arms with nothing to hold.

"Only a poet would think that a guitar stand could be sad," Joon-Ho said later when I shared the thought with him. Though he hadn't meant it as a compliment, his comment made me happy. He'd been spending a lot of time in the store, helping my dad reorganize and rewire the older part that hadn't yet been renovated. Sometimes he even worked at the cash, covering Josh's shifts. My mother offered to pay him, but Joon-Ho politely declined, letting her know he didn't need the money, and welcomed the opportunity to improve his English.

"The boy's a genius," my dad said. "The way he thinks—he's methodical, innovative, creative even."

It irritated me that my dad, just like my friends, thought so highly of Joon-Ho. "He's an engineer," I'd remind him. "He's trained to think that way."

It was late afternoon but still blazing hot outside. All the plants my mother kept against the window behind the store counter were wilting except for the cacti. *It's only mid-July*, I thought. *The real heat hasn't even hit us yet.* My mother was upstairs preparing dinner. I was at the cash, ringing in a flow of cold drinks and ice cream. Joon-Ho and my dad were fixing a shelf that had come off the wall, causing a row of cereal boxes to fall onto stacks of tuna cans before they all crashed to the floor. I was thankful no customers were under it at the time; they might have threatened to sue over a concussion from a direct hit with a box of Post Honey Bunches of Oats. Something like that had happened in Mr. Young's variety store.

Mona (I'd finally stopped thinking of her as Suzie X) came into the store, fanning her face with her hand. "I hate this weather," she said. "The guys stink worse than a bucket of rotten fish." She set a box of condoms on the counter and then pointed to her brand of cigarettes behind me.

As I placed them next to the condoms, I caught a glimpse of my dad in the security mirror hanging off the ceiling. He was using two plastic milk crates as a stepping stone to get on top of a stack of four crates. *That can't be good*, I thought. They needed another ladder. Why wasn't Joon-Ho on the crates instead? The aisles were so narrow. If my dad fell . . .

Then, as if reading my mind, he wobbled. My heart jerked, but he found his balance. He even gave Joon-Ho a quick thumbs-up. He turned and tugged on the bracket he wanted to reposition, and suddenly became all arms and legs, crashing into a shelf of canned vegetables, stews, and gravy.

"Ohmigod," Mona gasped. "Is he okay?"

I dialed 911.

"Don't move him," I yelled to Joon-Ho, repeating what the dispatcher was telling me. "They want to know if he has a pulse."

"He's unconscious, but breathing."

"Any sign of blood?"

"No."

The dispatcher asked how old my dad was. I couldn't think straight.

"Get my mother," I told Mona. She grabbed the condoms and cigarettes and ran out. "He was born in 1936. How old would that make him?" I asked. I squeezed my eyes shut and struggled to calculate as the voice on the phone told me to remain calm.

My mother ran down, her kimchi-stained apron still on. She cried out when she saw my dad, and ran to him, grabbing and tossing the cans from under his body. Joon-Ho had to pull her away. Her panic had me on the verge of tears.

The ambulance came with sirens blasting, its red lights streaming into the store. My mother took a deep breath, then another, and as the paramedics tended to my dad, she left to go upstairs. Minutes later, she returned, the apron gone, her purse in hand. There was a coolness about her now, a resolve, and I felt better.

As the ambulance drove my parents away, I stood in the doorway, desperately wishing Josh was home.

"He'll be fine," Joon-Ho said, though he avoided eye contact.

I wanted him to reassure me again, but he silently looked over the damage. Then he went to work, fixing the shelves my dad had fallen on.

"Were you robbed or something?" Mato had come in to purchase his usual thirteen lottery tickets while we were still cleaning up.

"No."

"Tonight's the night," he said, kissing his lottery picks before handing them to me.

"My dad fell," I said, "trying to fix that shelf."

Mato turned. Eyeing the top shelf, sloped and threatening to fall, he asked Joon-Ho, "Do you need a hand?"

Joon-Ho said he could manage.

Turning back to me, Mato asked, "Is your dad all right? I told him I'd share my winnings if I ever won big."

As I rang in the lottery purchases, I caught a glimpse of Joon-Ho getting on top of the crates. "No!" I yelled. "Don't go climbing those yourself." I thought of his bad leg and in a flash saw him falling, just as my dad had. But he was already on top, asking Mato to hand him a screwdriver.

The shelf was secured within minutes, and Mato and I handed Joon-Ho the cereal boxes to put back in place. Soon everything looked as it always did.

"Maybe tonight I'll win for sure," Mato said. "For doing a good deed." He smiled and waved as he headed for the door. "No more driving all day in a taxi for Mato."

I took a can of Coke from the cooler and offered it to Joon-Ho. "You're good with your hands," I told him, and realized I was repeating my dad's words. But I wanted to let him know his efforts were appreciated.

My mother called a while later. My dad was conscious but had injured his back. He'd be fine, she reassured me, though he had to stay in the hospital overnight. "I'm on my way back now to lock up the store," she said.

"Joon-Ho's still here," I told her. "We can do that. You should stay there."

I hung up and took a deep breath before sharing the good news.

At exactly 11:00 p.m., we turned off the store sign. Joon-Ho mopped up the floor, just as my dad would have, and I washed down the counter and removed all the money from the cash, just as my mother would have. I'd never closed the store without my parents before; I didn't even know the alarm code, but I had a key to lock up.

The air outside was now cooler and more welcoming. I invited Joon-Ho upstairs for something to eat. We'd managed the store on our own and my dad would be okay. The heavy scent of garlic and cabbage filled the apartment. My mother had left kimchi out on the cutting board and lotus roots marinating in soy sauce. I placed them in two small bowls with some rice and took the food over to the coffee table.

"What a day," Joon-Ho said, before taking a bite.

I offered him *soju*. He seemed surprised when I poured myself a shot too, but didn't say anything. We turned on the TV and saw a news clip about the Olympic Games, which would begin in September.

I glanced over at Joon-Ho. It was nice to see him so relaxed and unassuming, his body slouched deep into the sofa, his head tossed back.

"Yu-Rhee-ah," he said, "life is strange." His eyes closed, he continued. "A few years ago, I would never have imagined I would be in Canada when Korea was hosting the Olympic Games. I would never have thought of leaving Korea."

I had not heard my Korean name in a very long time. It was like hearing a lost tune, haunting and lovely.

"Say it again." The words came out before I could stop them.

He opened his eyes. "Say what?"

"My name."

"It's a beautiful name," he said. "Yu-Rhee."

I breathed it in, suddenly conscious that we were completely alone. I wasn't sure if it was the *soju* or something else stirring in me, but I felt light-headed.

"Well, you can watch the games here," I said. "You could root for the Koreans, and I'll root for the Canadians. It'll be fun." I looked down at his hand resting on the sofa between us and wished he would hold mine. If I moved in even just slightly, our legs would touch. He still owed me a kiss from prom night.

Joon-Ho asked, "If two athletes were competing for the gold, a Korean and a Canadian, who would you want to win?"

"I'd be happy if either won," I said, sensing a trap.

He sat up and faced me. "I got injured serving our country."

"You got injured during basic training."

"Combat training—with weapons." He grabbed an invisible stick, holding it like a baseball bat. "My leg was broken in seven places." He sat back so hard his head banged against the wall. I could have laughed, but didn't; he'd ruined my happy moment.

"You should have seen your face when I said your name," he said. "You can't deny who you are."

"Now you sound like my mother," I said. "You should go now."

"I'm not leaving you alone. I'll sleep in your brother's bed and help you open the store in the morning."

"Fine," I said, annoyed yet relieved. "You'd better get some sleep. The store opens at 7 a.m.—sharp."

"I know."

I left the empty bowls on the coffee table, but took the two shot glasses and rinsed them before putting them away. Going to my room, I shut the door and collapsed on the bed.

I woke up around 3 a.m. to go to the bathroom. Peeking into Josh's room, I saw Joon-Ho fast asleep on top of the covers. "At least you don't snore," I muttered. I grabbed a light blanket from the closet and took it to him. I thought back to him calling me by my Korean name. I traced a finger along his arm to his shoulder, and then gently touched his lips. What would I say if he woke up? I leaned in and brushed my lips against his, part of me wishing he'd wake up and kiss me back. My first kiss. But he didn't stir. I wondered if I'd be willing to pay the price of marrying a Korean man just to hear my birth name again.

The phone was ringing. I rubbed my eyes awake and saw the time: 8:27. *Ohmigod*, I thought. *The store.*

I ran into Josh's room. Joon-Ho was gone, and the blanket I'd covered him with was folded neatly into a square at the foot of the bed.

In the living room, I saw that the black money bag I'd left on the coffee table was gone too.

I raced downstairs to find that the flowers and plants had been laid out in front of the store as usual. My heart calming, I entered the store. Joon-Ho was restocking the drink cooler.

"We went through a lot of this yesterday," he said when he saw me.

I looked around. The newspapers had been laid out and the coffeepot sat two-thirds full.

"Did you call upstairs?" I asked.

Joon-Ho shook his head. He turned to face me, and I laughed when I realized he was wearing one of Josh's T-shirts, one with a Calvin and Hobbes cartoon on it.

"You look good in that," I told him. "Not so serious like in your own clothes." Though he was usually in jeans, his shirts always had collars.

A cab pulled up and my mother got out.

"He's fine, but the doctors want to keep him another day or two to run some tests. The taxi's waiting. I'm just going to get some of his things." She looked around the store and nodded. "It's Sunday—no deliveries today, you'll be fine." Then to Joon-Ho, she said, "Thank you for being here so early to help Mary. Our family appreciates all your help." She patted his arm, and he bowed his head. As she left, my mother said to me, "Good job with the store."

"I'll tell her later that you opened the store," I said.

"There's no need." And with that Joon-Ho disappeared to the basement to get more cases of pop.

The phone rang. It was Erin. "I forgot you were working this morning. I called upstairs a few times. I hope I didn't wake your parents."

I was about to explain what had happened when she blurted out, "I'm in trouble."

"Like, *trouble* trouble?" I asked.

"I think so," Erin whispered.

Stupid girl! I thought. "You should make sure. Have you taken a pregnancy test yet?"

"No," she said. "I'm just late—almost two months as of today."

"Does Jake know?" I wondered how much money he made selling movie tickets at the Cineplex. Would he offer to marry her?

"Are you frigging kidding me?" Erin shot back. "You're not helping."

"Well, we sell the test if you want to come over."

She arrived within half an hour. I slipped a pregnancy-test kit into a paper bag. It felt as if I were stealing from Joon-Ho's store instead of my parents'.

"Why's he here anyway?" Erin asked as we went upstairs. I explained what had happened.

"So you guys were here alone all night?" Erin said. "So . . . did you? You know . . ."

I shook my head. "I don't think of him that way."

"You should. *I* would!" she teased.

Of course you would, I thought. *That's why you're here on a Sunday morning taking a pregnancy test.*

When the test showed a negative reading, Erin let out a long breath. "Maybe it's all just stress and stuff. You know—graduation, university. Wow. Thank God, because I always thought it'd be me, you know, messing up first, because Rubina and Linda, well, they'll probably die virgins—and you . . ." Her voice trailed off, but then she said, "Sean's a good catch. I'm being serious now. You should give him a chance."

"He's sooo Korean," I said. An image of us dressed in traditional wedding attire flashed through my mind: me, a Christmas tree, in a bright red wrap-around skirt with a giant ribbon keeping my apple green jacket closed, wearing a gold crown headpiece; Joon-Ho, a giant blue package complete with a black bow sitting on his head—not exactly the gift I wanted.

"That's why he's perfect for you. He's the same as you. He's smart, really cute, and it's obvious he likes you."

I shook my head. I refused to think of a life spent elbow-deep in kimchi.

"Don't tell me you're still thinking about Mr. Allen."

I bit my lower lip and shook my head. *Would it be so crazy?* A life spent baking chocolate chip cupcakes and banana bread.

"You're eighteen. You need to move on. God knows, you don't want to end up like Linda or Rubina. You know, girls who accept their fate without question. Sex is great. You oughta try it sometime."

Easy to say, I thought, *now you know you aren't pregnant.*

"You know what your problem is? You Asian girls—you always need permission before you can do anything."

I wanted to be offended, but realized she was right.

"Well, I'm giving you permission. A licence, not to sleep around but to sleep with *one* guy—in your case, Sean—so you can join the rest of the living world."

Back in the store, I realized Erin had been successful in planting her idea. For the rest of the afternoon, I thought about how I would feel lying under Joon-Ho, his weight pressing into me, his voice a whisper, calling out my lost name.

A week had passed since my dad returned home. A Chinese doctor, who did acupuncture and who Kate's mother swore had cured her husband of drinking, had started to visit regularly. I squirmed each time I thought of my dad's back looking like a porcupine's.

"If he was meant to fall, the timing is good. It's summer. You're home. There's no snow to shovel," my mother said as we stood in the kitchen.

She was brewing a scary concoction of traditional Chinese medicine made of an assortment of plant roots, wild mushrooms, ginger, and other ingredients I didn't know. The longer it boiled, the worse it smelled, until finally the whole apartment reeked like things were dying in it.

"But Josh isn't around."

"Better he doesn't see your father in his condition," my mother said. She looked at the clock. The store would have to be opened in ten minutes. "Joon-Ho has been a huge help. Your father and I have really seen what kind of man that boy is."

I shrugged. Unfortunately, the more my parents praised him, the less attractive he became—which was too bad because I had been thinking more and more about him.

"Let this cool and then take it to your father," my mother said. She took off her apron, grabbed her keys and bag, and rushed downstairs.

I went around the apartment and made sure every window was as wide open as possible. I stalled by checking on the plants, watering the ferns, Chinese evergreen, and cacti. My mother was a firm believer that plants were necessary in each room to promote good health. Then, dutifully, I put on my mother's apron to strain the tea. It was still hot, and I struggled to keep the roots and herbs in the centre of the cloth I'd placed over the bowl. Finally, I picked up the four corners of the cloth and made a knot before gently lifting it. I used a spoon to press as much liquid out of it as possible, ready to pass out from the pungent smell.

"If you think it smells so stinky, how do you think it tastes?" my dad joked when I brought the cooled tea to him in his bedroom. "It's worse than a thousand skunks bathing in an outhouse."

I laughed. "As long as it helps you," I said.

"It helps me because it helps your mother stay calm. She needs to believe she's doing something to make things better."

"She needs to feel in control, you mean."

"Yes, but we both know that being in control can often be an illusion. If one person thinks he's in control but the other knows that he's being controlled *and* allows it, who's really in control?"

I looked down at the apron I was wearing. It was marked with faded stains in spite of my mother's obsessive need to have things clean. *You can't control everything,* I thought, *sometimes despite your best efforts.* I sat on the bed and looked up at the small lotus lantern hanging by the open window. The sun gleamed through the translucent pink paper. Remembering I'd been wondering how my parents met, I asked.

"Your mother was nineteen years old. I came to her village looking for work. I was an old man at twenty-seven, but then again, I

never looked my age." He winked. "There was a card game everyone used to play, a Korean version of bingo. One day, she had a card
but no pencil to mark out the letters on it. I had a pencil but no card.
I asked her if we could play together. She said no, but when another
girl called me over to play with her, your mother quickly changed
her mind."

"Control," my dad and I said together.

"Yes," my dad said, "but it was I who asked her in the first place.
I got what I wanted. I still do." He laughed and winced. "You're a
smart girl. Figure out what you want and the world will conspire to
make it happen."

I realized I didn't *know* what I wanted. What would the universe
do with me?

I was alone in the store one day when Erin dropped by. She had such
a goofy smile on her face, I thought she might be high.

"I have something for you," she said in a singsong voice. She
placed a slip of paper in my hand and curled my fingers around it.
"It's *his* number. Don't ask me how I got it."

I thought at first she was talking about Joon-Ho, but obviously I
already had his number.

"Mr. Allen—Mr. *William* Allen—that's his home number. Now
you can call him."

I didn't know how to respond.

Her smile fading, she said, "What? You're not his student anymore;
you're a grad now. You can do anything. Think about Mrs. Robb."

Megan Robb had been a student at our school and now supply-taught there regularly. She was married to the assistant head of science. Her nickname was Mrs. Twenty-nine—because that was how many years younger she was than Mr. Robb.

I entertained the possibilities but said, "You're crazy. What about Sean?"

Erin shook her head. "You're not into him."

I wanted to tell her she was wrong. I'd thought plenty about sex and Joon-Ho. Still, I looked down at the intriguing piece of paper. The number was easy enough to memorize.

"What am I supposed to say?"

"That's up to you." Erin was smiling again. "I just want you to be happy. I just want the whole world to be happy."

"You're amazing," I said. "I'm so glad you changed your mind about Western."

"Yeah, you can thank Jake for that," she said. "You're stuck with me for another four years at U of T."

She was crazy, I thought, but at least she was in love, if only with a guy whose sole aspiration was to be the manager of a movie theatre and sneak his friends in for free.

At exactly 4:00 p.m.—*a good time,* I thought, since it was before dinner—I willed myself to make the call. My plan was to hang up as soon as Mr. Allen answered. *Hearing his voice would be enough,* I told myself.

But it wasn't, and I responded to his hello.

"How'd you get this number?" he asked.

His voice was gentle, but I panicked at the question and blurted out, "My father was in an accident—he fell off a ladder." Obviously not the entire truth, but it sounded better. I explained my dad's injuries. I even went on to quote the Chinese doctor and his views on Western medicine.

"How are *you* doing?" Mr. Allen asked.

His voice was filled with such warmth and concern. My insides ached, as if they were being attacked by a thousand flying acupuncture needles, and I started to cry. *Stop it*, I told myself. *You're making a complete fool of yourself.*

There was a silence.

Then Mr. Allen said, "Maybe we could meet. I hate to hear you so upset."

I heard a voice inside me whisper softly: *Breathe. Be calm. Say something—say yes.*

We made plans to meet the next day at Second Cup, a coffee shop a few blocks away.

I said goodbye and hung up, wiping the tears from my face. My hands were trembling. Taking a deep breath, I leaned out the open window. The sun felt wonderfully hot against my face. I closed my eyes and vanished into its heat.

Chapter 10

$\mathcal{I}$ didn't recognize Mr. Allen as I walked towards the café. Dressed in jeans, sneakers, and a navy T-shirt, he was sitting under a brown awning, reading a book. His sandy brown hair seemed lighter than usual. He looked up and flashed his perfect teeth at me. His eyes were as blue as his shirt. Maybe it was the hot sun or maybe it was nerves, but I swayed in my sandals.

"What're you reading?" I asked as I sat across from him. I was trying to sound casual as my mind flipped through the list of things I'd rehearsed in anticipation of our meeting.

"*Aspects of the Novel* by E. M. Forster—the same writer who wrote *A Passage to India*."

So much for sounding smart and sophisticated.

"Could I get you something to drink?" he asked. I noticed he was drinking iced tea and told him I'd have the same. He went inside to get one for me.

I picked up the book on the table and thumbed through it. My hands were shaking.

"Ever read *A Room with a View?*" he asked, returning with my drink.

"Wasn't that a movie?"

"Yes. But this is a non-fiction piece, and quite interesting. I'm reading it as part of a creative writing course that I'm taking."

"You're taking a writing class?" I asked, surprised and suddenly happy. He'd once said that at my age he'd considered journalism, but he'd never mentioned he was writing too. I realized in that moment that none of our conversations in school had been about his personal life. I had a hard time containing my excitement. I asked him what he was working on now.

As he talked, everything seemed to take on a new clarity. The street and the shops that lined it looked as if they'd been given a fresh coat of paint and I could detect every shade. I listened to his witty anecdotes and his amusing tales of classroom mishaps—many of which he said he tried to incorporate into his short stories.

"I'd love to read something you've written," I said.

"Have you had a chance to do any writing?"

I took a notebook out of my purse and placed it in front of him. "I'd love your opinion—when you have time."

"Gosh, Mary, you put me to shame. I can barely bring myself to complete my writing assignments on time and here you are—another completed notebook." He picked it up and flipped the pages. "Have you given any more thought to getting published?"

I shook my head. Since he'd initially suggested submitting my poems to literary magazines more than a year ago, I'd received nothing but rejections. But a couple letters had been encouraging and I was still determined to get published to impress him.

"I'll drop it off at your store when I'm done reading it."

My heart sank. I might miss him again. How could I ask him when he'd come by without seeming anxious? He glanced at his watch, a cue I took to finish my iced tea. Though I wanted nothing more than for the afternoon to go on, I didn't want this perfect meeting to end awkwardly.

We were about to get up when a tall blonde appeared from behind me.

"Will!" she said. "It's been a long time." She took off her sunglasses and leaned over so that he could kiss her cheek.

A wave of expensive perfume filled the space around us. He stood but I remained sitting, remembering prom night. Why was it that every woman this man knew was so damn beautiful?

"Laura, this is Mary, one of my students," he said, and smiled. He placed a hand on my shoulder. "We were just getting ready to leave."

Former student, I wanted to correct him.

The blonde looked down at me. She smiled, though she showed no teeth. Her nails were painted the same sapphire blue as her eyes. How confident did a grown woman need to be to paint her nails blue? Her makeup was flawless. I stared at the black dots on my red dress and felt like a giant watermelon.

She put her sunglasses back on. "Let's go for a drink. I'm buying," she said.

I continued to sit, her confidence and beauty weighing me down like dumbbells resting on my lap.

"Sure," Mr. Allen said, then turned to me. "Thanks for this." He placed my notebook under the Forster book.

"Here, I'll put them in my bag," she offered, and before I knew it, eighteen of my poems, all inspired by Mr. Allen, were in her hot, manicured hands and disappearing into her Louis Vuitton bag.

I imagined myself leaping to rescue my work, her designer bag overturning, its precious contents flying into the air, the mirror in her compact shattering as it hit the sidewalk.

I watched them walk away, her arm linked through his. A police car, siren blasting, streaked by and caught my attention. A few intersections away, emergency vehicles were gathering. When I turned back, Will Allen and Laura were gone.

Even before we got to the nightclub, Erin and Jake were so wrapped up in each other that both Joon-Ho and I kept as far away from them as possible. I was envious of their spontaneous bursts of affection and wondered how it would feel to experience that with Mr. Allen.

The last time Joon-Ho and I had danced was at the prom, but here in a nightclub, with no teachers' eyes to spy on us, he seemed more relaxed, assertive, and bold. When a slow song played, his arms wrapped around me and pulled me into him. There was a shine in his eyes, and when the song ended, he pressed his lips first gently, then passionately against mine. Just as I was getting into it, Erin appeared, pulling at my arm. She was crying, makeup streaming down her cheeks. Reluctantly I pulled away from Joon-Ho, and Erin and I elbowed our way to the washroom.

"I hate him." She spat out the words.

I grabbed a handful of toilet paper and handed it to her. This wasn't the first time she'd lost it because Jake had flirted with another girl. Nothing I could say would matter at this point, so I just waited it out.

By the time we returned to the table, the guys had ordered more drinks for us. Erin quickly finished her strawberry daiquiri and stuck the oversized straw in my glass.

"It's not a Big Gulp," Jake told her. "Take it easy."

"Let's get outta here," she said. "I need air."

It didn't take long for Erin and Jake to make up, as the four of us walked along Bloor Street. We strolled by Honest Ed's, its huge yellow-and-red sign lit up by thousands of light bulbs like a theatre marquee. Then we were in Koreatown with its travel agencies, bakeries, and grocery stores.

We stopped outside a *no-rae-bang*, wedged between a walnut cake shop and a beauty supply store. Kate's family's restaurant was at the end of the block.

"I've never been to one of these," Jake said as we checked in. "I always thought you sang in front of a bunch of people when you sang karaoke."

"No, it's different with a Korean karaoke place. You can get private rooms, so you only sing with the people you came with. You pay by the hour," I explained.

Room 9 was no bigger than my bedroom and smelled of cigarette smoke and stale sex. It contained two black fake-leather loveseats, a coffee table, TV, and karaoke system. On the table were two songbooks; Erin grabbed the one with the English songs, and Joon-Ho, the one with Korean.

"I've never heard you sing," I said to him. "This should be fun."

As we busied ourselves putting a series of song choices into the system, Jake played with a remote that controlled the lighting. Soon we were all swaying to Erin's song, "Red Red Wine," a disco strobe light casting bright white bursts into the dark room. Jake then sang "Born to Be Wild."

Joon-Ho picked a Korean love ballad. As he sang, he turned to face me. His eyes were warm, and I found myself moved by the beautiful lyrics. Even Erin seemed affected, and when she put her hand on his thigh and told him he'd done a good job, I felt a pang of jealousy.

Jake wasn't impressed either. He sent her a look that made her shoot back, "So it's okay when *you* do it."

"I'm outta here," he said. He nodded at Joon-Ho. "Later." He didn't acknowledge me at all.

Erin, her cheeks red, whispered, "Sorry," before running after him.

"But we just got here," I yelled. I thought of chasing after her. I was upset with her for ending the night this way.

"Truly," the Lionel Richie song I'd chosen to sing, began to play. Joon-Ho handed me the mike.

"This is the first song we slow-danced to," I said.

He nodded. "I remember." Then he took my hand, and we were dancing.

My hips moved rhythmically against his. He kissed me, his breath smelling of spearmint and alcohol. As we danced, I tried to focus on the moment, but as hard as I tried, I couldn't help but think of Mr. Allen and how it might feel to be this close to him. I pressed into Joon-Ho.

"I want you," he whispered in my ear. "Yu-Rhee-ah."

The sound of my name snapped me back into the moment. I looked up into Joon-Ho's eyes, rose on my tiptoes, and kissed him. Our song played in the background and the strobe lights whirled around the tiny room. We fell onto the sofa. Gently, but firmly, I guided his hands along my body.

"Are you sure?" Joon-Ho asked.

I kissed him again.

I was in the washroom, rinsing my underwear, when Kate walked in. A love song played in the distance. It had been almost a year since I last saw her with her boyfriend, at a restaurant having dinner. She'd cut her hair and put on weight. I wondered if her father was still drinking and how her parents had taken to her having a black boyfriend.

"I thought it was you," she said. "I saw you coming in with your friends." She looked at the sink, at the bloody water, and shook her head.

"I hate when that happens," she said.

It took me a second to realize she probably thought I'd got my period. She went into a stall.

"So, how have you been?" I asked. I was panicked that someone I knew had seen me. I was embarrassed at the thought of the world knowing I'd had sex for the first time—in a Korean karaoke bar no less. The toilet flushed.

"You look sick," she said when she came out. "Are you okay?" When I didn't answer, she asked suspiciously, "Did you just do what I think you did?"

I looked in the mirror over the sink. My face was bright red. Kate ran her hands under the cold water. "I hope you used protection."

My mind was spinning. *Forget stupid Erin. Stupid me!* I thought.

"Don't worry, your secret's safe with me. My first time was here too—in good ol' Room 9," she said. "Just be careful. You know what happened to me."

I didn't. I shook my head.

"I thought every Korean person knew. I had a baby. A girl. With my ex-boyfriend. My parents freaked out, but they made me have the baby anyway. I never told them Jordon was black, so when I had the baby, they had another heart attack and made me give it up."

"Kate, I had no idea. My mother still talks to yours—she never said anything."

The washroom door opened and the distant music became loud for a moment. Two girls, dressed like the women on my street corner, walked in and headed for the stalls. Kate and I remained silent. She poked at her hair. I stared at my wrung-out panties, wondering what to do with them.

As soon as the two girls left, Kate continued. "I left home. Couldn't take it anymore. My parents came after me though. My father kept threatening to kill me or send me to Korea. Had to get a restraining order against them."

"Oh my God! Where are you living now?"

"With my new boyfriend, Alan. He's white. We work together. I'm still doing cash at Loblaws. We're unionized, so the pay's pretty amazing."

"What about school?" I couldn't imagine a Korean life without it.

"What about it?" she repeated. "That was never my thing anyway. I told my parents I wanted to go to college, study photography, but my mom said college was for losers." She rubbed at a clump of mascara. "So, you're seeing someone. Korean, no doubt."

I was offended by her know-it-all attitude.

"Well, be careful," she said.

"It was good seeing you again."

"Yeah, right." She applied another coat of lipstick, pursed her lips, and dropped the tube into her purse. As she pulled the door open, she looked over as if she wanted to say something else. But she didn't.

I sighed. She was the only Korean friend I'd ever had. I hesitated, then tossed my wet underwear into the garbage before rushing back to Joon-Ho.

Chapter 11

Two weeks passed, and although Josh was back, Joon-Ho continued to show up at the store every afternoon after his English class at a nearby language academy. My family never had to ask him to do anything. He'd go straight to work, lugging crates of pop up from the basement, washing our windows, even dusting everything on our shelves from top to bottom.

It was around three o'clock one afternoon when Mr. Allen unexpectedly walked in, dressed in a T-shirt and jeans. He'd dropped by to return my notebook of poems. As much as it thrilled me to see him, I was nervous. I saw Joon-Ho look at me. When I realized they didn't recognize each other out of the suits and ties they'd been wearing at my prom, I felt a wave of relief.

"This is my teacher," I said. I don't know what possessed me, but I wrapped a loose arm around Joon-Ho's and introduced him as Sean. When I saw his face relax, I let go.

Joon-Ho agreed to watch the cash so Mr. Allen and I could talk. We left the store and started walking. The sun was hot, but a cool breeze made it pleasant.

"Your poems were lovely," Mr. Allen said. "You remind me of a modern-day Elizabeth Barrett Browning."

Having just received yet another rejection letter from a poetry magazine to which I'd submitted several of my poems, I couldn't help but shake my head at his compliment. Rejection was the one thing they never taught you in any class. I thought back to my first— a standard form letter that baffled me. I'd never imagined I couldn't write prior to submitting the poems, because Mr. Allen had always made me feel like a gifted writer. The initial shock had been devastating, but after spending hours in the library reading about famous writers and their publishing experiences, I came to realize that rejection was part of the process. I also got lucky because a couple of the letters shed light on what the publishers wanted and it encouraged me to keep writing and submitting.

When I asked him about his own writing, he remarked that it was progressing slowly.

"My trouble is, I'm lacking a muse," he said. "Unlike you, who seem quite inspired."

Had he guessed my feelings for him from my poems? Maybe having the truth out in the open was better.

But then he asked, "So how long have you known Sean?"

Ohmigod, I thought, *does he think I'm in love with Joon-Ho? Should I tell him the truth—that I was in love with* him *and had been since I had him for English in grade nine?*

"I met Sean in Korea," I said instead, feeling like a coward.

We continued to walk north of our store, through the quiet residential streets, talking about books and our writing. I was amazed at how easily our conversation flowed. We talked about everything from the weather, to British writers, to the pros and cons of drinking cow's milk.

Eventually Mr. Allen stopped in front of a narrow red-brick house with a tiny front yard.

"This is my home," he said. "I rent the top floor."

I looked at my watch. It was a twenty-minute walk from our store.

"Do you need to rush back? I hadn't intended for us to walk all the way back here. I could give you a lift," Mr. Allen offered.

"Could I use your bathroom first?" I asked.

It was just as I had pictured it—cozy, the walls lined with bookcases filled with novels. I felt comfortable immediately.

"I love your place," I said, walking back into the living room from the bathroom.

"Yeah, pretty much everything is from IKEA." He laughed. "I'm not much of a decorator."

"You've got some amazing books," I said. "I could live here forever and not be bored."

"A lot of them I inherited from my mother. She was a librarian."

"You must have been exposed to all sorts of books growing up." I wondered if any of them were by Asian writers. I doubted it—everything I saw was by the usual suspects: Joyce, Hemingway, Steinbeck.

Mr. Allen offered me a Coke, and we sat side by side on his sofa as he told me about his latest writing assignment. "I need to write about a character who makes an important life decision," he said.

"I've been going crazy with ideas. I've killed a small tree trying to write something." He paused. "I'm hoping to turn it into a novel eventually."

I wondered if he was envisioning an entire forest disappearing.

"I'd love to see whatever you've got," I said.

He hesitated a moment, then disappeared into his room.

While he was gone, I tried to take in as many details of the living room as possible so that I could imagine it later: the new-looking brown rug under my feet; three stacks of old copies of *The New Yorker*, *Esquire*, and the *New England Review* piled several feet high in one corner of the room. There were no plants.

Mr. Allen came back and handed me some sheets of paper. The top one was a patchwork of crossed-out words and messy white blobs where Liquid Paper had been used.

"Yeah, I can't really type," he admitted. "Call me old-fashioned, but I prefer to write everything out longhand."

"You don't have an electric typewriter?" I asked.

"No, just an old manual one. The only thing is I need to hand in typed work."

"I could type this up for you," I offered. "We have a computer and I can type."

"I can't ask you to do that," he said. "Unless I paid you."

I shrugged. Anything to make him say yes.

"How quickly do you think you could do this?"

"I'll get on it right away and call you when I'm done."

"That's great," he said. He looked as if he might hug me, but didn't. Glancing at the clock, he said, "Let me drive you back. Your boyfriend's probably worried about you by now."

*   *   *

As he ate his rice, Joon-Ho asked, "So, what did you and your teacher talk about?"

We were in my kitchen having the dinner my mother had made for us before going down to the store. My dad was taking a nap in his bedroom. I knew I should have felt guilty for leaving Joon-Ho alone in the store, but he didn't say anything.

"He's writing a book. He's paying me to type up his work." I eyed the grocery bag with the manuscript on the counter.

"Are you in love with him?" The question came out of nowhere.

"No," I exclaimed. I looked at him as if he had lost his mind.

"Liar!" he said. "I read the things you wrote about him." He was trying to keep his voice down so as not to wake my dad.

I panicked and thought about the notebook with my poems in it. I'd left it behind on the store counter after Mr. Allen dropped it off. Joon-Ho must have seen him handing it to me and been curious.

"They were all love poems—in your writing! Are you in love with him?"

I wanted to say no, but the word got caught somewhere deep in me. My mouth opened again, and when nothing came out, Joon-Ho got up abruptly, grabbed the grocery bag, and took out the paper. As he flipped through the pages, I noticed that Mr. Allen had written on both sides. To my shock, he ripped the papers in half, then shredded them into smaller pieces.

"How do you know that the poems aren't about you?" I asked. My stunned mind was picking up speed. "Doesn't that make more sense? He's my *san-sang-neem*, for God's sake!" I used the Korean word for "teacher" to emphasize my point. Somehow, the Korean word made it seem less likely a student could have an affair with a teacher.

Joon-Ho's face froze. I could see he was trying to regain his composure. He sighed before collapsing into his chair.

"You're right," he said slowly. "He is your teacher." He looked up into my eyes. "I feel the same way about you. I want to marry you one day, when we're both done with our studies."

I was speechless. But I was feeling too guilty to be upset with Joon-Ho. After all, I'd slept with him and let him believe I liked him. And he was helping us out so much that my entire family had come to believe we owed him something.

I worked long into the night, first to sort out the puzzle pieces of the torn paper, then to type up Mr. Allen's work. His story was about a married man with three young children who wanted to sail around the world alone with the intention of never returning home. I read it over twice before I started typing it. It was interesting, though surprisingly not very well written. I couldn't help but feel disappointed as I racked my brain to come up with something meaningful to say about it, while avoiding the urge to rewrite parts of it.

Now that I actually had a life with men in it, I found myself writing long diary entries about love, its anticipations and disappointments. I preferred my bedroom door closed. That annoyed my mother—she wasn't used to knocking.

"You're holding the book too close to your eyes," she said one day. The smell of seaweed soup filled the room as she entered. "What man would want to marry a girl who wears glasses?" She dropped a load of clean laundry on my desk. "Why do you do every-thing on your bed when you have a perfectly good desk right here?" She knocked on the wood to make her point.

I looked around my unmade bed, a few books, spiral notepads, and my pencil case strewn on it. A part of the blue scarf Rubina had given me after my attack peeked from under my pillow. I refused to let my mother wash it. I'd told her it was my good luck charm, but the truth was I couldn't sleep without it around my neck or at least near me.

She read the title of the book I held. "*Invisible Man*. What kind of foolishness is that?"

"It's not really about an invisible man," I said. "It's about a black man who feels invisible because of the way white people treat him. It's a famous book by Ralph Ellison. Mr. Allen loved it."

"You and your Mr. Allen, and all the black and white people you read about." She bent down to pick up a pair of jeans and some shirts off the floor. "You never read books about Korean characters or even Chinese ones."

"That's because there aren't any books about them," I said, "Or at least I don't know about them." I thought back to all the books Mr. Allen had ever mentioned. None of them had been by Asian writers or about Asian characters.

"You want to know about feeling invisible?" my mother asked. She sat on the chair by the desk and rubbed her right knee. "It's always black and white in Canada. The Koreans, Chinese, Japanese, anyone from Asia are the true invisibles." Realizing she had me thinking, she went on. "Do you think anyone really sees us when they throw pennies at us for a newspaper?"

"There must be writers out there. I just don't know them."

"There are so many wonderful writers back in Korea."

"But they write about life in Korea and they write in Korean."

"Wouldn't you still be interested?"

Not really, I thought. Why was she bringing all this up again? When Josh and I were young, she'd tried to teach us to read and write in Korean. Her crazy work hours led her to give up. She told us to focus on mastering English instead.

"I want to major in English," I said. "At university."

My mother said nothing for a moment, then, "Maybe it wouldn't be too bad if you become an English teacher. Steady job. Have your summers off. Have children."

"You're missing the point," I said. I wanted to study English because I loved books and the written word.

"Yes, become an English teacher." She nodded to herself. "Make sure your students realize there are writers out there who aren't just black and white. Make sure they don't miss the point like you did."

I wanted to say something, but realized I'd graduated high school never having studied Asian culture, history, or literature. I couldn't think of one Asian writer, scientist, or great thinker. When I called Erin after dinner and asked her to name someone, anyone she knew who was Asian and had contributed to society, she said Confucius, which impressed me until she confessed that she knew the name only because her neighbour had named his dog after China's greatest thinker.

*   *   *

A couple of days later, I called Mr. Allen and invited myself over to his place. When he opened the door, I was caught off guard by his boyish look, handsome in a plain white T-shirt and khaki cargo shorts. I'd only ever seen him in pants before.

Focus, I reminded myself. *And breathe.* When I suggested that a first-person point of view might be more effective for his story, he seemed genuinely interested in hearing why I thought so. As we went over my ideas and talked more about E. M. Forster's *Aspects of the Novel*, I imagined how it would feel to be kissed by Mr. Allen, whom I had—at his urging—begun to call Will. Was he the type that planted short, soft kisses on a woman's lips, cheeks, and neck before kissing her passionately? Or would he take her aggressively, swept away by his desires?

"You'll be published long before I will," he said.

Thinking about the growing pile of rejection letters under my bed, I shook my head. As I looked up, our eyes met. There were so many lovely shades of blue in his eyes: sky, aqua, and cobalt. I leaned into him and kissed him lightly on the lips. Once, twice . . . He pulled away, but then kissed me back, his tongue suddenly in my mouth.

"Mary, I'm so sorry. This is all my fault," he said. He got up. "Can I get you something to drink? Sorry, I didn't even offer you anything." Without waiting for my response, he disappeared and returned with two cans of Coke and a package of Oreo cookies.

"Would you like some?" he asked, and sat back down.

"No, Will." I pressed my fingers against his lips to quiet him. It thrilled me to be calling him by his first name. My newfound confidence excited me. "This is what I want." I gently licked his lower lip, but he pulled back.

"What about Sean?" he asked.

"He's just a friend."

"Mary . . . I'm seeing someone."

For a moment I couldn't speak.

"Is it Laura?" I asked finally, unable to hide my disappointment. I had a flashback of her Louis Vuitton bag hijacking my precious poems.

He frowned. "No, it's Yuki," he said, then, seeing my confusion, "Ms. Nakamura. She's in Japan teaching this summer."

Great, I thought, *he's sleeping with the music teacher!* An image of her in her short cherry red prom dress popped into my head.

"Sorry, Mary," he said. "Really."

My eyes filled with tears as the truth burned its way into my brain.

"Mary," he said, "don't get me wrong. To be honest, I'm quite attracted to the writer in you. You have such a way with words. Your poems reflect a maturity I've never seen in any student, and your writing evokes such powerful emotions. I love talking with you. But Mary . . ."

I kissed him again. This time he didn't stop me. After all, Ms. Nakamura was a thousand miles away.

PART II

Missing People

Chapter 12

$\mathcal{R}$ubina stunned us with her news just one week before our much anticipated first day of university. She was being sent back to Pakistan—a country she'd left thirteen years ago—to marry her first cousin, someone she hadn't seen since.

"Do you have any say in this? Will you be able to come back?" Linda asked. Her lips quivered.

The four of us were at our favourite restaurant in Little Italy. Rubina set her fork down before shaking her head. I couldn't even form a response.

"Well, this sucks," Erin said. "So much for love and happiness. How could you let your parents do this to you?" She was fighting back tears.

After spending five years together, in and out of classrooms and cafeterias, hanging out in hallways and stairwells, we were going our separate ways. Rubina was leaving the country. Linda was going to York University to study nursing. At least Erin and I were together at the University of Toronto. By the time our bill arrived, we were all in tears, our faces streaked with mascara, our noses red.

"Ladies? Are we ready to move on?" our waiter asked, his eyes darting towards the other customers in the restaurant.

I thought back to the night we sat around the Ouija board, pledging our friendship and swearing we'd surrender our virginity only to our true loves. I'd already betrayed that oath by sleeping with Joon-Ho and now was starting a secret relationship with Will. Rubina would be on the other side of the earth, swept away like Dorothy and her dog, Toto. What would become of us? We were all caught in Rubina's tornado, forced to face the unknowns in the next chapter of our lives.

We're finally here, I told myself as Erin and I stood in front of Victoria College at the University of Toronto. It was a new beginning and I couldn't help but smile. When my family first arrived in the city, a neighbor had taken us sightseeing. My mother had stared out the car window, taking in the Royal Ontario Museum and the McLaughlin Planetarium with semi-interest. When she was told we were on university campus grounds, however, she rolled down the window and pointed to random buildings, statues, and monuments, asking our neighbour questions he couldn't answer. And as we drove by Queen's Park, with its Ontario Legislative Building, my mother asked me, "What do you think it means to have the university surround the most important government buildings in the entire province?" As far as she was concerned, high school had been merely a stepping stone to get here.

Erin and I were on our way to Convocation Hall, where our psychology class would be held. The campus felt massive. We walked in a stream of excited students crisscrossing Queen's Park. We'd been warned by a perky red-headed senior during Frosh Week to never be in the park alone at night. She also touched on sexual assault, date rape, and drug and alcohol abuse, told us that self-defense courses were offered through the Campus Police Office, and that counselling was available through Psychological Services. My parents would have been horrified. Her final piece of advice was "Don't feed the squirrels. Those bushy-tailed critters will come after you if they think you have food." She was right; they were everywhere—the fattest squirrels I'd ever seen. I was amazed they didn't run away, afraid of the hundreds of feet that could crush them. We avoided them.

"Leave it to Rubina to accept her fate so unconditionally," Erin said.

I glanced at her. I too had been thinking about Rubina, missing her, wondering about her new life married to a man she barely knew.

"God, I don't know how you people do it. You're like trained animals. Even with your cages unlocked, you refuse to escape."

I knew it must be impossible for her to understand the chains that kept immigrant girls—especially Asian ones—in place, but I was still irritated. Besides, where would we go? I envisioned a cell full of Asian girls, waves of black hair and piercing brown eyes staring out into nothing through steel bars.

The mob propelled us to King's College Circle. A cloud slowly crossed the sun, allowing us to admire the ivy-draped buildings and the quadrangle of green without shading our eyes. It looked just like a university campus in the movies. And Erin, with her dyed strawberry blonde hair, seemed to fit right in, although I thought she was trying a little too hard with her expensive silk blouse and Italian designer jeans.

"You've got to appreciate the Romanesque and Gothic Revival—

style of these buildings," she said, an attempt to impress anyone within earshot of her.

Though she hadn't said it, I knew she was proud to be the first person in her family to attend university.

"Only if you're an architecture major," a deep male voice responded.

Erin stopped to look around for the person who'd spoken. I tugged her along; we were late.

"But he sounded cute," she insisted. "He could be the father of my future kids."

Something hit my leg from behind. It was a white cane. The girl holding it had run into me when I had stopped abruptly.

"Excuse me," she said.

Her red backpack, blue jeans, and T-shirt told us she was a student like us. Erin and I watched her walk away with precision and turn to enter a building.

"At least she knows where she's going," Erin said, then, "I think that's Con Hall there." She pointed to a domed rotunda.

We started running towards it.

Four more years, I thought, as I glanced at the ivy-clad buildings around us. My parents' great expectations would be met and I could escape my cage.

I was watching the cash and trying to do psychology homework with Erin at the same time. Josh and my dad were at a wholesaler and my mother was upstairs cooking. Increasingly I was fed up with working in the store and resentful that girls like her weren't burdened in the same way, and yet could afford brand labels on everything they wore. Bored with her reading, she flipped through the credit-card application forms she'd picked up for us.

"I can't believe how easy it is to apply for these credit cards. You don't even need a job!" The glossy brochures promised they were designed specifically for students.

Unlike Erin, who was already complaining about school, I was enjoying my courses, especially Sociology. Whereas my English and history intro classes felt like an extension of high school, the social sciences—psychology, anthropology, and sociology—were new to me. Their subjective nature left room for vast interpretations, unlike the pure sciences and math courses I'd had to take in high school. The idea of a single right answer had never appealed to me.

My favourite instructor was my sociology prof, who, unlike the rest of my white male professors in their forties and fifties, had invited us to call her by her first name, Rusaline. Her eyes and skin were the colour of chestnuts, her youth and her beauty enough to have made her a successful model. Instead, she stood in front of two hundred students, most of them white, in a windowless lecture room at New College, trying to get us to think about power dynamics within modern society.

There was a lot of chatter the first day about why people had signed up for SOC101: to fulfill their breadth requirement; it was a bird course; the prof was hot. One kid slept through the entire lecture. But by the third class, I'd moved from the back to the front row, genuinely interested in learning about Max Weber, Émile Durkheim, and Auguste Comte.

"Are there any social thinkers out there who aren't white and male?" I asked. I couldn't believe I'd interrupted the lecture, and felt my face getting hot.

Instead of being annoyed, Rusaline smiled. "Great question," she said. "Inequity is ubiquitous. It exists in every human society, which means that across this planet, there are social scientists of every skin colour examining the same issues."

I felt my brain expanding at the thought.

Two weeks later four credit cards arrived in the mail. When my mother asked me about them, I told her all the students automatically got them. Erin, who was with me, flashed her set of cards.

Suddenly I had money. I bought clothes, shoes, and a bunch of other things from the university bookstore that I could have taken from our store instead, except they didn't have the cool U of T crest on them: notebooks, binders, and pens. I even bought a silk scarf with a historical map of the campus on it. I had no use for it, unlike my blue cotton scarf, and ended up giving it to Linda for her birthday.

Reality hit the next month when the credit-card bills arrived.

"Just pay the monthly minimum," Erin said.

I asked her how she was managing and couldn't believe it when she told me she had a trust fund.

"My mom told me my dad wanted me to be, like, forty before I could have it," she said. "In case I met up with some loser guy. Thank God he changed his mind before he died."

I wanted to ask her how much she had, but didn't have the nerve.

"You could always ask your parents," Erin suggested.

I shook my head. They'd kill me. I thought of asking Joon-Ho, but changed my mind. The last thing I needed was another reason to feel grateful to him.

"You need to get a job," Josh said when I told him. He leaned over the low shelf where he was stacking cans and dropped his voice. "A real job that pays money. Not like working here."

Shaking my head, I continued sticking price tags on the canned vegetables. "*Omma* would never let me—not now that I'm in university. All she'd do is yell." I didn't know why I was whispering; she couldn't hear us from the front counter.

"So get a job, and whenever you need to work, tell them you have class or need to go to the library. I've been working at Taste of Thai for almost three months now. Pay sucks. Tips are usually good though."

"Wow," I said. I felt betrayed he hadn't shared his deception with me earlier. He let out a low whistle when I told him how much I needed just to make the minimum payments.

"I'll lend you the money. Get rid of your cards, okay?"

I was so relieved I could have hugged him.

"I'll get a job," I promised. I just didn't know what I could do. I wasn't qualified to do anything.

"I want a tattoo," I said.

Will turned his head to look at the tattoo on the arm of the guy sitting behind him. We were at the café where we'd first met a couple of months earlier. He took a careful sip of his coffee before asking why.

"I don't know. It's art. It's taboo—if you're Korean anyway."

"Give it some real thought first. It's not exactly cheap or painless."

I thought of my credit cards. "What would you get if you ever got a tattoo?" I asked.

"Well, funny you should ask," he said. He rolled up his sleeve and showed me a small blue maple leaf on his left upper arm. "I got it during my second year. I played rugby. I only agreed to it because everyone else on the team had one. I did it for the team."

"Really?" I was delighted he'd allow his perfect white body to be mutilated. It made him more desirable. I stared into his eyes.

"So, how's the writing going?" he asked.

I sat up and reached for more sugar. I was still getting used to the taste of coffee. "Good. And you?"

"It's not." He let out a long sigh. "I have an OAC English class from hell—a third of them are ESL—some of them can barely string an essay together, never mind think about going off to university in a year's time. I've been meeting with so many of them after school for extra help, I might as well become a private tutor."

"My mother wants me to be a teacher," I said.

"If you want to write, write. Don't make the same mistake I did."

"So quit. Write instead."

He made a face at me. I thought he was going to tell me to grow up, but instead he said, "I thought about it. Yuki thinks I'm crazy. We even fought about me taking all these writing classes. She wants me to finish my Master of Education instead. Become a principal. Rule the world."

"Why doesn't she go for it herself?" I asked, annoyed by Ms. Nakamura in her cherry red dress casting a shadow on the moment.

"She wants to get married. Spend our summer months travelling. Then have kids. As far as she's concerned, everything's set. I just

need to do my part. But you know, Mary, I'm thirty-two years old—
if I don't do what I want to do now with my life, when?"

"You're thirty-two?" I asked, caught off guard. I'd been enjoying
hearing the intimate details of his incompatibility with Ms. Nakamura. "How old is she?"

"Twenty-eight. And she thinks she knows exactly what she wants
out of life. She's happy doing what she's doing."

I pretended to drink my coffee. I was afraid to ask him if he loved
her, if he wanted to spend the rest of his life with her.

"She'd be better off without me," he said.

I let out a deep breath, but said nothing. He apologized for his
bad mood, then asked about my classes.

"I'm the only Asian person in my English class."

He didn't seem surprised. "Are you okay with that?"

I rolled my eyes and smiled. "I'm used to it. My brother and I
were the only Asians—not Koreans—the only *Asians* in the entire
school when we first came to Canada."

"What was that like?"

"You get used to it. We got picked on a lot till a black kid started
school." I'd forgotten about Winston Anderson and the day his
mother showed up at school, a copy of *The Adventures of Huckleberry
Finn* in her hand. She demanded to know why the school library had
a copy of it.

"Have you ever read it?" Mrs. Rushin had asked. "The book is a
classic and quite sympathetic to the plight of your people."

"What. The. Fuck?" Mrs. Anderson said, emphasizing each
word.

I thought she was going to throw the book at Mrs. Rushin.

Instead, she grabbed Winston's hand and left. He never came back. But the teacher stopped picking on us after that.

"There are no black students in my class either," I mumbled. Then, to lighten the mood, I said, "My first paper's on Eliot's use of symbolism in *The Waste Land*."

He laughed. "I guess universities, like high schools, recycle the same curriculum every year."

When Will offered to lend me all his old essays to look over, I was so happy, I could have gotten up and danced.

"You could swing by any Sunday afternoon. Call first," he said.

It would be my first time back in his house since the afternoon we kissed.

Linda, who was always telling me she prayed for me, helped me get my first job interview. It was at a daycare she worked at part-time. I was so thrilled, I called Will to share the news.

"Why didn't you tell me you were looking for a job?" he asked. "I've been looking for someone to tutor my ESL students. You would have been perfect."

"I can still do it," I said. I wanted to be as involved in Will's life as possible. "How many students did you have in mind?"

"There are a few visa students—from Korea, actually. You'd be the ideal tutor for them." He invited me to come by the following Sunday afternoon. Sundays, he said, were when Yuki visited her sick mother in Orangeville.

I felt conspiratorial. It was only a matter of time before he realized what I already knew—that I could make him happy in a way

Ms. Nakamura never could. Unlike her, with her grand plans to control his life through marriage and babies, I simply wanted him to be who he wanted to be—a writer, like me.

The next few weeks of university passed quickly as I settled into a routine and juggled my commitments. Unlike in high school, where I was in classes from 9:00 a.m. to 3:30 p.m. five days a week, in university I only had ten hours of lectures and two tutorials. This allowed me to work the 3:00-to-6:00 p.m. shift every day at the daycare and tutor four hours on Saturday mornings. I spent Saturday nights with Joon-Ho, Sunday afternoons with Will, and helped out in the store every minute in between.

"She's at the University of Toronto now," my mother told all our regular customers.

"They don't care," I said. "Stop talking about me." It was embarrassing to hear everyone wish me well.

"She's proud of you," Mrs. O'Doherty said. "She's a mother. Give her the chance to be happy for you."

When I asked her about her own children, she said two of them had passed away and that one daughter was living in Vancouver. She didn't elaborate.

My mother wasn't happy for me, I thought bitterly. She was proud of herself. Proud she'd been a good mother who'd helped me through my studies so far. My accomplishments were merely a report card on her performance to date. We got into a fight when I told her I was quitting piano just before school started. I told her I'd be too busy with university studies.

"It's not like you cared enough to show up at any of my recitals," I said.

"Somebody had to watch the store," she shot back.

"But you and *Appa* always made it a point to go to Josh's tournaments!"

"Only the big ones," she said.

"So you could collect all the medals to show off, and tell people what a great mother you are."

She didn't say anything, and for a while things were cool between us. *The missed recitals hardly mattered now,* I thought. I was no longer a kid. I had two jobs, financial obligations, university studies, and men to juggle. I threw my credit cards behind my dresser, which was too heavy for me to move on my own, ready to be the grown-up I longed to be.

It was almost four in the afternoon when a red Coca-Cola delivery truck pulled up in front of the store and the driver jumped out.

"He's kinda cute," Erin said.

I nodded. I'd had a slight crush on Owen since he first started making deliveries a year ago. As I tended to the customers and kept track of the number of new cases coming in and empty cases going out, Erin made her way outside to talk with Owen. It annoyed me that she'd abandoned me. Several customers bought Lotto Super 7 tickets because the jackpot was at an all-time high.

At my first opportunity, I looked outside. Erin was smiling and twirling her newly blonde hair, which fell like a delicate scarf over her green dress. I envied her ability to charm men with her false modesty. Her eyes locked on to his, she accepted the slip of paper he passed her and carefully folded it in half.

I hadn't realized until I heard the chirping that a bird had flown into the store. It zoomed past my head and crashed into the glass behind me. I screamed, but not loudly enough for Erin and Owen to hear me, and ran out from behind the counter. When it flew past me again, I screamed louder. This time both of them came running.

"There's a bird in the store!" I yelled.

Owen laughed. We looked around, but there wasn't a bird in sight.

"Wish I could stay and help," he said, "but we've gotta get the deliveries done." He waved a hand at me, then, trying to hide an obvious smile, he said to Erin, "See you."

"Are you gonna go out with him?" I asked after he left.

Erin shrugged. "He *is* sort of cute." Her back was to me as she watched Owen board the truck and drive away.

"What about Jake?"

"What *about* Jake? You're the last person in the world who should be talking."

I was surprised at her sharp tone, but she was right. I hadn't seen Joon-Ho in a few weeks, nor had I seen Will, although I hadn't been able to stop thinking about our kiss. Our various commitments had thrown all of us into different routines.

Mrs. O'Doherty walked in. Her top was the same shade of shamrock green as Erin's dress. "How's school going, Mary?" she asked as she walked over to the milk cooler. She stopped halfway and turned. "Do I hear a bird? Where's it coming from?"

"Ohmigod, it's in the basement," I said. The delivery men had left the door open and the lights on. I hated the basement, with its cold, dungeon-like rooms. Half the lights didn't turn on. The thought of something living trapped down there sent a wave of panic through me.

"A wild bird in a house is bad luck," Mrs. O'Doherty said, "a sure sign of death in the family—if you believe in such things." She picked up a newspaper and shook her head. "Another suicide on the Bloor Viaduct. They really need to do something about that."

I'd heard the news about the suicide. But right now, I was more concerned about the trapped bird.

"Can you go down and look for it?" I asked Erin. "I can't leave the cash." I placed the milk and newspaper into a bag and wished Mrs. O'Doherty a good day. The truth was I was too terrified to do it myself. It was a tiny bird, but knowing it was downstairs, flying blindly, desperately seeking freedom, sent shivers down my spine. Erin looked just as freaked out.

"We can't just leave it down there," I said. I wished my parents were around, but they were in Brampton attending yet another one of Josh's tae-kwon-do tournaments.

"So call someone," she said. "Call Sean."

I hesitated. But I couldn't think of anything else to do so I dialed his number. He arrived in twenty minutes, and within five minutes he'd returned upstairs.

"Why isn't it moving?" I asked, looking at the bag he was holding.

"It's dead."

"You *killed* it?"

He nodded. "I'll take it outside."

You didn't have to kill it, I thought, feeling sad and guilty the poor bird had died in our store.

When he returned, Erin kissed his right cheek and called him her hero—a gesture that irked me more than I wanted to admit. She went behind the counter, collected her textbooks, and stuffed them in her backpack.

"I'll see you guys later."

"How's it going?" I asked Joon-Ho. "It's been a while since you've been by the store."

"My studies are more demanding than I could have imagined." He paused. "There's a lot of catching up, because I did my degree in Korea. It's like I'm relearning everything—even how to think—but in English this time." He changed the subject, asking about my parents, and finally how I was doing.

As I answered his questions, I wanted to tell him I'd missed him. Finally I said, "Thanks for being around when I need you."

He smiled. "Once things settle down, I'll be back," he promised. "We'll do things again." Then, without another word and without a kiss, he left.

I was alone again in the store, hating its relentless demands, the thought of the dead bird giving me chills.

Chapter 13

The week before Christmas, Joon-Ho called to tell me that his parents were visiting. "My mother's looking forward to meeting you and your family," he said.

I wondered how long he'd known about this visit. They were expected to arrive at the end of the week.

"It's the holidays, my parents get pretty busy," I said.

"They know my parents are coming. My mother's already spoken with your mother. Everything's set."

I was outraged. When I confronted my mother, she insisted it was a harmless introductory meeting and that we weren't committed to anything. "You need to be smart about these things," she said as we worked together behind the counter, "and keep all your options open. A good marriage match requires more strategy than a game of chess."

"I don't play chess," I said, deliberately being difficult.

A stream of customers came through, and I had to wait for them to leave before my mother continued.

"Joon-Ho's family is very well-to-do, and Joon-Ho's an only child. He's also hardworking and intelligent. He's a fire dragon.

With a little work, your marriage can work quite well." Apparently fire dragons and earth roosters weren't the ideal match, but compatible nevertheless.

"But you never mentioned marriage before," I said.

"Joon-Ho's mother called me. I didn't call her. What was I supposed to say?"

"What you've always told me: that I have to finish university first, then think about marriage."

"You never said you didn't like him," she said. "Besides, it's not like we're expecting a wedding in the new year."

The new year? I thought.

She paused to think. "No, definitely not in the year of the snake."

It was pointless to argue any further with her.

As Joon-Ho and I got off the elevator at the Four Seasons Hotel and walked to his parents' suite, I wondered aloud how much money his father had had to make in Korean *won* to afford such a fancy hotel.

"Your uncle's doing just as well," Joon-Ho said.

He would know, I told myself, and thought back to my aunt's luxury condo in Seoul, the one we'd stayed at during our visit to Korea. Though Joon-Ho's parents lived next door, I hadn't met them. My aunt was living the high life as my mother laboured in our store. I suddenly felt sorry for my mother, remembering how she'd cried in Korea. I took a deep breath as Joon-Ho knocked on the door, and decided I wanted to make a good first impression. Keep all my options open.

As we entered, we removed our shoes, and as soon as Joon-Ho and I sat on the sofa opposite his parents, his mother began talking.

She was wiry, with shiny black hair that made her look like a Korean version of Morticia, the mother from the Addams Family. She wore a long black dress with black beading along the V neckline. A ruby teardrop pendant hung from a gold chain around her neck. Her husband, who wore a black suit, sat like her shadow, dark and silent. The more Joon-Ho's mother talked, the less I heard, her words spinning in my head like clothes in a dryer. In her eyes, I was a Canadian bride being trained as a Korean wife. My mother had warned me to be agreeable. Did I know that Joon-Ho ate only Korean food? Did I know how to cook Korean food? Was I a good cook? Better than his own mother?

I nodded, and kept nodding: Yes, I would bear a grandson. Two. Three. Family—his—would always come first. My own life, last. In my imagination, a woman's head, severed from the rest of her body—a result of excessive nodding—flew high into the air against a backdrop of blue sky, and landed in a nest in a tree, hidden from view.

Joon-Ho tapped my shoulder.

"We'll see you and your family at dinner tomorrow night," his mother said, dismissing me.

I bowed and walked towards the door. Joon-Ho and I put our shoes on. I turned and bowed to his parents again, and we left.

There were maids with cleaning carts in the halls. I wished we had more privacy.

"Thank you for coming," Joon-Ho said as we got into the elevator and the doors closed.

"How could your parents think we'd get married when you and I have never talked about it ourselves?"

He said nothing.

"We need to talk," I said. We stepped out of the elevator into the lobby. "Now."

Joon-Ho told me he needed to get back to his parents. He turned and left me standing alone under a stream of blinking Christmas lights.

Kate's mother's restaurant, one of the oldest in Little Korea, had opened in the mid-seventies. It was known for its *bibimbap*, Korean-style fried rice, and *bulgoki*, marinated prime beef grilled right at your table. We sat, my mother facing Joon-Ho's mother, the two fathers facing each other, and Joon-Ho facing me. Dressed smartly in a white shirt with the black-and-blue checkered tie I'd given him for Christmas, Joon-Ho was busy studying the menu. Would it be so bad marrying a Korean man? Having Korean children? A Korean life in Canada? If only Will didn't have a girlfriend. If only he'd told me he was in love with *me*, instead of the writer in me. I looked down at the white holiday dress my mother had bought on sale at a dress shop. Red lacing ran along the sleeve and hemline. I hated white; I could never keep it clean. Ignoring my menu, I allowed myself to become distracted by the Korean folk songs playing in the background.

"Too bad it wasn't with *my* boy," Mrs. Kim teased as she brought generous servings of *banchan*—complimentary side dishes of bean sprout salad, spicy steamed tofu, and green onion pancakes—to the table. She placed the kimchi, which could make or break Korean restaurants, in front of Joon-Ho's mother.

As she picked up her chopsticks, she sniffed the kimchi. I couldn't help but frown—I'd never seen anyone do that before. She bit into the pickled cabbage and chewed slowly.

"It isn't the same when you use local ingredients." She did nothing to hide her look of disapproval.

Mrs. Kim's eyes flashed as she held a fixed smile. She turned to look at my mother, who appeared distracted by the contents of her purse. I sensed Mrs. Kim must be feeling sorry for her, because as she walked by, she patted my mother's shoulder—not once, but three times.

My dad broke the tension by asking Joon-Ho's father, whom I'd begun to think of as Gomez Addams, if he played golf. The man's face lit up.

Joon-Ho's mother sliced the air with her hand to stop their discussion. "We've checked with the best fortune-tellers," she said. "They're a respectable match: fire dragon and earth rooster. While we would have preferred an earth monkey, Joon-Ho's ideal match, this will do."

The more she talked, the more I concentrated on the music. As much as I'd rejected most Korean things, I'd always been fond of Korean stringed instruments. The music reminded me of my *harmony*, and I wondered how she would have reacted if she were here. The restaurant was packed. A few people were standing by the door waiting for a table or to pick up food they'd ordered to take home. It had been Kate's mother who'd insisted we have dinner there. Now I wondered if my mother was having regrets. We were clearly overdressed. The dark mahogany tables and chairs had seen better days and all the little knick-knacks—figurines of brides and grooms in traditional Korean attire, and decorated paper fans—looked gimmicky hanging against faded floral wallpaper.

Though we'd ordered after several of the guests around us, our food began to arrive quickly. "At least I can't complain about the service," Joon-Ho's mother said, surveying the piping-hot plates in front of us. "But that music is too loud." She looked at Mrs. Kim and pointed to a speaker semi-hidden by artificial plants hanging from the ceiling.

"They're planning a wedding engagement," Mrs. Kim told customers sitting around us, as if she hadn't heard Joon-Ho's mother. A few of the guests raised their glasses to us and nodded their heads politely.

I felt my face burn. I whispered to my mother, "You told me this was just a simple dinner to see if the families liked each other—nothing more."

She brushed me off. I looked at Joon-Ho, but he was engrossed in a feast of short ribs, ox tongue, and liver, all dripping soy marinade. I kicked him under the table. He looked at me confused, and continued eating.

"I wish we had a private room," Joon-Ho's mother said. The restaurant was getting noisier. Then she asked Joon-Ho how the food was.

"Please have some," my mother said. The table was crammed with dishes we would never normally order.

But she shook her head. "I can't imagine it'll come close to what I'm used to back home."

I knew my mother must be disappointed. But Joon-Ho's mother, my Morticia, was doing such a fine job antagonizing her and destroying our perfect marriage match, I was delighted. I allowed myself to relax and slid back into my chair.

"Sit up," Morticia snapped.

I couldn't believe she was telling me what to do. I looked at my mother, hoping she'd say something. But she didn't. My dad was busy talking about baseball, which apparently had become a national obsession in Korea. Both he and Joon-Ho's father were drinking sake. I suddenly craved the sensation of *soju* burning down my throat.

"We've already purchased some excellent pieces of jewelry for the wedding," Morticia said. "While we were in Hong Kong. The best jade."

"You're too generous," my mother said.

I felt dizzy. The words *subservience*, *obedience*, and *silence* hovered like ghosts around the table. I looked down at my white dress. I was already a ghost. I thought about Rubina. I wondered what she might be doing right at that moment, halfway across the world. I thought back to when we first met in Mr. Mills's class. I remembered telling her about Delia and her awful scar. Now Rubina was in Pakistan somewhere. When she first told us about her arranged marriage, I'd felt nothing but pity for her, and wondered how she could allow herself to be controlled like that. I'd been annoyed by her lack of strength. But now I wondered how my fate would be any different from hers, any different from that of Delia—who had to sleep with men she didn't love to survive. We each in our own way had surrendered our lives.

"He was such a difficult delivery." Joon-Ho's mother was describing her labour. "It was enough never to consider a second child. But I had produced a boy. I was done."

Through a haze, I heard my parents talking and sensed Kate's mother watching us from a distance. I forced myself to turn and look at a little boy who was seated right by the window at the next table. He blew on the glass then wrote his name in bold letters in the condensation: *Jung-Soo*. It made me think about my own Korean name. Did it need to stay lost? Was there no other way to get it back than chaining myself to a Korean man? Perhaps it was time to surrender. I remembered what my dad had once told me: *Figure out what you want and the world will conspire to make it happen.*

Then it hit me: I could claim my name myself. I could have *everyone* call me Yu-Rhee. I didn't need Joon-Ho and his crazy Addams family. I sat up, straightening my back.

"You need to eat a lot of kimchi," I heard Joon-Ho's mother say. "But garlic grown on Canadian soil isn't quite the same—which makes me think of how my grandson will be raised here."

An old Korean folk song I hadn't heard since I was a child was playing. I started humming along. My mother looked horrified. It was about *Kap doli* and *Kap suni*, a boy and a girl who secretly loved each other but pretended to be indifferent. They both married someone else, and cried as they thought of each other on their wedding night.

"I can't believe they're playing this ridiculous music," Morticia said under her breath, but still loud enough for us to hear. "I feel like we're trapped in some time warp."

The word *trapped* set me free.

"I can't do this," I said, first to myself, then again for everyone to hear. Even I was surprised by the strength of my voice. "You haven't even told me you love me," I said, looking at Joon-Ho.

His mouth was too full of food for him to answer. His mother didn't look concerned. My mother placed her hand on my lap and whispered for me to keep quiet. This angered me even more.

"You lied to me," I said. "This was a set-up. You've gone and planned a marriage without me."

I knocked my rice bowl over standing up. Food spilled down my dress. I wanted my mother to say something, but I knew her well enough to be sure she'd suffer any humiliation quietly rather than make a scene.

"I can't marry you," I told Joon-Ho.

"But we—"

"Had sex! So? I'm in love with someone else."

Joon-Ho's mother said something in Korean I didn't understand, a muffled word that sounded like a curse. Joon-Ho turned to her, his mouth dripping with tempura sauce. My parents were speechless.

I rushed away from the table. Kate's mother chased after me, catching my arm as I reached the door.

"You'll catch a cold," she said.

Was she smiling? I fled, a trail of whispers following me into the night.

Chapter 14

$\mathcal{M}$y parents and I went on as if nothing had happened. It was no different from Leon's attack or me finding out about my mother's missing sister. On TV, black and white families talked about their feelings all the time. But that wasn't our way, and I was glad. My mother didn't ask who I was in love with. For all I knew, she thought my overly dramatic attempt to sabotage the night was a lie. I wondered if she might secretly be relieved.

"Focus on your studies," she said. "It was a mistake to plan too far ahead. There's a time for all things, and an order for all things: birth, education, marriage, children, death."

To my relief, Joon-Ho didn't come by.

"I'm so glad you weren't there," I told Josh as we restocked shelves. "I never want to see him again."

"I guess we should have seen it coming," he said, taking boxes of tissues from me. "Think how much he used to help out in the store and how much time you guys spent hanging out."

Was he suggesting this was all my fault?

"He's not a bad guy," Josh said. "I sort of miss having him around. He was doing an amazing job fixing the basement. It's bright—you can actually see the inventory we have now. He wanted to put in new shelving and finish off the lighting system."

It annoyed me that he liked Joon-Ho. The two had even gone to the arcades a few times together during the summer. "Well, *Appa* misses him even more than you," I said. Although my dad hadn't spoken about him, I knew he had been the fondest of Joon-Ho, his mechanically adept, hardworking, Korean-speaking sidekick.

Will was changing before my very eyes. He'd gone from being the cool, sophisticated teacher to the stereotypical suffering artist. He seemed more discontented each time I saw him. His last story—one I'd proofread and told him was brilliant even if it wasn't, because I loved him—had been trashed during a creative-writing workshop.

"It was brutal," he said, staring down at an avalanche of unflattering, even hostile comments buried within fourteen critiqued copies of his story.

"Not all of it is bad," I said. "This one says it's sentimental and whimsical."

"Maybe Yuki's right," he said. I felt his despair deepen. "I thought I could taste the book I was meant to write. Now I have doubts about everything. I feel like my mind has turned to . . ." He searched for the right word, then gave up.

I seized the moment to relate what my English professor had shared with us earlier that week.

"Did you know that the ancient Romans used to believe every person had his own genius, a divine soul, and that it was this genius who would grant a writer his creative and intellectual prowess?"

Will looked at me as if I'd lost my mind, but I continued, trying to remember the details. "Somewhere along the line, the genius moved from being an outside entity—a guardian angel of sorts—to becoming the writer himself. My prof says it's just too much pressure to put on one person. That's why so many writers end up insane, or dead."

I didn't know where I was going with all of this, but I'd begun thinking about my own genius, my "inner poet," and the strength and clarity of thought she had been providing me recently.

Will collapsed on the sofa and threw an arm over his eyes. In the window the two small geraniums I'd given him had begun to wilt, so I went to fetch a glass of water. As I tended them, I thought I saw Joon-Ho drive by. I leaned against the pane to get a better look, but the car sped away.

"Why is she so opposed to me being a writer?" I asked as my dad and I shopped for cigarettes at a wholesaler. I pulled the trolley along as he went through his list and found the brands we needed.

"Your mother was a gifted writer herself," he said, adding varieties of Benson & Hedges—regular, menthol, and deluxe—to the trolley. "She won every writing contest in her village for years and even made it to the district level."

"Really?" She'd never mentioned she used to write. I recalled Joon-Ho telling me about my *harmony* writing poetry.

"I'm sure one of her life regrets is that she never pursued it."

That's her *problem,* I thought. She'd chosen to get married, have kids, move halfway around the world. "It seems like it's in our family history to write."

"Well, it's what you both picked at your *tol*." He folded his list in half, took the trolley from me, and headed towards the checkout.

I'd only attended one *tol*, which had been for the grandson of a family friend. It was held in a large condo party room with seventy-five people, which I thought was excessive for a baby's birthday, and led by a monk. Everyone, even the non-Buddhists, prayed to San-shin and Samshin, the mountain god and birth goddess, before a table full of food: colourful rice cakes stacked a foot high, apples, Asian pears and other fruit, including whole pineapples and watermelon.

We had photos of Josh at his *tol*, dressed in a pink jacket with a blue vest and grey pants, a black hat with a long tail on his head. My own *tol* photo had been in black-and-white, and my mother had to tell me that my skirt was poppy-red, and my jacket striped red, blue, and white. My hat was gold and silver. Each of us had a long silk sash wrapped around our waist to symbolize longevity.

The highlight of the *tol* was when the child participated in the destiny ceremony. Laid out on the floor or table would be several items: money to symbolize wealth, yarn for a long life, a brush or a pen for scholarly pursuits, rice cakes to show that the child would never be without food, and a ruler to show that the child would make a living using his or her hands. The item that the baby picked up first would determine his or her future. I had selected a pen. And now I had learned that my mother too had chosen a pen.

"So, it's in our fate. It was our destiny," I said.

Our conversation was interrupted by Mr. Park, who owned a convenience store in the Vaughan and Oakwood area. "Did you hear about the Cha robbery?" he asked, rushing towards us.

My dad nodded. Word got out quickly in the Korean community.

"That's the third time they've been robbed at gunpoint this month," he said. "But what's Cha going to do? He can't even give that store away—too many blacks in that neighbourhood." He continued his rant by complaining about the rising cost of cigarettes. "Forget the blacks, it'll be the high taxes that kills my business first. I wish a giant bomb would fall and kill off all the blacks—then at least half my worries would be gone." He walked back to his trolley.

"How many times a week do you think a store gets robbed in Toronto?" I asked my dad.

"It's better here than in L.A. or New York. There's twice as many Koreans out there trying to run a business." My dad looked at his watch. "We need to get going." He paused. "Don't worry about what Mr. Park just said. If he were in Korea, he'd be complaining about the Japanese or the Chinese. If he had it his way, he'd be the only man left standing. You just remember to always treat everyone the way you want to be treated, and you'll be okay."

Of course, because Mr. Park was older, my dad had no choice but to stand and listen. One could never openly challenge the thinking of anyone older. That much I understood.

Before he started the engine, my dad said, "Don't mention to your *omma* that I talked about her writing. Your *harmony* knew how talented your mother was and didn't want her to marry me."

"Why?"

"Your *harmony* didn't approve of me. She thought I was too old—and I was! I was twenty-seven when I first met your mother. She hadn't even reached twenty. And I had no money. That's why I went to work in Germany for three years." He pulled out a pack of Chiclets, popped two pieces into his mouth, and offered me some.

He'd quit smoking after my *harmony*'s death, but the sight of all those cigarettes must have set off a craving. I'd known about his time in Germany working the mines, a popular thing to do in the 1960s for Korean men needing work.

"It seemed like a good idea at the time," he said. "Like Korea, Germany was politically divided. Unfortunately, I didn't make the huge amounts of money your *harmony* wanted, but I couldn't be away from your mother any longer. I was sure that if I were gone too long, she'd meet someone else, although she wrote to me faithfully, and I her. When it started to snow the morning of our wedding, your *harmony* was sure the gods were sending us a sign. And one might agree: It had never snowed in April before—cherry blossoms were blooming! I didn't know what to do. But your mother did. She told me the gods were blessing us, that we should be grateful for their beautiful gift. The snow was beautiful! And magically, by afternoon it was gone, and the sun came out. She had calmed my soul with her words and her faith." His eyes grew misty. "The difference between true love and infatuation is that while infatuation is about you and what you want, true love is always about the other person and what he or she needs. Remember that. It's the lesson your mother taught me, and one I'm passing on to you."

I thought of Will. From the moment I'd first walked into his classroom, he'd made my heart race. Could something that had begun with infatuation turn into true love?

"Your *harmony* never forgave me for being poor and not giving your mother the life she thought she deserved. Her sisters married rich husbands, but your mother has her pride. It was her idea to come to Canada and make our money here. How could I disagree? She was willing to give up everything for a life with me." With that, he started the car and raised the volume on the song that was playing.

Was it worth it? I felt like asking my mother. *To live chained to our store, your burdens passed on to your children? To live behind a counter day in and day out, floating in and out of boredom and the ever-present fear of being robbed?* I looked at my dad. He was chewing his gum happily and gently tapping his fingers to the music.

"I can't believe I won!" Mato, our cab-driver customer, said, his hands outstretched. "After all these years. It's not the million, but still!"

"Seventy-eight thousand dollars is a lot of money," my mother said. She patted his back.

Mato's eyes glazed over as if he were envisioning his future. "Yes, yes. I'll invest it in some sort of business—and that's how I'll make my million. Maybe I'll buy a store like this." He looked around. "I could be my own boss. No more taxi driving for me. I'd sit behind the counter all day—or better yet, hire someone to do that for me." He laughed.

"You'll never make your millions that way," I said.

My mother shook her head. "No, no," she began. "This business is too hard—too much stress. Better you focus on real estate, buy and sell. Be a businessman."

Mato continued to look around the store. "I haven't really noticed it before, but you people have put a lot into this place. I remember before you got here. The store was half the size—dingy, dusty, and dreary. How's that for poetry?"

I smiled, appreciating his attempt to amuse me. He looked up at the ceiling and the new lights that hung there. "It's so bright—but not too bright. I like the way you've redone everything."

I knew my mother was thinking about Joon-Ho as Mato talked, because it was Joon-Ho who'd spent so much time helping with the store's renovations.

"This is a lucky store," Mato said. "And you're like my second family. When I get my money, I'll take everyone out to dinner to celebrate."

We smiled and nodded, though we had no expectations he'd follow through. There had been previous winners in our store, but he'd won the largest amount by far.

After Mato left, my mother said, "This store is my life. Or rather, I gave up my life for this store."

I thought of what my father had told me about her hope on their wedding day.

"Have you heard from Joon-Ho?" she asked.

I shook my head. It had been almost a month since our breakup and I was relieved with each passing day that I didn't hear from him, wanting to believe that it was all over, that he had no further expectations of me.

I left the store to head upstairs. When I stepped into the apartment, I heard the toilet flushing.

"Joon-Ho called. He wants you to call him back," Josh, who must have realized it was me, called out from the bathroom.

My heart sank. The timing was eerie. "How'd he sound?" I asked.

"Fine."

"I think he's been following me around."

"That sounds like your overactive imagination," Josh said as he emerged. "Anyway, he told me he was really busy with school and stuff."

"You don't think he's scheming some sort of way to get back at me or anything?"

"No. Do you?"

I'd wondered ever since I thought I saw him outside Will's place. Even as I walked around campus, I sometimes felt his presence, though I could never prove anything. The last time I'd felt this way was after Leon's attack. I still cringed whenever I thought about that night and the months that followed, although I did my best to bury those memories. I sometimes wondered if I should have taken up the female police officer's advice to contact Victim Services. Maybe if I'd done that years ago, I could now leave the curtains to my bedroom window open or fall asleep without Rubina's blue scarf around my neck, a habit that had evolved into a compulsion.

I tried to reason with myself: Joon-Ho and I attended the same university—it would only be coincidence if we bumped into each other.

"He probably just wants to tie up loose ends so he can move on," Josh said. "I wouldn't worry about it. The guy's been like a cousin to us more than anything. I bet *Appa*'ll miss him more than all of us combined."

I knew that was true. In my dad's eyes, Joon-Ho was a genius. And sadly for me, still the ideal son-in-law.

Joon-Ho picked up after a single ring. "It's me," I said. To my surprise and relief, his voice sounded warm. We agreed to meet at Robarts Library on campus the next day.

"I'm looking forward to seeing you," he said.

"Me too." The words were an automatic response, and I regretted them.

I sat outside the library cafeteria, partly hidden by student artwork on display in the lobby. In the distance but still within view was a group of Korean students huddled together, waiting for others. I recognized them as members of the largest Korean-Canadian student organization on campus. Joon-Ho had expressed interest in joining the group and we'd even attended one of the dances they'd organized. I admit, I didn't try hard to fit in—they were a tight bunch who demanded I also go to their church and hang out with other Koreans. Now I avoided them.

I took out my sociology books and a highlighter. Things had recently taken a disastrous turn in Rusaline's class after a heated discussion on whether blacks could be racist towards whites. According to an article we read, racism, by definition, meant the ability of one group to subjugate another. Since our governments and business leaders were still predominantly white, it wasn't possible for blacks to be considered racist. In 1989 it was still about white power and privilege.

"So, if you have a black guy in management refusing to hire some dude 'cause he's white, he's not being a racist?" a white male student asked.

"Technically not," Rusaline said. "That's discrimination, yes. But no, technically he is not a racist because—"

"That's bullshit," he said, and the class broke into individual or group rants. Some students even walked out.

I regretted that things had gone so badly for Rusaline. It would have been interesting to expand on the idea of power and privilege, to go beyond the black and white issues to include other minority groups—the Asians, Canada's First Nations. We continued to remain the "true invisibles" my mother had once talked about.

I looked up from my reading to see Joon-Ho had arrived. Seeing his tight smile, I felt a sudden need to apologize, "I'm sorry about everything."

Joon-Ho's face relaxed. He sat next to me.

"How have you been?" I asked, my voice tentative. I really didn't want to know.

He opened his mouth as if to speak, but didn't. Finally he said, "Things are better now. I'm working very hard. If all goes well, I'll graduate as planned."

"That's great," I said. I smiled, though I still stared off at some art displayed in the distance.

"Yu-Rhee-ah," he said, trying to get my attention. "I still want to marry you."

My heart stopped.

"I want to start over again," he said. "I'm giving you a chance to make it all right again. I've had a long talk with my mother. She's back in Korea now, but you could call her and apologize."

The thought of apologizing to his mother for rejecting her need to mould me into a Korean bride filled me with a disgust I couldn't conceal. Joon-Ho pulled back when he saw my face.

"I can't be with you. I told you, I'm in love with someone else. I'm in love with Will—"

"No, I don't believe that. He's your teacher. It's an infatuation."

"No it's not!" I objected.

"He hasn't said he loved you. You haven't slept with him."

"How do you know that? What, are you spying on me?" I was stunned he would know such things.

"I have my ways," he said. There was menace in his voice. "Let's just get through this school year," he said.

"I don't want to marry you."

"Let's just get through this school year," Joon-Ho said as if I had missed the point entirely.

"I don't want to marry you," I repeated.

Joon-Ho ran his fingers through his hair and moaned, as if he were dealing with an annoying four-year-old. "No, you'd rather be with some *white* man." He looked at me, as if repulsed. My throat tightened at the memory of our last kiss, the taste of his lips.

"I just want you to leave me alone. Please."

The colour left his face. Without another word, he got up and left.

Chapter 15

"You don't look so good," I said.

Will ran his hand across the stubble on his chin. "It's been a hell of a week." He took my coat and hung it up.

"Well, guess what!" I said, my voice a song. I reached into my bag and pulled out a copy of *Arc*, a poetry magazine. "They've published three of my poems! I've known for a while that they would, but I wanted to surprise you." I flipped through the pages, then held it up for him to see.

It had been his idea for me to submit poems to the magazine, so I even dedicated one of them to him: "For W.A." He looked over the pages, offering a weak "Wow" before clearing his throat. "That's great," he said. He hugged me, his unshaven chin scratching my cheeks. "Thanks—for the dedication."

The two neglected plants by the window looked beyond saving. I should have moved them out of the sun, I thought, and debated with myself whether to throw them out.

"Have you had a chance to do any writing?" I asked as I drew the curtains back and looked outside. Nothing. I'd been nervous the entire walk over.

I turned to Will. He was sitting on the sofa, staring at a pile of student essays on his coffee table, a blank look on his face.

"Yuki broke up with me—yesterday."

I was so overcome with happiness, I couldn't stop myself from smiling. I turned away to regain my composure.

"I'm sorry," I said, and moved towards the sofa to sit next to him.

"It's for the best anyway," he said. His face crumpled and he went from sitting to lying down, his arm swung over his head in his usual way.

I stood by his feet, wondering if I could move them to sit down.

"I've been getting the worst headaches," he said.

I took that as a cue to make him some tea and went to the kitchen.

"Maybe I should try meditating," I heard him say. I'd noticed a red book on the floor next to him, *Buddhist Meditations on Writing*. "Aren't your parents Buddhists?"

"Yeah," I replied, searching through his cutlery tray for a clean spoon. A cardboard box sat on the countertop; in it were a few framed photos. I picked one up. As much as it pained me, I had to admit they made an attractive couple: Ms. Nakamura with her lovely raven black hair, almond-shaped eyes, and gentle smile; Will, his arm wrapped around her waist—their bodies like pieces in a completed jigsaw puzzle.

Will sat up again when I handed him the tea. "She just flipped out. Told me we were through. Wouldn't even tell me what was going on." When I didn't say anything, he continued. "Last week, she told me to announce my retirement from the literary world after she saw the feedback from my last workshop. Now she freaks out. Maybe she's right; I should give up writing."

I sat facing Will, cross-legged. *One crisis at a time*, I thought. First, I needed to repair the broken writer's soul in front of me.

"You know, up until now, all you've done is academic writing. Creative writing's a completely different thing. It's intuitive." I took the mug from him and sipped a bit of tea to calm my nerves. Relieved he seemed to be listening, I went on. "It's like a story chooses you and you write it. It's a creative process you haven't really done a lot of, right? The last major thing you wrote was your master's thesis. A research paper." I handed him the mug back.

"Yeah." Will's face brightened. "Yuki doesn't get it—that I need time to construct the narrative—the images in my head. Writing's a compulsion. I can't help myself. She was only getting in the way. Her and her ambitions for me."

It pleased me, I confess, that he was blaming his writing failures on her.

"I can do this. I was meant to do this." He looked at me, searching for reassurance.

I nodded, happy to give it.

"You're wonderful," he said. He leaned over to kiss me.

It was so incredible I didn't even flinch when I felt hot tea splash onto my lap. I'd never felt so happy in my life. We were both finally free.

I'd just left a Korean herbal shop with a bag of ginseng I'd picked up for my mother, who was complaining more and more about her aches and pains, when I ran into Kate outside Bathurst subway station.

"You look tired," she said.

Juggling the daycare, tutoring, and school was taking its toll on me. Instead of responding, I asked her how she was doing and she told me everything was all right, though her voice said otherwise.

"How are you?" she asked.

"Great."

"Really? I heard about what happened in my mother's restaurant."

"Things are fine now," I said. I wasn't ready to tell her about Will.

"You're okay with Joon-Ho dating your friend now?"

I looked at her, confused.

"The one with the wavy blonde hair."

"Erin?"

"Yeah, that's the one. I saw them the other day by the Second Cup, where I work. They looked pretty cozy, if you know what I mean."

"Are you sure?" I couldn't believe it.

She nodded. "I've got to go."

Something was wrong. "Kate," I said, touching her shoulder. "Call me if you ever want to talk."

"It's not like we're friends or anything."

"Well, sometimes it's easier to talk to a stranger," I replied.

"You're not that either," she said, though she smiled before rushing off.

The TV was louder than usual so I knew Mrs. Young was visiting. She was hard of hearing.

"It's easy to say, but I have no place to go," I heard her say as I stood awkwardly in the tiny foyer, wondering if I should leave or make a noise to let them know I was home. "I always thought once Peter left for school, I could go back to Korea, but how would I support myself? I don't know what's worse—either way, I'll die a beaten woman instead of an old woman like you."

The phone rang and my mother turned off the TV to answer it. I took the opportunity to open and close the front door, being louder than necessary.

"*Annyeonghaseyo*," I greeted Mrs. Young.

Pink, white, and green pieces of paper were stacked on the coffee table. Mrs. Young was holding some wires. She and my mother were making paper lanterns for Buddha's birthday celebration while watching Korean soap operas.

"How are your studies?" Mrs. Young asked in Korean. "Did you choose a major yet?"

"I'm still taking intro classes," I said. "I'm enjoying sociology and psychology quite a bit."

"What do you learn in psychology?" she asked. She picked up pliers to bend the wires into a frame.

"Right now, we're looking at personality disorders."

She grabbed wire-cutters. "What's that?" she asked. I was impressed by how skillfully her hands manipulated the wires.

"It's a little complicated." Since I'd started the course, I'd begun to feel like I had every mental illness mentioned in the textbook, including obsessive-compulsive disorder, for needing my scarf to sleep with every night.

"Would you like to help us?" Mrs. Young asked.

"Sorry. I've got to use the phone," I said. I took it from my mother when she was done and went to my room. The TV came back on as I closed my door.

Erin confirmed she and Joon-Ho had met a couple of times.

"It was only because he wanted to see how you were doing," she said.

I thought about Joon-Ho telling me he had a way of finding out about my life. It had never dawned on me his source was Erin.

"What's the big deal?" Erin said. Her calm tone was getting on my nerves. "He'll get over you. I was gonna tell you at some point."

"You're so pathetically stupid," I said, and hung up. Didn't she realize she was being used? What was Joon-Ho hoping to find out? Details about Will? Was he crazy enough to contact Ms. Nakamura and tell her I was behind their breakup? Couldn't he just leave me alone?

When Josh came upstairs, we asked each other at the same time, "What's wrong?"

Mrs. O'Doherty had died. Her granddaughter was downstairs and wanted to see me.

Kathleen O'Doherty was the spitting image of her grandmother. She extended a slender hand, which I'd barely touched before she withdrew it.

"I'm very sorry to hear about your grandmother," I said.

"Thank you," she said. "Unfortunately, I didn't really get a chance to know her. I live in Vancouver, as does most of my family." She hesitated. "My mother and my grandmother didn't get along. In fact, they haven't spoken in years."

It was true Mrs. O'Doherty had rarely mentioned her family in the five years I'd known her.

"Anyway, I found these and thought you might want them." She handed me a grocery bag filled with old diaries. "I've gone through some of them. It didn't take me long to figure out who you were. She mentions you quite often. She was clearly very fond of you."

I pulled a diary out of the bag. Her handwriting reminded me of my grade-three teacher's—the one who'd taught me cursive. The lettering was neat and elegant. As Josh offered Kathleen a drink, I scanned a few entries and stopped at May 15, 1988. *Mary is getting ready for her prom. Today, I got the greatest pleasure helping her shape her eyebrows of all things! It reminded me of Rosemary and how excited she was at her own prom.*

My eyes watered. "Are you sure you don't want these?"

Kathleen took a sip of Mountain Dew. She shook her head. "Neither does my mother."

I wanted to ask her what had happened between the two that caused such animosity, but it wasn't appropriate. *There's a sad story here*, I thought. I would have jumped at the opportunity to get to know my *harmony*. She too had been separated from her daughters—the one lost to her and the one who'd left, putting more than ten thousand kilometres of ocean and land between them.

"I thought, though, that my grandmother might want you to have them. You can throw them out if you don't."

I shook my head. They were precious. Mrs. O'Doherty was a writer, even if all she wrote was her diaries. I had an image of her arriving home, her usual box of instant oatmeal, loaf of bread, and canned tuna in her shopping bag. She sat at the tiny desk in the corner of her living room, her antique brass reading lamp lit, her diary opened, and Rachmaninoff playing in the background.

"She loved Russian composers," I said. "She used to lend me her records." I thought about the small collection that had accumulated over the years, still resting by my record player. She'd never asked for any of them back.

Kathleen looked at her watch, thanked us for the drink, and left without looking back.

I wanted to call in sick, but I'd already missed a day last week and another the week before, so I went to work at the daycare. As soon as I arrived, Maura, my supervisor, called me into her office. I was nervous and began scripting what I might tell her so I could hold on to the job. I still had balances owing on all my credit cards.

"There's a man who's been hanging out in the parking lot," she said. "I asked Linda, and she said it was a friend of yours." She pointed to the small monitor on her filing cabinet. The security tape showed Joon-Ho, smoking a cigarette as he sat on the hood of his car. I wasn't losing my mind; he *was* following me around.

"Tell your friend this is a daycare within a school. Seeing strangers hanging around makes our parents nervous."

"He's not my friend," I said.

"Well, if he continues, I'll have to call the police."

"I'll talk to him," I said.

Mato, who still drove a cab in spite of his lottery win, gave me a ride to Joon-Ho's house, which was near the university campus. "I can't quit driving just yet," he said. "It's not like I won a million dollars." He didn't charge me.

I hadn't called Joon-Ho to say I was coming. I was too angry. But when I got there, he wasn't home. His landlady, Mrs. Henry, let me in. Although she must have been in her seventies, she looked much younger in a white blouse, black skirt, and wide black belt. Her grey hair was cut short, like a boy's. I'd met her only once, when Joon-Ho first moved in. She greeted me with a wide smile and gestured me inside.

"You're Sean's girlfriend . . . ?" she said, trying to recall my name.

I didn't correct her. "You have a lovely home," I said, although there was nothing in it I cared for. The living room was decorated with antiques: a coffee table, a corner cupboard crammed with colourful crystal and china ornaments, and next to it an old-fashioned cabinet writing desk, which felt too dark and heavy for the space. Hung above the damask sofa was a painting of yellow roses and lilies. It would have been pretty if not for the gaudy gold frame.

"My Roger painted that for our thirtieth anniversary, God rest his soul," Mrs. Henry said. "It's a painting of my wedding bouquet. It used to hang downstairs in the guest room before Sean moved into it . . ." She rubbed her wedding ring. "I've been blessed. You too, my dear. Sean is a good man. It was his idea to hang the flowers here, so I could see them every day. He's been a great help. This house is falling apart faster than I am." She put her hand to her cheek and closed her eyes for a moment. "My Roger, he was the same—could fix anything."

A tea kettle whistled from the kitchen at the same time the grandfather clock at the end of the hall struck four. Mrs. Henry frowned, and said, "I didn't realize it was so late. I'm expecting company." She disappeared into the kitchen, but kept talking. "Would you mind waiting for Sean in his room? I'll let you in. If he was expecting you, I'm sure he'll be along in no time."

I was about to tell her he wasn't expecting me, then changed my mind. "Yes, that'll be fine."

It had been a while since I'd been in Joon-Ho's room. When I flicked on the light switch, I was startled to see a bulletin board full of images of me. Twelve photos arranged in three rows, pinned according to the time and date stamped on them. The first had been taken back in Korea. My face was makeup-free and bruised, my hair pulled back in a tight ponytail. *It looks like a damn mug shot*, I thought. When had he taken all the other photos? There were shots of me at the prom, at my nineteenth-birthday dinner, even one of me on campus.

No wonder Mrs. Henry thought I was his girlfriend. I felt annoyed and thought of removing them, but decided against it, afraid of Joon-Ho's reaction. I searched for a piece of paper to write a note on. His desk, also an antique, was covered with textbooks and binders. I noticed an essay Joon-Ho had written and picked it up. *At least he's keeping up with his studies*, I thought. I flipped to the back, curious about the mark he'd received. In black marker, his prof had written, "Plagiarism is a serious breach of the university code of behaviour and will lead to charges of academic misconduct. Because this is a draft version of your paper, I'm letting it go with this written warning. Please see me as soon as possible."

I was suddenly afraid for him, and thought with a pang of guilt about what I'd done for my own last essay, a comparison of three major works of satire in English literature—virtually Will's old paper retyped with my name on it. I hadn't even read *Moll Flanders*, the third book discussed in my essay. I looked in the drawer. There were letters, all in Korean. I read the top one, dated a couple of weeks before his parents' visit.

Glad to hear school is going well. Looking forward to meeting your girlfriend. Have prepared the appropriate gifts for her and her family. A wedding after your graduation would be ideal. You'd have to find work immediately and then you can begin our immigration paperwork. Your father has not been able to stop talking about retiring in Canada. He has become obsessed with golf, and has already heard that golfing conditions there are excellent.

My heart skipped a beat. What was going on? I searched through the drawer and found guides on Canadian citizenship and immigration. And I thought *my* mother had huge expectations of me! Joon-Ho's mother wanted him not only to get a Canadian education, but to use that to get a job and get her out of Korea. Typical. If I'd entertained even the remotest possibility of marrying Joon-Ho, knowing his dreadful mother would soon be breathing the same air on the same continent was enough to quash any residual romantic feelings.

I stuffed everything back into the drawer and looked at the alarm clock by Joon-Ho's bed. 4:15 p.m. Where was he? There was a copy of *Arc* next to the clock. I flipped to the pages with my poems. A pencil had been used to scratch out my dedication to Will—all that was left was a small hole in the page.

"What're you doing here?"

I turned and saw Joon-Ho at the door. It took a second to catch my breath. "Mrs. Henry let me in. I just got here."

Joon-Ho threw his coat on the bed.

"My supervisor—at the daycare—has you on video hanging out

in the parking lot. She told me she'd call the police if you did it again. I came to tell you that, because I didn't want you to get into trouble."

His whole body relaxed. "Thanks," he said. "Is that all?" He didn't seem concerned.

"Yeah," I said. "You've got to stop this. You've got to leave me alone. You've got to leave *my friends* alone."

Joon-Ho sat on his bed, and wrapped his hands around his head. "Okay, but I need your help."

"What?"

"I'm having trouble writing my papers. I have all the ideas—in my head—but I need help getting them on paper. English isn't my first language, and it's becoming more obvious as the work gets more complex. And I keep getting these bad headaches." He rubbed his ear.

"If I help you, you'll leave me alone?" I felt as if I were making a pact with the devil, but I didn't know what else to do. There was a part of me that felt sorry for him. But I still remembered the bird that had been trapped in the store basement.

Joon-Ho nodded. Then in Korean, he said, *"Yak-sok,"* before repeating it in English. "I promise."

Chapter 16

$\mathcal{I}$ got fired from the daycare the same day my mother handed me a thousand-dollar check from the lottery corporation—the amount shopkeepers got for selling a winning ticket. I made a mental note to thank Mato for coming into the store and purchasing his thirteen lottery tickets when I happened to be working. The money would be enough to pay off the rest of my credit-card debts.

Later that night, alone in the apartment, I stared at the phone and debated whether or not to call Linda. I needed to apologize to her. She must have been regretting the day she'd recommended me for the daycare position. Even I had been surprised to hear how many days of work I'd missed since starting there five months earlier. I thought about calling Erin, but I was still angry at her for not telling me about Joon-Ho. As for Rubina, I didn't even have a way to contact her. She hadn't bothered to call or write since moving to Pakistan. For all I knew, she was six months pregnant with triplets.

My friends are useless, I thought. I was exhausted. It was almost a relief to be fired, especially now that my debts were gone. Still, it was crushing to know I'd messed up so badly.

Pushing my final psychology essay to the side, I picked up the grocery bag stuffed with Mrs. O'Doherty's diaries. They carried faint traces of the homemade potpourri that used to scent her apartment. As I breathed in the fragrance of lavender and citrus, tears fell down my cheeks. I thought back to her comment, "A wild bird in a house is bad luck—a sure sign of death in the family." She'd been more like a grandmother to me than the two in Korea I barely knew.

I took a deep breath, blew my nose, and started reading one of the diaries. It felt awkward at first, like going through the unlocked door of a friend's home. I stopped when I found a passage about me. Mrs. O'Doherty had written that I had "a constant look of longing."

What had she meant by that? It was disturbing to know I was a character in someone's book, even if there was no intended audience for it. The idea of someone watching me had haunted me since the night of my attack. I searched through the grocery bag and found her diary entries around the time of that night. She'd been told I fell down the stairs, but she'd guessed what had happened. She wrote: *The police came by asking questions. There's been an attack in the neighbourhood. Oddly, Mary's nowhere to be found, her mother telling me she has taken a bad fall.* Then, a few days later: *Josh has confirmed my worst suspicions: Mary was attacked by a pimp named Leon. She didn't fall. I swore on my life I wouldn't say anything. He seemed relieved to tell me. What a burden to hold such secrets.*

She'd known the truth all along. I felt stupid now. And Josh. I'd never even stopped to think about the impact my attack could have had on him. *What a burden to hold such secrets.* I was glad he'd been able to turn to her. Mrs. O'Doherty had been like a guardian angel, watching over us, protecting us in her own way.

The diaries chronicled not only my life, but the lives of several others in our neighbourhood. I picked up another diary. Mr. Martin, who owned the shoe store below the apartment where Mrs. O'Doherty lived, had apparently tried to convert his store to a convenience store after he saw my parents expand theirs, but my mother had stopped him. How could Mrs. O'Doherty have known this when I hadn't? In another entry, she wrote about an "odd homeless man with a horn around his neck." I looked up to see Josh standing in the doorway.

"She wrote about Tico," I told him. "Did you know that his real name was Tracy? How'd she find that out? Ever wonder why he wears that horn—?"

"Kate's on the phone," he said. "She doesn't sound good."

Josh drove me to Christie Pits and waited in the car. I found Kate sitting on a swing. She didn't look up, so I sat on the swing next to her. On a night when I'd been feeling utterly friendless, I was grateful she'd thought of me.

"I hate my mother," she said, then looked up at the darkening sky.

Wow, I thought to myself. I would never have the courage to speak so honestly—especially about my mother. Neither would Joon-Ho. I admired her.

She started crying. "I hate my mother, and one day, my kid's gonna say the same thing about me." She turned to me. "She'll hate me for giving her up. My mother's given up on me."

I looked at the empty field. I wished I knew what to say to make her feel better.

"You're one of the strongest people I know."

She laughed and grabbed the swing's chains, pushing off gently.

"I don't know why I even care," she said. "I tried going back home—after my boyfriend kicked me out. But I can't win with my mother. It's always, 'Why can't you be more like Bridget? Or Angela? Or Mary?' " She shook her head. "Do you know what it's like to be a constant disappointment to everyone?" She dragged her feet to stop swinging. "My mother tried to set me up on all these blind dates, get me married off. She's even resorted to calling guys up in Korea. She's hoping someone will be desperate enough to see me as a free ticket to Canada." She began swinging again.

It was growing dark, and the night air was chilly. Kate had only a thin black jacket on. Looking at her made me feel colder, even though I was wearing a coat with a turtleneck under it. The park seemed large and dangerous. I was glad Josh wasn't far away.

"My mom set me up with a cop—a Korean cop," she said, staring at the ground. "Weeks ago. I was so desperate for him to like me I let him do pretty much anything he wanted—not just him but one of his friends too—" She stopped swinging and burst into tears again. "How could I be such a total fuck-up? I hope she drops dead."

"You know, my mother and I were sitting on a bench outside a train station in Korea. My mother was a mess, because she'd just found out some awful stuff about my dad's family, when your mother appeared—like magic out of nowhere. She knew just how to make my mother feel better."

"It's nice to hear she's good for something," Kate said between sniffles.

"She's been a really good friend to my mother. I wish I could be the same for you. I just don't know how."

"Well, you're here now." She finally looked up at me. "How're you doing, anyway?"

"I got fired today—from a daycare of all places. I apparently missed thirty-two days of work in five months. How's that even possible?"

She laughed. "I guess I'm not the only fuck-up in K-Town."

I smiled. "Kate, no one I know isn't messed up somehow, some way. Some even more than you." I thought of Joon-Ho. I even thought of Will, who'd long been threatening to make major changes in his life. No one I knew seemed free of complications.

I got up, stretched, and reached out my hand for Kate to take. She looked unconvinced, but when she wrapped her fingers, cold as stone, around mine, I knew she was grateful for whatever lies she presumed I was telling her. We walked to the car in silence.

It felt wonderful to be able to meet Will during a weekday, even if it meant missing a couple of classes. It was the last Friday of his March break and we'd decided to take the day off and drive up north with no real destination in mind. The morning was lovely with clear blue skies—perfect as a poem. I imagined that this was what it would be like if I were Will's girlfriend. Maybe I would become a teacher after all, and we would have our March break together, our summers too.

But it looked more and more like winter the farther we drove away from Toronto, and though the snow was beautiful on the open fields, I couldn't help but think it must be bitterly cold outside. Still, the sun was radiant. Will didn't talk as he drove, so I listened to the radio. When Bobby McFerrin's song "Don't Worry, Be Happy" came on, I took it to heart, and did just that.

When I needed to use the washroom, we stopped at a little restaurant in the middle of nowhere. A gust of wind whipped against us as we got out of the car. Even though the restaurant was empty, it was several minutes before the waitress sat us. I ordered the breakfast special before rushing to the washroom. On my way back, I passed the kitchen, where I heard our waitress talking to another woman. "Why's a handsome guy like him wasting his time with a skinny little Oriental? I could drown in eyes as ocean blue as his."

"Maybe there ain't enough of us smart, sophisticated types wherever they blew in from," the other woman said, and laughed.

I felt as if I had just been punched in the stomach. I sat down, wondering if I should tell Will I wanted to leave. He didn't give me a chance.

"I've requested a leave of absence for next year," he said, breaking into a smile.

"You can do that?"

"I was thinking of doing some travelling. Paris—isn't that the ideal place to be writing?"

If you're French, I thought, but smiled back.

"I've been giving this real thought. You were right. I need a change of environment. A new scene to write a new scene, ha-ha."

Our food arrived at the same time as our coffee.

"Come with me," he said.

I was about to ask him where, when it dawned on me he meant Paris. I stopped stirring my coffee.

"What about school—for me, I mean?"

"Take a year off. We could write together."

"What about money?"

"I've got some savings—Yuki made me put aside money for the wedding and the down payment on a house. I told you—she had my whole life planned."

The last time I'd seen him this alive and animated was in the classroom. I allowed myself to indulge his fantasies. *Don't worry, be happy.* He put his fork down and reached over to touch my hand, sending the most wonderful sensations through me. I wanted to say yes.

"It'll be amazing. Come with me. I don't want to do this alone."

I should have been delighted, but there was something about the way he said he didn't want to go alone.

"I'll think about it."

That night, I lay awake, excited by the thought of being halfway around the world with Will. I would be free of Joon-Ho. Still, I couldn't shake the comments the waitresses had made. I'd snatched back the tip Will had left, though I'd done it behind his back. Maybe life would be easier with a Korean man. We certainly wouldn't draw any attention.

I was exhausted when my mother woke me up early the next morning. Joon-Ho was on the phone.

"Where have you been?" He sounded furious.

I rubbed my eyes and looked at my alarm clock: 7:30.

"What's wrong?" I was afraid he'd found out I'd spent the day with Will.

"I tried calling you all day yesterday. The chair of engineering wanted to see me. He asked me all these questions about my undergrad paperwork, about the courses I'd taken in Korea, if all my paperwork was real. I told him of course. But I don't think he believed me, because now I need to meet with the dean. The chair told me I could bring counsel. What does that mean?"

I was relieved his panic had nothing to do with me.

"Counsel—like, a lawyer?" I asked.

"I don't know. I didn't want to ask any questions."

"Well, I'm sure there's nothing to worry about. Just tell them the truth."

"Can you come with me?" He sounded like a little boy.

Though I dreaded being dragged into his mess, I agreed to meet him at the dean's office on Tuesday morning. I'd be missing even more of my classes. *Too many needy people in my life,* I thought as I hung up.

I could tell by Joon-Ho's silence as he walked out of his dean's office that things hadn't gone well. We walked outside together.

"It's all over for me."

"I'm sure it'll be fine," I assured him. "Once they go through your records and verify them, everything will be fine." I touched his arm.

He turned away.

"It will be fine, right?" I asked, needing to hear it from him.

I almost lost my balance as he slumped over me, shaking.

"What have I done?" His cry was muffled. "What have I done?"

I tried to push him off me gently. His mouth was trembling and tears rolled down his cheeks. I took his face in my hands and tried to calm him so I could find out what was going on. As if the feel of my hands had helped him, Joon-Ho seemed to regain composure. He drew a deep breath and told me the truth about everything.

We sat in Joon-Ho's bedroom trying to figure out a game plan. His case was set to go to the Trial Division of the University Tribunal. Although he'd initially thought of pleading "not guilty," he changed his mind after consulting a lawyer he found in the Yellow Pages.

"Maybe you should have gone with a Korean lawyer," I said, looking at the *Code of Academic Behaviour* he'd been given and feeling overwhelmed by the legal jargon. I had no idea the university had such a strict protocol on academic misconduct. Since Joon-Ho had told me he'd never graduated from a university in Korea, nor taken any of the graduate-level classes he claimed he'd completed to get into the master's program, I knew he'd never be allowed to stay. Still, he seemed determined to see this through.

"The last thing I want is for any Koreans here to find out," he said. "You have no idea what lengths my father went to or just how much he spent to get me here." He was highlighting the charges against him, and looking up the words he didn't know in a Korean–English dictionary. There were several charges, all related to forged and falsified documents. Words such as *cheat*, *fraud*, and *misrepresentation* alarmed me more each time I read them.

"I can't believe he betrayed me," Joon-Ho said, and handed me a sheet of paper. His hand turned into a fist that pounded his desk so hard that several items, including a tiny framed photo of his parents, crashed to the hardwood floor. I bit my lower lip as I read the page.

One of his professors had provided the university with a written statement that Joon-Ho had been warned about plagiarism regarding parts of his draft thesis. Once his academic records had been inspected, the truth about his past in Korea was exposed.

Joon-Ho asked me to help him write a personal statement expressing his deep regret. He wanted me to mention that, since his arrival, he'd been under a tremendous amount of pressure to excel and that his health had been compromised as a result. Though I thought this an irrelevant detail, I told him I'd do as he asked, desperately hoping that once everything was settled, he'd go back to Korea and be out of my life for good.

While Will had helped me out with my English and history papers, I still had my social science papers to write, but I began working on Joon-Ho's statement later that night. I was resentful because I'd really been getting into some of the research I was doing for my courses. Some of it had horrified me: In anthropology, I learned about female genital mutilation as a cultural practice; in sociology, I was stunned to learn about the high rate of elderly abuse in Canadian society; and in psychology, I witnessed the human capacity for cruelty as we watched documentaries about famous experiments conducted by psychologists over the years. Walking into an English class and escaping into Virginia Woolf's *To the Lighthouse* made me feel like Alice in Wonderland.

The phone rang. I ignored it. It could have been Joon-Ho wanting an update. The phone kept ringing. Finally I went to get it. It was my mother calling from downstairs.

"Why didn't you pick up?" she demanded. Mr. Young had been robbed again, and this time he'd been shot. His store was several blocks north of ours—the shooter was still out there.

"You need to watch the store. I need to get over to see Mrs. Young. Your father's already gone over," my mother said and hung up.

"Maybe we should close early," I said when I got downstairs. I didn't want to be alone in the store. Josh was out celebrating a friend's birthday and not expected back till much later.

"You'll be fine," she said. "I've already called Joon-Ho, and he'll be here in a few minutes."

I had to admit I was relieved he was coming—better he get shot than me.

The papers reported the robbery the next day: "Shopkeeper Shot Several Times During Armed Robbery." My mother and I were behind the store counter and I read the story to her. "An unidenti- fied male, armed with a gun . . ." I stopped and scanned the rest of the article. "It says Mr. Young's in stable condition. He'll be fine. Does Peter know?" I thought of Mr. Young's son. He was my age and studying in Kingston. "He's still out there, you know," I said, referring to the robber.

My mother nodded.

"This isn't the most flattering photo of Mr. Young," I said, point- ing to the black-and-white head shot of him in the paper. "It looks like a passport photo."

"The reporters demanded a photo of him," my mother explained. "It was either that or a photo of the store—which no store owner would want." She looked around our place. "Who would ever buy a store with a known history of violence? Mr. Young was stupid to fight back. Remember, if you're ever robbed, just give them everything they want."

Or play dead, I thought, remembering what I'd done with Leon.

My mother folded the newspaper and put it back on the rack. *The advice she gave me had worked for her*, I thought. I had long ago lost count of the number of times we'd been robbed, unarmed or otherwise, and we'd never made the local newspapers.

Over the next few weeks, I thought more and more about Joon-Ho's upcoming hearing and the importance of one's reputation. I couldn't help but recall a scene from Shakespeare's *Othello*. The good Cassio laments to the evil Iago, after getting drunk and attacking an innocent Montano, "Reputation, reputation, reputation! O, I have lost my reputation. I have lost the immortal part of me . . ." I'd felt such pity for Cassio.

Awareness of the importance of a good reputation had prompted me to maintain the lie that I'd fallen down a flight of stairs rather than let it get out that a man had nearly raped me—although my public declaration at a restaurant that I'd lost my virginity was certainly a hiccup. Thankfully, my mother had never mentioned this incident since, even though I knew I'd severely complicated her hope of finding a proper Korean man for me.

Perhaps even more significant, because our livelihood depended on it so much, was our store's reputation. Our pride and misery. My mother's third child. Her baby.

I wondered about Joon-Ho's reputation. What would my mother think if she found out he was about to be kicked out of school? My reputation was my responsibility—when had Joon-Ho's become mine as well?

On one hand, I wanted to expose him, especially to my family, who adored him. I suspected my dad still wanted me to marry him. But a sympathetic part of me understood Joon-Ho's overwhelming pressure to succeed in the eyes of his parents. I feared the dark side of him, but knew it came from being born Korean, an only child and a boy, raised to believe he was destined for greatness (and therefore allowed to exercise authority over women). But I hoped beneath that was a gentle spirit, a boy who'd given me my first kiss, who'd whispered my lost name. I remembered the origami swan he'd made me, and his comment about swans mating for life. I'd freely surrendered my first time to him, but he couldn't hold that against me. Could he?

"It's a beautiful love story," Mrs. O'Doherty had said as she handed me Tchaikovsky's *Swan Lake*. On the album cover was a drawing of a ballerina. "It has everything you'd want in a good story: a distressed princess, a brave prince, and an evil magician."

If I was Odette and Will was my prince, what did that make Joon-Ho? I looked at the ballerina's face. Her eyes were downcast, her lips a thin line with no hint of a smile.

Chapter 17

According to the clock that hung over the Council Chamber doorway at the university, it was 4:30 when I arrived for Joon-Ho's hearing. I was half an hour early. I'd brought one of Mrs. O'Doherty's diaries with me, but I was too nervous to read it. Instead, I sat on a bench in the little foyer outside the chamber, anxiously waiting for Joon-Ho.

Of all the buildings I'd been in on campus, Simcoe Hall, which housed the offices of the president and other administrators, was the most intimidating with its white marble floors, and huge portraits of past presidents and council chairs, draped in robes, lining the walls. They were all white, although I was happy to see some of them were women.

I held my breath and counted each second that went by until it was exactly five. A clerk walked out, and as he struggled to pronounce Joon-Ho's name, it hit me that Joon-Ho, who'd never been late for anything, wasn't going to show up. I told the clerk I was there on Joon-Ho's behalf.

The sight of the Board Room took my breath away. It was huge, with a glass dome and arched windows. In the middle was a giant round wooden table with a hole in the centre. It reminded me of a lifesaver. I counted eighteen chairs around it. Did they deliberately meet in such a large room to intimidate students?

As I sat down, my hands trembled and I tucked them under my legs. From reading the guides Joon-Ho had been given, I knew the Tribunal Hearing Panel consisted of three people: a student representative, a faculty member, and the tribunal chair. It was easy to figure out who the student was. A Canadianized version of Joon-Ho, with the same haircut and build. A math or science major, I thought. When the chair asked me to state my name, I noticed the tape recorder in front of the clerk, a tiny bright green light indicating it was on. Did I have to give them my real name? The realization that my presence would be permanently recorded sent a new wave of panic through me. Though I was doing nothing wrong, I still felt guilty. I wondered if the university would now look into *my* records, verify all *my* paperwork.

The chair outlined the details of the charges and then asked if Joon-Ho was guilty.

"Innocent," I said, unsure what else I could say.

The legal representative for the university, Allison Roy, began to speak. She was a stylish woman in her mid-thirties, whose short blonde hair and slender build reminded me of one of the lawyers on the TV show *L.A. Law*. Her opening comments began with the university's need to protect its integrity. As she talked, I tried to think where Joon-Ho could be. How had I not foreseen this?

Ms. Roy's hands never stopped gesturing. "This was not a spontaneous, random act, but a methodically planned and executed scheme, whereby the student deliberately and intentionally set out to defraud the university."

I swallowed. She was making Joon-Ho out to be some sort of monster. I felt like standing up and saying, *He's not as horrible as you think. You have no idea what kind of pressure he's been under.*

Ms. Roy picked up some papers. "These were submitted as part of the student's application. Forged and falsified documents, dated May 8, 1987; June 10, 1987; June . . ."

Ohmigod! I thought. I had absolutely no paperwork with me. Joon-Ho had everything. I didn't even have the personal statement I'd laboured to write for him, pleading for leniency.

After Ms. Roy outlined what she felt were the appropriate sanctions against Joon-Ho, I was asked if I wanted to say anything. I was so angry at him for abandoning me and so disappointed in him for not being man enough to show up, I wanted to say no. But I felt sorry for him at the same time. I wanted everyone in the room to know he wasn't the scheming, pathological liar out to "pervert the course of justice" Ms. Roy had called him in her closing remarks. I forced myself to stand up, every part of my body shaking.

"Joon-Ho wanted me to express his sincere regret for everything that has happened." As I tried to remember the details of his statement, I became aware of everyone watching me. I imagined the round table as a giant flotation device and I could hear myself speaking as if from a distance. "As the only son of a highly successful and accomplished father, there has always been tremendous pressure on Joon-Ho to excel." How long could I go on before passing out?

I talked about the burdens, the great expectations we—immigrant students, visa students—shouldered, when my eyes caught those of the student rep. There was something there. Compassion? Understanding? It was enough to anchor me, and I was able to continue. I added that I'd known Joon-Ho for several years as a close personal friend.

"In spite of everything said here today, Joon-Ho isn't some horrible mastermind who set out to hurt anyone, especially this university. Coming to Canada—studying at the University of Toronto—had been a lifelong dream, not just for him, but for his family, and he truly regrets his actions. They will haunt him for the rest of his life."

I felt tears coming to my eyes as I sat down. I tucked my hands back under my legs, relieved my role in this was over.

The chair advised that the panel would deliberate and asked everyone else to leave the room.

I found a pay phone and called Joon-Ho's number. No answer. I could picture him drunk. He was sprawled on the floor of his room, hopelessly muddled. Then my thoughts turned graver. Josh had told me that Koreans now had one of the highest suicide rates in the world, and that leaping from buildings together was becoming common for mothers and children who'd failed.

"Reverend Shim talked about it in church," Josh said. "A mother and her son who was expelled from Seoul National jumped from a campus library." I thought of Robarts Library, standing fourteen storeys high, right in the middle of campus. Joon-Ho had once told me he thought it looked like a swan, although I'd read somewhere it had been designed to look like a turkey, or even a peacock. I imagined the shadows of a mother and son falling, like leaves blowing in the wind. It happened slowly, soundlessly, almost peacefully—until the bodies landed with heavy thumps. I shuddered and went back into the chamber.

The chair explained that the tribunal would make a recommendation to the Governing Council for Joon-Ho's expulsion. His academic records and transcripts would record that sanction so he'd be barred from ever applying to the university again.

How was I going to break the news to Joon-Ho?

I was coming out of the ladies' washroom when I almost bumped into the young man who'd sat as the student rep. He mumbled, "Excuse me."

"I'm glad you were on the panel," I said. He turned back. "You even look like Joon-Ho." I didn't smile; I was too exhausted to be friendly.

"I can't talk to you."

"No, I get that. I'm just trying to understand everything that's happened. I feel sorry for him. All he wanted was to be successful here. You get that, right? He never meant to hurt anyone."

"Well, he did," the young man said coolly.

I looked at him, confused.

"He makes the rest of us look bad. Like we're all a bunch of idiots who can't make it here." His face turned red. "Don't *you* get it? People like him make *them* suspicious of all of us." He pointed at a portrait on the wall. "God knows, we all cheat—but what he did crossed the line. At least if you're gonna lie big-time, do it right."

"But we don't all cheat." How could I have mistaken compassion in those eyes? "And there's a big difference between doing things right and doing the right thing."

"Grow up. You're so naive. Let me guess—you're a music major. You got here on your musical merit. Well, some of us need to get places in the real world." He walked away.

I was stunned. I'd expected him to be sympathetic. What had

he meant when he said *we all cheat*? Asians? Or everyone? I'd used some of Will's essays to help me, but did that make me as bad as Joon-Ho? I thought of Linda at York University and the gold cross she always wore. She was the most honest person I knew. I could never imagine her lifting the hem of her skirt to check for answers during a test. And Kate. If she'd cheated and lied, she would have gotten into a university.

The Koreans had a saying: "It is better to fail with honour than to win with dishonour." When had things become so complicated?

I walked out into the evening air. Ms. Roy came out the same doors but ignored me. I walked behind her as she headed towards St. George Street, watching her move confidently in her navy blue suit, her head held high, her black briefcase telling the world she was not only beautiful but smart. Was she flawed in any way? Did she have any scars like Delia, who used to wear the same black heels? What would it feel like to have her blonde hair, her figure that turned heads, and her brain that got her into law school? If I had all that, would it be enough for Will to fall in love with me?

A gust of wind sent the smell of Chinese sticky buns our way. I couldn't envision Ms. Roy eating greasy noodles from a food truck, but I was wrong. She stopped, and I kept walking.

Chapter 18

Mrs. Henry answered the door. This time she seemed annoyed.

"Sorry, Sean isn't answering his phone, and I'm worried."

"Yes, yes," she said, but didn't seem concerned.

I heard voices as soon as I stepped into the foyer. The living room was full of women dressed like Mrs. Henry and sipping tea. It was ten in the morning. Who entertained this early?

Downstairs, I knocked before I tried the door. I was sure I'd find Joon-Ho passed out or hungover. But he was sitting at his desk, his palms resting flat on the wooden finish. The desk lamp was on, the room light turned off. He was staring at the bulletin board on the wall. Seeing him eye the photos of me, I could have kicked myself for not having removed them when I had the chance.

"Have you been drinking?" I asked, sniffing the air. There were a few empty cans of Labatt Blue on the floor by his bed. "Where were you? I tried calling last night . . . this morning . . . I was worried about you."

Silence.

I resorted to small talk. "Mrs. Henry has a ton of ladies here." Unlike the room upstairs, filled with chatter and the clicking of porcelain cups against saucers, this room was filled with a sense of doom.

Joon-Ho nodded. "Some of her church friends practically live here," he mumbled.

"I was told it might be months before you get official word of your expulsion. Apparently these things move very slowly. There's always the appeal, although that's not really an option given what happened."

"Really? So I still have time . . ." He stared at the bulletin board again, his fingers drumming on the desk then closing around a water bottle.

He was wearing Josh's Calvin and Hobbes T-shirt, and I remembered the first time I'd seen him in it, how attractive he'd looked then—clean-cut, fit, ready to tackle any challenges. Now, much like the T-shirt itself, Joon-Ho seemed faded.

"Have you told your parents?" I asked.

"Why? So my father can save me again?" He sat on the bed and rubbed his temples. "My headaches won't stop. They're getting worse." He took some aspirin out of his drawer. "Damn it!" He shook the empty bottle and whipped it against the wall.

Before I could say anything, he continued in Korean. "The only thing he ever asked of me was to make it in Canada so we could all be together here. He's already made these big plans for his retirement here. He thinks this country is like paradise—" His voice cracked. "Remember the reason I left the army? My broken leg? My mother was so mad at my early discharge—it was just another thing I never finished right in her eyes. You'd think she'd be happy I could walk again." He hugged his pillow.

I stood there awkwardly.

"The army was supposed to save me. It was keeping me from attending university." He looked at me. "The truth is I failed Seoul National twice. So when I got discharged early—and had no place to go—my father came up with a plan to send me to Canada." He drew a deep breath. "My father has lied and covered for me my entire life. I was even starting to believe the lies. I really believed I could do this. I was so close." He fell back on the bed.

I looked around the room, regretting that there were no windows to let in some natural light. I debated whether I should turn on the room light.

Joon-Ho shot back up. His eyes narrowed. "Have you told anyone?"

I shook my head. "I haven't told a soul," I said. Who would I tell? Who would care?

"I can't let my father save me again. Besides, I still want to marry you."

It took me several seconds to speak. "I'm in love with someone else. We're not having this discussion again."

"No. It's not natural. He's your teacher. He's not Korean."

"I'm in love with him."

"Have you slept with him yet?" His voice was strangely calm.

My cheeks were burning.

He grinned at my obvious discomfort. "I'm the only man you've been with," he said. He reached into his bottom desk drawer and pulled out a turquoise ring box. "I was going to ask you on my graduation day."

He held the box out for me, but when I didn't take it, he pulled me onto the bed next to him. The ring reminded me of the one I'd seen on Kate's mother's hand when I first met her. Only this diamond was real, I realized, reading the *Tiffany & Co.* engraved on the inside of the band.

"It's a two-karat diamond solitaire. My mother brought it with her when she visited. She chose platinum instead of gold, because she said it complemented the Korean skin tone better. She can be very thoughtful sometimes." He carefully placed the ring back in its box and set it on his night table before flopping back on the bed. "It's going to be okay. We can still get married . . ." he mumbled over and over, like a prayer.

I noticed the Canadian immigration guide on the floor next to the bed. It was the same one I'd seen weeks ago when I was going through his desk. Now that he was no longer able to study and get a job in Canada, the only way he could stay in the country was through marriage—through me. All this time, I'd felt sorry for him. I'd told myself that I understood his plight because I understood what it meant to shoulder the expectations of Korean parents.

"I'm not going to let you use me," I said, snatching the ring box and shaking it in front of him. "I never want to see you again." I threw the box at him.

Joon-Ho grabbed my arm from behind and twisted it.

"Let go of me. You're hurting me."

He pushed me onto the bed. His foul breath was overwhelming. His tongue invaded my mouth, his teeth biting, his lips sucking my lips, cheeks, and tongue. I couldn't make a sound.

No, I thought, *this can't be happening.* His weight was on me, and I felt his hands undo my jeans.

"Stop," I said, trying to push him away.

"Why? Because you're not the one in control this time? I'm so tired of you leading me on."

I cried out as he grabbed a fistful of hair. He rolled me onto my stomach and pulled my pants down. He was faster and stronger than I was. Then I thought of Mrs. Henry and the living room full of women upstairs.

"I'll scream," I said. "Mrs. Henry has her friends over. They'll hear. You'll go to jail—"

He stopped and curled into a ball, his fingertips pressing into his temples.

"You really are insane." I struggled to free myself. He didn't move as I raced to do my jeans back up, grab my purse, and get to the door. "If you ever touch me again, I'll make sure the whole world knows every little secret about you."

I was dazed by the sunlight as I stormed past the room crowded with women in prayer and out the front door. It wasn't until I was several blocks away that I allowed myself to stop and catch my breath. I collapsed against a mailbox and burst into tears. I could still feel Joon-Ho's hands on my skin and taste him on my lips. I closed my eyes and covered my ears with my hands. I felt so stupid for thinking I could help him. That I *should* help him.

"You okay?" a woman asked. Her dog sniffed me. She pulled it away, but when I reached to pet it, she relaxed the leash.

"What's your dog's name?" I asked through my tears.

"Princess. After Princess Diana." The woman smiled. "She's a golden retriever."

"I always wanted a dog," I said. I wondered how Will would feel about getting a dog, then remembered he was allergic to them.

"She likes you," the woman said, seeing the dog's wagging tail. She petted her. "I tell you, they're more friendly and loyal than any human's capable of being." Princess barked and licked my face.

Maybe I should give up on men, I thought, *and get a dog*.

I showered as soon as I got home. The hot water splashed on the bruises already appearing on my arms, the same raw reddish colour as those I'd suffered when I was attacked by Leon. In a couple of days they'd turn blue, then within a week, green, before turning yellowish brown. I tried to remember the spectrum of colours on Delia's face when I last saw her. The bruises were purple and green, which meant she'd come into the store a few days after her attack and not right away like I'd thought. It felt strange to be making that connection now.

My mother came upstairs from the store. She was practically dancing. I'd never seen her so excited. "My sister—Mi-Ra *oni*—we've found her. She's been living in the U.S. all this time. Can you believe it? New York City. How is it possible we could have been living so close to each other all this time and not have known it?" She looked exasperated by my blank reaction and switched to English. "My sister—the one who disappeared before the war?" Then, speaking Korean again, she said, "It's been forty years. I barely remember."

The black-and-white photos I'd taken from my aunt's collection were sitting in a box under my bed. When I went to my room to fetch it, I found Joon-Ho's letters to me in the same box. I tossed them in the garbage. When my mother saw the old photos of her, her three sisters, and her mother, she threw her arms around me—a gesture so unexpected, I didn't move. Moments later, I realized I should have hugged her back.

"If only my mother were alive to see this moment. To have a sister living in North America—it's only an hour flight." Her eyes became dreamlike. "She's planning to visit. Aren't you excited about meeting your aunt?"

I nodded. I was numb from my encounter with Joon-Ho. But I was happy to see my mother so pleased about something.

"There's so much I need to do," she cried. "I have to get ready. You need to help me clean up. This place. The store. I can't wait till she sees everything we've done with the store."

It seemed a random thought, but I remembered what I'd read in Mrs. O'Doherty's diary about how my mother had stopped Mr. Martin from opening a variety store of his own, so I asked how she'd done it.

She seemed momentarily puzzled by my question but answered, "Zoning laws. My lawyer, he's a brilliant man." She laughed, then became serious. "You would have made such a good lawyer."

I thought of Allison Roy in her blue suit and high heels eating a Chinese sticky bun on St. George Street. Not wanting to hear another speech from my mother about studying law, I said, "I'm thinking of taking some time away from school and going to France."

"Why would you say such a ridiculous thing? Where would you get the money?"

"That's not the point. I've been giving it some serious thought."
Which wasn't entirely true.

"You're going to finish university. We haven't come this far
for you to start destroying everything with your crazy fantasies.
Besides, what would my sister think? Why would you ruin my perfect moment by saying such things?"

"Your sister, more than anyone, would understand. She's the one
who left you and my *harmony* to do what she wanted."

I thought my mother was going to hit me, but she went into her
room instead, slamming the door.

She'd stopped a businessman in his tracks and she'd do everything to stop me, too. She always had. France seemed more of a
long shot than ever. I stood there without moving. If I'd wanted to,
I could really have spoiled the moment for her. I could have told her
my dad's beloved Joon-Ho had just tried to rape me.

It was almost the end of April, and I closed my eyes to shield them
from the sun as I sat on Will's front steps, humming along to Air
Supply's "All Out of Love" on my Walkman. The sun felt good. It
had been a long time since I'd felt so calm and relaxed. I was singing along to the next song when I sensed a shadow fall across me. It
was Will, smiling the same goofy smile I'd fallen in love with back
in grade nine.

"Sorry I'm late," he said. "Long line at the grocery store . . ."

I took one of the shopping bags and followed him inside. The
music had me feeling good, playful even. I popped the cassette into
Will's stereo while he got some soda.

"Have you given any more thought to France?" he asked.

I practically threw myself at him, wrapping my arms around his neck. I continued dancing. Will hesitated, but then I felt his fingers in my hair. His other hand pressed into my back and I guided it under my skirt.

"Are you sure you want to do this now?" he asked.

I pulled back briefly and flung my top off.

"Does this mean you're coming with me?" he asked before he gently bit into my nipple.

Later, with our bodies still intertwined and me feeling simultaneously high and sleepy, I found myself wanting to hear my Korean name. Will tried to say it, but his tongue tripped over it. He was reluctant to try again, for which I was grateful.

My psychology exam was at ten in the morning, and I was almost out the door when the phone rang. After hesitating for a split second, I ran back and picked it up. It was a nurse at St. Michael's Hospital. My "sister Kate" was asking for me. I knew right away she was in trouble. An abortion? When I asked what had happened, the nurse would only say it was an emergency and that I needed to get to the hospital immediately. As worried as I was, I was still angry at Kate, and cursed her under my breath on the way over as I wondered how I was going to explain missing my psych exam to my professor.

When I was directed to the Psychiatric Emergency Services, I felt real panic. And when I saw Kate lying there, her hair matted and her wrist bandaged, I almost threw up.

She tried to smile. Her lips were badly cracked.

"Thanks for coming. It's not as bad as it looks."

I helped her sit up, folding her pillow in half before sliding it behind her.

"So, I fucked up again."

I shook my head.

"No, I mean, I fucked up killing myself. I should have cut this way," she said, running her index finger up and down her arm, "instead of this way—" She traced where she'd cut herself. "They always cut this way," she said matter-of-factly. "I only realized that sitting in Emergency." Her voice dropped. "There was another cutter in Emerg. with me. Now, *she* was messed up. Her name was Mary too, but she was Hispanic. She cut too deep—ripped right through her tendons. Her parents found her screaming—the pain got to her. God, if only I'd done it right, I would have bled out faster. Glenn Close got it so wrong."

I swallowed hard.

"This wasn't some *Fatal Attraction* thing though," Kate said. "No, my only problem is my mother. God, I can't wait for her to die." She gave me a half-smile. "They're holding me for seventy-two hours. Apparently they can. I didn't want my mother around, so I told them my parents were out of town. They're gonna hook me up with some psychiatrist. Maybe that's a good thing. I'm just so tired of feeling bad all the time."

I was fond of Kate's mother, whom I still thought of as the Gucci Lady, outsmarting her in-laws with her fake jewels. But I understood Kate's frustrations because I didn't know any girl who didn't wish her own mother dead in some fleeting moments of fantasy. I'd often thought that a life without my own mother would bring me a freedom so vast yet unknown, it both scared and excited me. I could drop out of university, go to France with a white man, and write bilingual poems.

A voice came over the PA system announcing a Code White in progress. "That's a violent and aggressive patient," Kate said.

I avoided asking her how she knew.

"It could also be a violent visitor," a nurse said. She asked Kate how she was doing and said she'd be back soon with something for her to eat.

"Did you know today's my birthday?" Kate looked at me. "Some party, huh? It would've been kind of cool—to die on my birthday— like the Shakespeare guy you like so much."

I had to laugh. She'd remembered me telling her that bit of Shakespearean trivia years ago. I reached out and touched her hand, grateful for her friendship.

"So, what's up with you?" she asked.

I told her Will had asked me to go to France with him.

"So, he's in love with you. You know that now."

He'd never told me so, but I nodded anyway.

"You're so lucky," she said, "I should hate you."

"It's not like I can just drop everything and go—I have school—"

"Go. Defy your parents. I dare you for once to do what *you* want to do."

We continued talking about Will and me and our supposed bright future together. It seemed to give Kate pleasure. I was almost beginning to enjoy myself.

"He sounds like the type of guy who'd always give you the window seat on a plane," Kate said.

I nodded, and imagined Will and me, holding hands in the night air as we walked down the Champs Elysées, past the cafés and shops towards the Arc de Triomphe. I could even hear the cars honking on the busy street as other lovers walked past us.

"I've always wanted to photograph the Eiffel Tower," Kate said. "I used to have a book on France filled with photographs when I was a kid. I think that's when I first fell in love with photography— because all the people in the photos looked happy."

She fell asleep holding my hand.

As I left, two volunteers who introduced themselves as Sister Rosalind and Sister Suzette gave me brochures on suicide, and cupped my hands in theirs before letting me know they'd be praying for our family.

"God bless you, too," I told them, not knowing what else to say.

I skimmed through the brochures on the streetcar home, pausing to read the list of reasons why people attempt suicide. When I read over the danger signs to look out for, I thought back to the night I'd met Kate in the park, and felt guilty.

The last time I'd felt this helpless was when I struggled with what I could do for Delia. Images overwhelmed me: the jagged scar on Delia's hand, her valentine smile, her bruised face. I was so close to becoming sick on the streetcar, I got off and threw up behind a garbage can. A homeless woman with a shopping cart packed with black plastic garbage bags watched me and offered me several paper napkins. It was a small gesture, but it made me feel better.

As I walked along Queen Street West, I thought about Kate and took several deep breaths. A poster of Jodie Foster and Kelly McGillis hung in the window of Queen Video. I'd meant to see *The*

Accused when it had come out, but had never gotten around to it. I read the captions. The idea of a broken woman seeking justice intrigued me.

A street musician smiled at me as he strummed "Penny Lane" on his guitar, and soon I could hear Tico's horn in the distance. By the time I got home, I was feeling better. After all, Kate had reached out to me, had even made me her sister.

When Josh told me Joon-Ho had been by the store to speak with my parents, an alarm went off inside me.

"What did he want?" I demanded. Josh was in his room playing a game on his new computer. A computer we were supposed to share.

"I dunno," he said. It annoyed me that my parents always relented when Josh wanted something pricey—first his five-hundred-dollar guitar and now a Commodore 64 that probably cost a lot more. He'd told them he needed it for homework, but all he ever did was play Commando on it.

"Did he even bother asking for me?"

"Yeah. I told him you weren't home." He continued shooting at enemy soldiers.

"This game is so stupid. What kind of gun never runs out of ammunition?"

He didn't respond.

I sighed. "We're supposed to be sharing this computer. That's what *Omma* said."

"It's in my room," he said, without looking up.

I pressed the on-off button until the screen went black, and I stormed out. I ran downstairs and asked my mother what had happened with Joon-Ho.

"We were so surprised his family still wanted the marriage," my mother said. "Because of what had happened at Christmas. We thought we'd never hear from them again."

My mother said Joon-Ho looked very upset when she told him they didn't want me to think about marriage—to anyone—until I graduated. That wouldn't be for another three years.

"Your father sympathized with him. He really likes Joon-Ho. Even invited him to help him finish with the basement renovation—which Joon-Ho agreed to."

I groaned. The last thing I wanted was for our family to owe him any more favours. But how could I tell my parents what had happened? "Anyway," my mother said, "he'll be back tomorrow to help, which is great timing. My sister will be visiting next week. I want this place to look perfect."

I wondered why she cared so much about impressing a sister she hadn't seen in four decades, a sister she didn't even know was alive until recently. Besides, she had nothing to prove. As far as the Korean community was concerned, my mother already had it all: a successful business and, more important, two children doing well in school, which, in turn, would secure good marriages.

"It's been so long since I've been this happy," she said. The woman who was chronically in pain and complained about the flight of stairs she had to climb each time she had to go from the store to the apartment was now talking about visiting the CN Tower, Niagara Falls, and the Royal Botanical Gardens out in Hamilton.

Then it hit me. Like me, she'd had a sister appear out of nowhere, and her sister was the real thing. Of course she'd care. I wanted to tell her I was happy for her, but felt awkward.

"I'll go clean my room," I said instead.

Tico came in. I took a deep breath to avoid smelling him, and smiled as he held the door open for me.

"Is your sister here yet?" he asked my mother.

She had told *him* about her?

"Not yet. Soon," said my mother. "Very soon."

"Never seen you so excited like this before," he said, accepting the loaf of bread. "I'm real happy for you."

I let the door close behind me and walked away.

It was close to ten thirty the next night when I got out of Will's car. I didn't bother to look back as Will drove away, recalling his words: *You're beginning to sound like Yuki.*

I'd suggested we try a new Korean fusion restaurant that had opened in the Yonge and Finch area. He complained that the drive there was too long and that there were never any parking spaces along Yonge Street. We ended up eating at the Keg instead.

"Did you get a chance to begin any of the books I got you?" I asked, biting into my Caesar salad. In my attempt to expand his reading repertoire, I'd bought him several books by Asian-American and Asian-Canadian writers.

"Damn it, Mary. I told you already—I've been really busy with work," he said. "You know I teach an OAC class. Besides, I'm not so keen on reading stuff that's been translated."

"None of the books I gave you were."

"Besides, I'm taking a poetry class right now, not novel studies."

"Joy Kogawa writes poetry." It was obvious he hadn't even looked at them. "I went to half a dozen different bookstores to find all those books for you—there's not a whole lot out there by Asian writers."

Maybe it was my fault; I was expecting him to embrace that part of me that was foreign to him—to leave the comforts of his white world and try to see things from the point of view of an Asian protagonist, or at least go to a restaurant that didn't require a steak knife. Ms. Nakamura had probably tried to do the same and failed.

Standing alone now on the sidewalk outside the store, I sighed and looked up at our apartment. Joon-Ho was standing by the window in the living room. I'd spent the day away from home to avoid seeing him, and wondered why he was still around. Instead of going upstairs, I went into the store, only to be told by my mother to go upstairs and get my dad so he could start cleaning up.

I saw two shot glasses and *soju* on the coffee table. The toilet flushed and Joon-Ho stepped out of the bathroom.

I did nothing to hide my annoyance. "What are you still doing here?" I asked.

"You've been gone all day," he said. "What have you been doing?"

"What do you think?" I snapped back.

My dad walked into the room. Oblivious to the tension, he patted Joon-Ho's arm and said they should get back to the store. Joon-Ho nodded.

After they left, I ran to the window. As they stepped onto the sidewalk, Joon-Ho looked up. I knew I should be afraid, though I wasn't sure of what. *Maybe I should have told my parents everything about him*, I thought.

I couldn't shake the bad feeling. When I finally fell asleep, I dreamed I was walking in the Han River in Korea. The water was only knee-high. I was using a tree branch as a walking stick, balancing myself as I stepped over small stones and algae. Tiny fish swam around my bare feet. I had looked up to watch the passing cars on Seongsan Bridge when I felt my stick jab into something. I tried to lift the stick but it was stuck. I yanked on it, then leaned down to pick up whatever it was stuck in. To my horror, I pulled up Leon's bloated head, his red hair matted with debris and mud.

I jerked awake, turned on the light, and reassured myself that it was just a dream. Why Leon? It didn't make any sense. If I was going to have a nightmare, it should have been about Joon-Ho. I stroked the blue scarf and tried hard to forget about Leon.

I closed my eyes and thought back to the first time I'd seen Will. He was wearing a white shirt with a blue tie that made his blue eyes look dreamy. Blue—the colour of blueberries, the sky, and the ocean. I tried to focus my mind on that but it refused to cooperate, and images of red—blood, a sinking sun, and Leon's hair—invaded my thoughts. I tried to focus again on Will and a life in Paris. I felt my body relax eventually, and soon I was in that strange place between sleep and consciousness, wondering if I was asleep or dreaming that I was.

The store alarm sounded, its intermittent blasts frightening me awake. It was 1 a.m.

"You can't go down there!" my dad yelled at my mother. "We should wait for the police."

They came within minutes and found the store secure. They wondered if some faulty wiring could have triggered the alarm, and asked my dad if he'd been doing work in the store lately. When he said yes, they left.

When the alarm went off again just before 3 a.m., both my parents went downstairs. I remember being half asleep, looking up at the clock and seeing it was 3:05, when a blast so strong it shook the bedroom walls and floor made me scream and cover my ears.

Josh and I ran downstairs. The store windows had been blown out, and clouds of dust and flames were everywhere. I saw someone in the phone booth across the street. It was Mona and she came running towards us.

"I called 911," she yelled. "Was anyone inside?"

Josh ran into the store. I started to follow, but Mona grabbed my arm and yelled, "Are you crazy?"

"Our parents are in there!" I screamed. I called out for Josh.

Police officers and firefighters appeared out of nowhere in the dark as if in slow motion—there were sirens and lights everywhere.

A police officer forced me back across the street. When I saw Josh and my dad being led out by firefighters, I was so relieved and happy, I turned and hugged Mona, who'd been standing next to me the whole time. I ran towards Josh and my dad, expecting to see my mother following them out, and when she didn't appear, I screamed at the firefighters, "Where's my mother?"

I looked at my dad, who was covered in blood. Paramedics ran over.

"Where's *Omma*?" I asked Josh. His face, smeared with dust and ashes, seemed frozen. Finally, two words escaped his lips: "She's gone."

I was back in that strange place between sleeping and being awake, unable to tell the difference. I heard muffled sounds—people yelling, a dog barking, car doors slamming. I saw flashing red lights, a streetcar, and a news truck behind a police barricade.

Josh pulled me to him but everything felt unreal. The burnt smell in his hair and clothes, the tears that fell against my cheeks.

"She's gone," he said again.

"I want to see her," I demanded. I needed to know, to make sure for myself, but Josh held me back. I fought and kicked, even biting his hand, and when I realized that I could not escape his grip, I tried desperately to see past the mess of firefighters, police officers, and paramedics standing in front of the store.

I yelled at Josh, "She could still be okay. She could still be alive!"

He held me so our eyes locked. "She's dead. Trust me—she's gone."

"How can you be so sure? She could still be okay!"

Josh shook me. "A beam fell on her—cut through her neck."

My legs collapsed. I felt Josh's arms cushion my fall as everything blurred and then went black.

When I woke up, I automatically reached for my blue scarf. It was around my neck as usual, and I thought for a moment I'd dreamt everything. But there was a framed photo of Peter and his parents on the wall. I was at the Youngs' apartment, in Peter's room. I had no memory of how I'd got there or how long I'd been out. Sunlight peeked through the window shade. Where was my dad? Josh? I ran for the door, crashing into Josh.

"Tell me," I pleaded. "*Omma*'s okay—it was all just a mistake." Tears ran down my face.

Josh helped me back to bed. "Mrs. Young is making you some tea," he said.

"Did you bring my scarf here?" I asked.

He nodded. Had he known all these years that I couldn't sleep without it? Not since the night of my attack? I picked it up and draped it over me, rocking myself, trying to escape into a place where none of this was real.

Chapter 19

The next few days were like a bad dream. Our apartment had sustained damage, and we had to wait for the fire marshal's approval before we could return. My dad, brother, and I ended up with Mr. Young's family. Mr. Young was still recovering from his gunshot wounds, his upper body stiff, his right arm in a sling.

Mrs. Young served *soju* to the men and orange juice to Josh and me. She placed a platter of food on the coffee table. She didn't take a seat. My dad helped Mr. Young light his cigarette. The strike of the match and the sight of the smoke and flame startled me. I blinked several times and told myself everything was all right; there was no chance of a fire starting here. *I'm losing my mind*, I thought, and sipped my juice.

My dad had escaped with minor cuts and scrapes. The blood I'd seen him covered with had been my mother's. He seemed remarkably calm. Too calm. His hand was steady as he lit another match. It was the first cigarette I'd seen him smoke in years, since my *harmony* died of cancer. He inhaled deeply and blew smoke out of his nose. Soon the room was filled with that smoke; the smell of tobacco mingling with the aroma of deep-fried dumplings and spicy rice cakes.

"It was a freak accident," Mr. Young said.

I thought of the work that my dad and Joon-Ho had been doing, all the supplies and equipment they kept near the washroom in the basement: red plastic containers with explosive symbols and flammable warnings on them, paint thinners, rags kept in a pail off to the side.

"Yes, an accident," Mrs. Young repeated sadly. "You mustn't blame yourself," she said to my dad.

Mr. Young cursed in Korean and told her to shut up. "Peter should be here."

Even though I knew Mrs. Young was a little hard of hearing, I hated that he talked as loudly as he did.

"But he's writing his final exams," Mrs. Young said.

Before Mr. Young could say anything, my dad gestured with his hand. "No, no . . . leave him where he is," he said.

"Boy doesn't even know what's happened to me yet," Mr. Young said, and puffed angrily on his cigarette.

I was stunned that they hadn't let Peter know about a robbery that had left his father with three gunshot wounds. He could have died.

Mrs. Young said, "It's his first year. We didn't want to do anything to upset him and disturb his studies. He'll find out soon enough."

I looked at Josh, but he was staring absently at the food on the coffee table. I'd wanted to attend Queen's University myself, and remembered my mother throwing away the brochures. I wondered for a second if my dad and brother would have kept my mother's death from me if I'd been away during the explosion. Mr. Young emptied his shot of *soju* and signalled for Mrs. Young to refill it. I could have used a shot myself.

"Boy's going to be shocked and pissed when he comes back," Mr. Young said, his voice low. He looked at his arm. "His old man's been shot up, your store's blown up, but no, his mother says that his studies have to come first."

He ground his cigarette into the ashtray and sighed. "What a life," he said. Then he asked Josh and me, "Do you know what I used to do back in Korea?"

"You were an architect," Josh answered.

"Did you also know I used to be an athlete? Judo middleweight. Was pretty good too. Lost to Kim Eui-Tae. He represented Korea in the '64 Olympics in Tokyo. Bastard actually won a bronze. That should have been me." He reached for another cigarette. "Now I can't even defend myself in this godforsaken country."

My dad lit another match. Mrs. Young returned with *soju* and more food even though we hadn't touched anything in front of us. Mr. Young's cigarette dangled carelessly from his mouth. It made me nervous.

I hadn't known Mr. Young had studied judo. When I started wondering what there was about my mother I'd never known and now never would, I stopped myself. What was Josh thinking? I wished we were at home. I wanted to talk him, alone. I needed to know I wasn't dreaming everything that was happening. I'd had bad dreams before—nightmares I'd willed myself to forget, had buried deep in the caverns of my mind. *I've had bad dreams before*, I repeated to myself. *I always wake up—eventually.*

I picked up my empty glass and excused myself. I went into the kitchen, hoping to find another bottle of *soju*. It sat on the counter as if waiting for me. I picked it up as Mrs. Young walked in. She went over to the cupboard and took out two glasses. I filled both and we drank in silence.

I was in the Youngs' store early the next morning, getting milk to take back upstairs, when I saw the newspaper headline, "Flames Rip Through Two-Storey Building Killing One." My heart skipped a beat. But at the same time, nothing felt real. After all the years my mother had feared our store would appear in the newspapers and draw negative attention, now we'd made headlines everywhere. Everything that had been a blur the night of the fire was in black and white for me to read: Even though our store had been destroyed, the business next door suffered minimal damages. There was an ongoing fire and police investigation. The estimated damage was $400,000, including loss of inventory.

How could the newspapers know everything? We hadn't told them anything. A vision of television reporters in the night, held behind the police barricade, flashed in my head. A reporter was talking with Tico. Had he seen anything? I wondered if she had assumed he'd seen something because he was homeless and had nothing to do but wander the streets at night.

Josh and I walked over to what was left of the store to find that neighbours, customers, and strangers had left fresh-cut flowers wrapped in paper or plastic on the sidewalk by the yellow police tape. The red, pink, and white flowers were a colourful contrast to the blackened store. Someone had even left a giant brown teddy bear.

I was surprised and touched by everyone's generosity. I noticed a note attached to the stuffed bear, and worked my way around the flowers to get it.

"Hey, you can't do that!" a voice called out.

I turned. It was a woman on the opposite side of the street. She pointed at the teddy bear.

"Put it back!"

"It's my store." I looked at the charred remains and started sobbing. The note pinned to the bear was from Mato. *I'm so sorry for your loss.*

"Mato said our store was lucky," I said to Josh. "Remember—when he won the lottery? Lucky? How? *Omma* was always complaining about her aches and pains. We worked stupid hours. Normal families eat dinner together. When was the last time we ever did anything together? All this time, we've been so afraid of the store being robbed, well, THIS STORE'S BEEN ROBBING FROM US ALL ALONG AND NOW, AND NOW IT'S GONE AND KILLED *OMMA*—" I screamed. I didn't care if people were looking. Another building could have exploded, and I'd have been oblivious to it.

Josh reached out, but I pulled away, clinging to the teddy bear. I didn't want to be consoled. Unlike my mother, I wanted the world to witness the pain and injustice that had struck my family. I turned to tell the woman across the street to mind her own goddamn business, but she was gone.

Chapter 20

Traffic on the 401 was slow. I sat in Mr. Young's van, which we'd borrowed, trying to find a radio station playing songs that I liked. My dad and I were on our way to the airport to pick up my mother's sisters who were flying in from Korea. Their flight was scheduled to arrive only two hours before the sister they'd lost as children would fly in from New York City.

My aunt Mi-Ra was still a mystery to us. She had been for thirty-nine years. I wondered if we'd have trouble picking her out in the crowd. I had a photo of her in my purse along with a letter to my mother, which had arrived only a few days ago. She'd be coming alone. Her husband, who had suffered another stroke, was unable to travel.

"She looks like your *harmony*," my mother had said. "She has her eyes, her nose. No wonder our mother loved her so much. If only she could have lived to see her again."

I trembled recalling her words and returned to the radio dials to distract myself. I had vowed I'd stay strong today; that I wouldn't unravel like I had outside our store. I would be the rock my mother had been for her sisters when their mother passed away.

"Such a big airport," my *jag-eun emoh* said, slightly out of breath as we got to the waiting area for Aunt Mi-Ra's flight.

She'd put on a lot of weight since I'd last seen her. Could she be pregnant?

"I read it was named after one of your presidents."

Prime minister, I thought, but didn't correct her.

"I need a drink," she said.

I offered to get her something, but she shook her head. "I'll fall asleep if I sit down. And I need the exercise." She wandered off with my dad following her.

"It's hard for her," my *kun emoh* said. "She cried during most of the flight. She's trying hard to put on a strong face. But she's devastated, as am I. We haven't really had a chance to think of *kun oni*." She was referring to my aunt Mi-Ra. "She's also embarrassed by all the weight she's put on. It's stress-related, I'm sure."

She wasn't pregnant after all. One of the luggage bags fell over and I straightened it. It was packed to capacity. I'd thought they were staying for just the week.

My aunt said, "Half the things in that are for Joon-Ho from his mother. Can you believe she had the nerve to ask?" She forced a smile. "I can still remember the day you and Joon-Ho met in my apartment. That seems ages ago now. How's he doing?"

"I don't know." I hadn't thought about him since the fire, and realized he might not know what happened, unless he'd read about it in the papers. I wondered if my dad or Josh had called him.

"His mother brags about his marks all the time. That and how happy he is here," my *kun emoh* said. "Maybe I should have sent my daughter here too."

"How is she doing?" I asked. I'd barely seen her in Korea.

"Still studying as hard as ever," my *kun emoh* said, and sighed. "She wants to do graduate work and refuses to let us help her find a husband. She needs to marry, or all that education will be for nothing. But I can't believe you'll be marrying Joon-Ho after his graduation next year, yes?"

It was as if she'd hit me over the head with her purse.

"What's wrong?" she asked.

I told her the truth—how Joon-Ho had been expelled from university for plagiarism and lying about having completed his undergrad studies in Korea. I also told her I had never agreed to marry him and that his mother knew this, because I had told her so during her visit.

It was my *kun emoh*'s turn to be stunned. "But I have a bag *full* of clothes for him and gifts for you from his mother," she said. "I think Joon-Ho's been lying to his mother since her visit . . ." her voice trailed off.

My dad and my *jag-eun emoh* returned. The four of us sat shoulder-to-shoulder, drinking our coffees in silence. Aunt Mi-Ra's plane was delayed, and eventually my other aunts fell asleep, the thirteen-hour time difference catching up with them. *Kun emoh* snored gently, the way my mother used to.

They were still sleeping when my dad and I spotted Aunt Mi-Ra coming through the gates. I recognized her right away—she looked like my mother—and burst into tears.

"Yu-Rhee-ah," she said. We hugged, clinging to each other, and soon were joined by my other *emoh*s. My dad, who'd collected the luggage and piled the bags onto a trolley, stood off to the side, waiting patiently.

Chapter 21

"This city is so clean," my *kun emoh* said, admiring the view of Toronto from her hotel suite. "You can actually see the blue sky."

My aunts and I had just returned from the funeral. My dad and Josh were downstairs at the bar, my dad having insisted that the women be left alone to talk. My *jag-eun emoh* and I were making tea, using the little hotel coffee maker to boil water.

Aunt Mi-Ra handed me a red box. It was a gold cross on a chain, similar to the one she was wearing. "My whole life changed when I found Jesus," she said. "He gave me purpose. Focus. Faith." She removed the necklace from the box and unclasped the little hook. "It's twenty-four-karat gold—the best that I could find. It'll help you get through the next little while—"

"*Omma* would kill me if she saw me wearing it," I said. I hadn't meant to be harsh—the words just tumbled out. Josh had openly been going to a Christian church for a while now, and neither of our parents had said anything. "We're Buddhists. *Omma* was a Buddhist."

"You don't have to wear it, of course," Aunt Mi-Ra said, blushing. She put the necklace back in the box.

We sat around the coffee table quietly sipping our tea. I wished

Josh were with me, that we were back in our little apartment. I wanted to close my eyes and hear a pot bubbling or a pan sizzling on the stove top while the smell of soup or onion pancakes pervaded the air. When a barking dog in the hallway broke the silence, my *jag-eun emoh*'s face lit up.

"Do you remember the time *Oni* convinced me that our dog was the reincarnation of my lost doll?" she asked. "I was only four years old. I can't believe she did that to me. I ended up dressing that poor dog in a rag diaper and carting it around in an old pram."

"No worse than what she did to me!" my *kun emoh* said. Turning to me, she explained, "Your mother was always better at Japanese than I was. One day, I didn't want to do my homework, so I made her do it for me. She had to read a story and answer questions. I should have caught on when she agreed so easily, but she convinced me she wanted to help. Well! She deliberately answered every question incorrectly! I got a mark of zero and the strap—fifteen strokes on my hands for each question. The teacher thought I was mocking him—the answers had been so ridiculous. Then when I got home, your *harmony* was so ashamed of me she beat me with a stick."

"I hated that stick!" Aunt Mi-Ra said.

"Your mother was a clever girl, and so convincing," my *kun emoh* said. "She was also very bold. She had the nerve to give the stick a name." She paused trying to remember the details. "Hae-Won—she named it after the meekest girl in school!"

"She'd tell your *harmony*: 'I hate Hae-Won—she's so mean to me! I hope she falls and snaps in two,'" my *jag-eun emoh* said. "Then the two of us started doing the same thing, complaining about Hae-Won and her horrible treatment of us."

"It was all very funny until your *harmony* showed up at school one day, demanding that our teacher beat Hae-Won for bullying the three of us so ruthlessly!" my *kun emoh* said, struggling to talk through her laughter. "Did the three of us get it then!"

"*Ai-goo-cham-neh!*" Aunt Mi-Ra said. "I wish I could have been there!" She turned to me. "Since she was a young girl, your *harmony* used to regret that your mother was born a girl, not because she wanted a son—which she desperately did—but because she saw how bright and capable your mother was. 'What a waste,' she'd say. 'She would have made a brilliant lawyer.'"

Was that why she'd wanted me to study law? At least she'd thought I was capable enough to pursue it.

It fascinated me to hear these stories of her childhood. Why hadn't she told me herself? Why hadn't I thought to ask?

Her ashes were in a black urn on the dining table. My aunts would take it back to Korea so the ashes could be scattered on the same mountain as those of my *harmony*. I thought about my *harmony*'s funeral procession—the ringing of little bells, the incense that filled the mountain air, and the colourful garments worn by the monks who exorcised the evil spirits. There'd been snow on the mountain-top then. I took comfort in thinking that now, in May, it would be green. I imagined the wind lifting fluffy dandelion heads high into the air and scattering them softly over my *harmony* and her daughter.

Waking up earlier that day at the Youngs' apartment, I'd hoped for rain to fall in torrents, a reflection of our pain and loss. But instead, the sun came out, trapping me and everyone else in its brilliant rays before we escaped into the darkness that was the funeral home. Hundreds of people, mostly Korean, showed up at the funeral. I had to wonder who was minding all the variety stores across Toronto.

"This is Mrs. Kim," I told my aunts when I introduced Kate's mother to them.

"She was my best friend," Mrs. Kim said with a trembling voice. Her eyes filled with tears. She'd worn the traditional white *hanbok*, causing several people to mistake her for one of my mother's sisters.

"She was like a sister to me," she whispered into my ear. All the women had dressed in white at my *harmony*'s funeral.

This was the first time in years that I'd seen Kate and her mother together. The idea that Mrs. Kim felt like my mother's sister reinforced the sense that Kate and I were like sisters. I was truly glad she was with me, even though her words about me only being free once my mother was gone still haunted me.

Unlike her sisters, my aunt Mi-Ra wore a stylish black suit—a reflection, no doubt, of her many years spent in America. I'd ended up wearing one of Kate's black dresses.

"Why did you wait until now to contact my mother?" I asked. Maybe it wasn't the right time or place to ask, but I wanted to know.

"It's a complicated story." She paused. "Your *harmony* made me choose—when I told her I was in love with Craig, she made me choose between him and her. Craig made me feel beautiful after your *harmony* did everything to keep me as ugly as possible."

I didn't understand, and said so.

"It was to keep me safe. All the beautiful girls in our village were taken away once they reached the age of sixteen to serve the Japanese soldiers. So your *harmony* kept me in rags once I showed signs of becoming a woman. My hair was cut to make me look like a boy. She would tell me I was hideous to reinforce the message that I was undesirable and should avoid any attempt to be vain. Your *emoh*s won't remember; they were little then but your mother would have remembered."

I was relieved when Mrs. Kim interrupted us. "I think we'll be starting soon." She took my hand in hers and squeezed tightly as we made our way to our seats. I did my best to avoid the looks on people's faces and used Erin, Linda, and Kate as shields. As I sat listening to the service, I deliberately tuned out the people who got up to speak. It was the only way I could keep myself from completely falling apart.

If only Rubina could have been here too, I thought. It would have been like being back in high school. I felt as if my friendships with Erin and Linda had changed significantly now that we were immersed in university. I felt betrayed by Erin for meeting Joon-Ho behind my back, though I didn't have the courage to tell her so. And I still felt guilty for getting myself fired from the daycare, although Linda had said nothing to make me feel that way. Maybe she was secretly angry at me but afraid to say so. She'd made new friends at York, and while I listened to her stories about them, I really didn't care. Being honest with friends, I was beginning to see, was never easy.

The scent of incense was gentle in the air, but I remembered the harsh smoke stinging my eyes and nose the night of the explosion. The feeling grew more oppressive, and I struggled to keep from choking. *You have to get through this. Just get through,* I thought. *Everyone is watching.*

*   *   *

The one person I wanted most at the funeral hadn't been there. Throughout the whole ceremony, I'd looked for Will, who'd promised he would come.

"He's a jerk. You need to cut him loose," Kate said.

Easy for her to think that, I thought. She'd never known him as Erin, Linda, and I had back in high school.

As the adults mingled and snacked on refreshments, my friends and I slipped out of the funeral home for some air. I knew Kate was right. Perhaps I'd invented a Will Allen who'd never existed in the first place. *My* Will had been a man who knew what he wanted, not a boy who flew about in every direction like a tattered flag flying in the wind.

"What about Sean? Where is he?" Erin asked.

Josh had mentioned that my dad had called Joon-Ho, but there was no answer.

"When's the last time you saw him?" Erin asked. "Isn't it weird that he isn't here today?"

"I haven't seen him since he was at the store helping my father with renovations," I said.

"What were they doing, anyway?" Erin said.

I shrugged. "I don't know," I said, growing annoyed. "Something to do with updating the wiring system and repainting the walls."

"Could Sean have accidentally done something wrong?" Linda asked.

"Or maybe he did it on purpose," Erin said.

I didn't know if she was serious or joking, but Linda snapped, "That's not funny." Her fingers picked at the trim of her dress.

Erin apologized, but her comment had raised a possibility. After all, Joon-Ho was the last person who'd worked on the wiring.

"You need to shake both guys from your life," Kate said. "They're driving you crazy. I wish you had the will to just let them go."

"My will has nothing to do with it," I said. As soon as the words escaped my lips, I thought of Will. My Will. I grew angrier. Why wasn't he there for me? I felt stupid and gullible.

Joon-Ho, on the other hand, was out of my life for good. My friends just didn't know that yet because I hadn't told them what had happened between us. And now I couldn't stop thinking: *Was he somehow responsible for what happened?*

"Was it worth it?" I asked Aunt Mi-Ra later that night. We were out on the hotel balcony, just the two of us. I stared off in the distance at the green light on the Canada Life Building's weather beacon. Steady green meant clear weather. I took it as a sign to press for answers. I looked into the living room, where my other aunts were watching TV. "Your sisters think you abandoned them. My mother died believing you broke your mother's heart."

"I suppose I did break it when I chose Craig," she said. "Your *harmony* was outraged—the thought of having a mixed grandson mortified her. She started beating me and I ran away. I spent a lifetime resenting her for making me choose. I didn't even get a chance to say goodbye to my sisters." She wiped tears from her eyes. "I didn't even know my mother had died until Craig and I visited Korea this spring. That's why I reached out to your mother."

I stared at the cross around her neck, glad she had her faith to lean on. I wished my mother were alive to hear the truth and to have back the relationship she was denied because of my *harmony*'s prejudice and pride. I thought of Will, knowing that my mother too would have fought me. In that way, she was no different from her own mother.

"You're young, Yu-Rhee-ah," Aunt Mi-Ra said. "You don't understand, yet, that with love comes sacrifice, and that true love inspires the greatest of sacrifices."

Chapter 22

"It says the store was deliberately sabotaged," I exclaimed. I was translating a letter we had received from the fire marshal's office. My heart raced. Had I been right about Joon-Ho? We were finally back in our apartment a month later.

"No," my dad said. "An accident." Was he trying to protect Joon-Ho? Himself?

Investigators had shown up with electrical safety authorities to inspect the wiring they suspected had caused the fire. They asked to speak with my dad, but as his English was so poor, I was told to translate. I led Ryan Faulkner, one of the detectives, upstairs and left him sitting with my dad in the living room to make coffee. When I returned, they were both smoking in silence.

"Joon-Ho was the last person working on the wiring," I told the detective when he asked.

"Is he a technician or a contractor?" he asked matter-of-factly. He was writing everything in a tiny spiral notebook.

"No." I shook my head. "He's an engineer, though, doing his master's degree in electrical engineering." As soon as I had said that, I wondered if I should tell him about Joon-Ho's expulsion and the truth about him never graduating in the first place. But the detective quickly moved on to his next question.

"Would he have any reason for wanting to sabotage your store?"

Before I could answer, Josh, who had just come home, said, "No."

Should I mention it? I opened my mouth, but closed it again. The detective saw my hesitation and asked me if I had something to say.

I shook my head.

He asked my dad if he had anything to add. My dad said no and gestured for the detective to have some coffee, which he hadn't touched.

"Here's my card," the detective said, handing it to me. "Call me if you have anything you'd like to share." With that, he took a quick, polite sip of coffee and got up to leave.

"I think Joon-Ho did it," I told Josh. We were in his room, the detective's card still in my hand. My dad was in the living room watching TV. "I think he set the store to blow up. I don't know how but he was the last one working on the wiring."

Josh flopped onto his bed. "I'm really tired," he said. He covered his eyes with his arm to block out the light.

I sat at the end of the bed. My heart was pounding, but I knew if I didn't tell him everything, I'd lose it.

"Joon-Ho was expelled from the university," I said, and rambled on, describing his plans to marry me to stay in Canada, his attempted rape, and the look he'd given me the night of the explosion—the one that should have told me immediately he was up to something. "It's all my fault," I said, trembling and close to tears.

Josh looked at me incredulously. "Why didn't you tell me . . . ?" He got up and began pacing. "I'm going to go see him," he said.

"No, don't." I was afraid of what might happen if Josh confronted Joon-Ho. If I was right, who knew what he might do. "I'll call the detective back," I said. "I'll tell him everything I told you. Let him deal with it. It's his job."

Josh didn't seem convinced. He'd been sleepy moments earlier, and now was wide awake.

"I may be wrong about everything," I said.

"But he tried to hurt you—"

"I'll tell the detective that too. Please, don't do anything that could make things worse."

My dad called us from the living room. He was out of cigarettes and wanted Josh to run to the Youngs' store for more.

"Promise me you won't do anything until we talk some more," I said to Josh as he left the apartment. He agreed.

I gave Josh five minutes, then went to my parents' room and called the Youngs'. Mr. Young answered. Josh hadn't shown up.

"Is he walking towards the store? Can you check?" I asked. The urgency in my voice was enough to make Mr. Young put the phone down and do as I asked.

"Don't see him," Mr. Young said a few moments later. "Is everything okay?"

"No," I said, and hung up. What had I done? Josh was surely on his way over to Joon-Ho's. Should I go over too? I was having trouble breathing. I went back into the living room. My dad had fallen asleep on the sofa. I dialed Joon-Ho's number. He picked up after the first ring.

"It's me," I said. "We haven't seen you lately. There was an explosion and a fire. My dad said he tried calling you. Did you know about our store?"

There was silence on the other end, but I could hear faint breathing, so I knew Joon-Ho was there and had heard me.

"You were the last one working with the wires, and the police told us that's what caused the explosion."

The silence was becoming more than I could bear.

"My mother's dead."

In a low voice, he said, "I'm sorry about your mother."

"Did you do it on purpose?" I screamed.

"I swear I never meant to hurt her." He was crying and stumbling over his words.

I was so shocked, I couldn't talk for several seconds. His sobs were pathetic, but he'd lied many times before. My mother, Josh, and my dad had treated him like family, and his lies had brought us one disaster after another.

"You killed my mother!"

"No, you don't understand. We can still fix things."

He was mad. "You'll go to jail!" I yelled.

"I'll deny everything." His voice was defiant.

I gasped. Then, my voice composed, I said, "My aunt's here from Korea. I've already told her everything. About your lies. Your secrets. She'll tell your mother everything if she hasn't already done so. Everyone in Korea will know. I've already told the police what I suspect—"

He hung up.

I was bluffing, but Joon-Ho wouldn't know that. Then I remembered Josh was on his way over. I was suddenly terrified. Josh knew tae-kwon-do. I dialed Ryan Faulkner's number, my heart was pounding. When he finally picked up, I told him about my argument with Joon-Ho.

"My brother's on his way there now," I said. "Josh has his black belt—" I stopped myself.

"Hold tight," he said. "Give me the address again."

He made me promise not to do anything—to wait for his call. But I couldn't just wait. Mato's cab was across the street. I ran to it, but there was a customer in the back seat, and Mato didn't even see me as he drove away. I woke my dad up and told him what had happened. Before I could finish, he grabbed his keys.

"There's nothing we can do now but wait," I said. As gently as I could, I took the keys away from him. We sat down. *It was Joon-Ho. All this time, it was Joon-Ho*, I thought. The look of shock on my dad's face made me feel like I was going to be sick. *Focus*, I told myself. I need to stay calm for *Appa*. I took a series of deep breaths, remembering my mother used to do the same to quell her panic.

Faulkner called me from Joon-Ho's place half an hour later. Neither Josh nor he had gotten there in time to catch Joon-Ho.

Chapter 23

"Where could he have gone?" Faulkner asked me.

My dad asked the same thing after I got off the phone.

Why did everyone expect me to know? I wondered, annoyed and frightened at the same time. For all I knew, he was on a plane back to Korea. It would be just like him—take the cowardly way out. He'd concoct some story and his parents would believe his lies because they'd have no choice. After all, they were the ones who'd taught him that he was incapable of living life without lying.

My dad, who'd held himself together throughout everything that had happened with my mother, withdrew into his room. Josh was remarkably stoic, and I wondered if the shock of everything hadn't sunk in yet.

Three days later, Joon-Ho was found. He'd jumped off the Bloor Viaduct. His body was discovered by a young couple who'd wandered into the ravine looking for privacy.

"They should put up a barrier," Mrs. O'Doherty had once said in our store, after reading a newspaper headline about a jumper. "The viaduct has the highest suicide rate next to the Golden Gate Bridge in San Francisco. Shame on us for not doing anything about it."

I was sure Joon-Ho had read about the viaduct too. I imagined his state of mind during his final moments. If I closed my eyes, I could hear him whisper, "Goodbye."

I was lying on my bed staring at the ceiling when the phone rang. Josh brought me the cordless. "It's Kate," he said.

"I heard about Joon-Ho," she said. His story had made the cover of the *Korea Times*. "You okay?"

"No, actually I'm not," I snapped. I hadn't intended to be curt. I took a breath and tried to explain. "I wanted to go down there—to the viaduct, but my dad and Josh wouldn't let me." It was no different from needing to see my mother. I wanted to make sure—to see with my own eyes.

Kate was quiet. I knew she was searching for the right words.

"I appreciate your call," I said, wanting to hang up. "I'll talk to you later."

"You're the one who's always telling me to look forward, not back," she said. "You finally have your answer about Joon-Ho. Listen to your own advice—move on now. I'm finally getting things back on track. It's weird but good to be home and I'll probably go back to school in the fall. I've been looking into colleges—they have some really neat programs I never even knew about. I'm thinking of Humber and their photography courses. My parents have come around to the idea."

"That's great," I said, happy for her. "How's your father?" Her mother had told me at the funeral that his health had taken a turn for the worse.

"It's complicated," she said. "Liver problems are never good. He's gonna die. It's a matter of when."

I wanted to tell her I was sorry, but my first thought was, *At least he's sick. You have time to prepare for his death.*

"It's so bad," Kate whispered, "watching someone die slowly. We can't even look him in the eyes anymore—they're a horrible yellow. His stomach looks like a balloon and he's always moaning. I swear it would be so much better if he got hit by a bus tomorrow and—" She stopped.

We let the silence fall between us.

Then Kate asked, "Do you think it's our fault? That we somehow brought all this on ourselves because we failed our parents in some way?"

Why would she think that? It wasn't supposed to be this way. The dream my mother had talked about *forever* never included parents dying before their children, before any of our dreams were realized, before there was proof that the sacrifices and hardships were worth it.

"I hate being Korean," I blurted out. My mother had been right in her accusations all along.

"Where'd that come from?"

"It sucks to be us!" I yelled. "Our parents never asked us if we wanted to come to Canada. They made the decision—then they bitch and complain about all the sacrifices they made for us. What the hell for? It's not like I could ever have lived up to my mother's expectations. She was always so demanding—my grades were never good enough, my friends weren't Korean enough, I didn't play the piano long enough. Well, I'm glad I quit that stupid instrument when

I did. And if I want to throw my life away by being a writer instead of a teacher, it's my life to throw away. My life, Kate. And it's gonna be a great life because unlike my mother, I'm going to *live* it. But you know what? My mother will never know because she had to go die on me just like your father will die on you—" I burst into tears. Kate was already crying.

The call-waiting signal beeped. I barely heard it the first time and ignored it the next time.

"Do you think we'll ever be okay again?" Kate asked.

"We have to be—it's the only way of ever getting back at our parents," I said, then added, "That's a joke." The knot in my chest slowly unravelled. "I'm so happy we're friends," I said.

"Best friends," Kate said. "Best friends forever."

Josh and I were sitting in his room. Two days had passed since our dad locked himself in his bedroom.

"What are we going to do about *Appa*?" I asked. "He refuses to eat anything I make him. I'm really worried."

"He needs time," Josh said. Then quietly, "I let him know everything—about Joon-Ho's school, his plans to use you. Us. Even about him trying to hurt you. He needed to know."

I looked over at the guitar in its stand next to the bed. It had been a long time since I had heard it being played. I missed the old days, when Josh would strum happily in his room and I'd be next door in my room trying to study, the smell of my mother's chicken or ox bone soup thick in the air. I used to think it was crazy that she made us eat hot soup on hot summer days, but she'd say, "Rice, kimchi, and hot soup," in English. "All necessary at each meal for good health and long life."

"I still can't believe it," said Josh.

I wasn't sure what he was referring to specifically—so much had happened in the past two weeks. At least my *emoh*s had gone, I thought. I was relieved they hadn't seen my dad in his present state. When they were leaving, Joon-Ho's fate was still unknown. My *kun emoh* had been beside herself. "What am I going to tell his mother?" she kept repeating. "That he's a missing person somewhere in Canada?" She ended up leaving everything Joon-Ho's mother had sent with Mrs. Henry, including the gifts intended for me. "Let her deal with it," I told my aunt. I didn't want the stuff at our place.

I got up to leave, intending to start dinner even if no one was going to eat it. "I'm going to make *jajangmyeon*," I said to Josh. "From scratch. Maybe *Appa* will eat that. I think we have black bean paste left and some noodles."

"Did you know he still blames himself for the night you were attacked years ago?" Josh asked. "He's never forgiven himself, and now—"

"Really?" I said. "But it wasn't his fault." The idea of my dad living with any guilt was absurd. "It wasn't his fault," I repeated. Tears welled in my eyes. That summer night felt like a lifetime ago.

"The hardest person to forgive is yourself," Josh said. "I still feel horrible I wasn't here for you that night either."

"There was nothing you could have done," I said. The idea that both my dad and my brother had shouldered such a burden all these years overwhelmed me. My knees buckled and I sank to the floor.

My dad must have heard us sobbing. He came in and threw his

arms around both of us. We'd never held one another before; it was something our family simply didn't do. But now the three of us clung to one another, gasping for breath. The sadness that had been trapped for so long broke free, shattering the silence that had stood like walls around us.

I stared at the paper swan and its reflection in my dresser mirror. It triggered a memory from grade three. I'd secretly worn my mother's prized necklace to school. The onyx gemstone pendant had a gold crane on it. Koreans are fond of birds, each symbolizing something different. A crane represents prosperity and happiness. A swan, purity and peace.

The necklace had been an engagement present—my dad couldn't afford a ring. I loved the sensation of having something so precious dangling from my neck. Somewhere between afternoon recess and the final bell, I lost the necklace. For days afterwards I struggled with what to do. I debated whether I even needed to tell my mother. *Wasn't it kinder,* I thought, *to spare her the truth?* Perhaps she'd never miss the necklace—she never wore it, and kept the silk pouch it was stored in out of sight at the back of her armoire. As time passed it became easier to push the guilt into a dark corner of my mind.

My mother never mentioned the necklace. I became convinced she'd guessed the truth and was punishing me with her silence—the way we always dealt with things—and over time, she too had forgotten.

Now I wondered what would have happened if I'd told her the truth right away. Would she have lashed out? Would she have shown compassion? Could I have learned something? If so, perhaps

I wouldn't have envied Linda and her cross, which allowed her to sin and keep sinning. All she had to do was ask for forgiveness and move on. What happens to those of us who have no one to forgive us?

The origami paper had faded over the years, as had the red ribbon around its neck. I had a flashback of Joon-Ho in his crisp white shirt as he handed it to me when we first met in Korea. Feeling a surge of anger, I tore the swan in half. He'd taken my mother and I could never forgive him. I looked at the broken swan. How much of that was my fault? I'd agreed to play his game by sleeping with him and fighting for him to stay at the university. It was easy now to pass judgment on myself, but did I need to feel bad for making choices I thought were right at the time? Was I selfish to want to live by my own standards? To strive to be happy and fulfilled? After all, wasn't that the Canadian way? I opened my window and allowed a gust of wind to sweep the paper and ribbon out of my hand, sending them swirling into the open air.

Chapter 24

"I couldn't go without you," Will said from the kitchen.

I sat on his sofa wishing he were going to France so we'd be forced to say goodbye. I had planned to tell him he was better off without me, but the truth was that I was better off without him. It was mid-June—time for this, like the school year, to end.

The small white birthday cake I'd picked up for Will sat on the coffee table, candleless. I looked around his apartment, my eyes tracing the layers of brown everywhere. A brown sofa on a brown rug. Wooden bookshelves and tables. Dead plants in different shades of brown by the window. This had once been my happy refuge. Now the place felt confining, a cell from which I needed to break free.

"You're still mad at me," Will said, returning with plates in one hand, forks in the other.

I didn't respond. He'd apologized endlessly throughout the past few weeks for missing my mother's funeral. But I was breaking up with him for larger reasons he didn't seem to grasp.

"I'm sorry, okay?" he said. "What would I have done there anyway? You had your family and friends. Like I said, there's just something about funerals—"

He extended a hand. I ignored it, so he placed it on my shoulder. "Talk to me," he said.

"You forgot a knife," I said, trying to keep my voice steady, my eyes focused on the cake.

"I've got an idea for a new book," he said as he walked away. "Got it from one of the kids in my grade-ten class. He'd probably benefit from having a tutor if you're still interested."

Will had been sending me a regular stream of kids. Now that we were about to break up, I'd need to find another job. That, and I'd have to write my own English papers.

"You know I care for you deeply," he said as he sat down. "I'm sorry, but I'll make it up to you." He handed me the knife.

"Cut your own damn cake," I blurted out.

Will froze, and then, in his usual way of attempting to defuse any uncomfortable moment, he kept talking as if he hadn't heard me. "Who knows, I may still write the next great novel. I may still become everything you want me to be."

"You're such a dreamer," I said, restraining a laugh. I was familiar enough with his romantic reveries to be bored and impatient. I pulled a white envelope out of my purse.

"Here. This is for you." He'd asked me to write him a poem for his birthday, saying he missed reading them. I felt foolish I'd spent so many hours writing them over the years.

He started to open the envelope, but I stopped him. He could read everything I'd wanted to yell and scream about after I left.

"I've got to go."

"But you haven't even had any cake."

"Happy birthday," I said, then mumbled, "Now grow up."

Will exhaled deeply. "I don't know why I thought you were any different. You sound just like her." I knew he meant Ms. Nakamura again. "Did it ever dawn on you that I have problems of my own?"

I had just lost my mother. Our store had been blown up, and Joon-Ho had killed himself. We were dealing with an inquest—our lives torn open so deeply, the sun could plummet into them and we'd still be in darkness. I stared at Will, stupefied by his utter disregard for my suffering.

"You complain so much about making sacrifices, Mary. Well, I have news for you—you're barely out of high school. You know jack shit about true sacrifices. I've spent every summer since I graduated buried in courses and every school year butting heads with admin who want me to coach every fucking team and chaperone every bloody dance." He got up and grabbed a bag by his briefcase. "I'll be lucky if they let me teach at all next year—they want me to learn how to use a damn computer! What the hell do I need a computer for to teach English?" He began throwing dozens of posters and prints into the air.

"I was told to take 'em down," Will said. "New principal only wants student work up on the walls."

The vintage movie posters! Images of beautiful women like Audrey Hepburn in *Breakfast at Tiffany's*, with her perfect figure and sultry pose, had intimidated and awed me. I'd never heard Will swear before, and I wondered to what extent, until now, he'd continued to see me as a kid in his class. I ached for Mr. Allen and the safe haven that had been our classroom. Mr. Allen with his white shirts, rolled-up sleeves, and quirky ties. I even missed the silly tassels on his loafers.

"You'll have next year off to write," I said. I looked around the room and now saw splashes of colour: old posters of *Casablanca*, *Gone With the Wind*, and *Citizen Kane*. A print of Sidney Poitier in the movie *Guess Who's Coming to Dinner* caught my eye. "It's your life. You don't owe anyone anything. You have to follow your passion, your desire to write." I remembered how empowered I'd felt when Will first shared those words and the Poitier movie with me. It saddened me to see him lose control like this. I truly felt sorry for him.

Will started to say something, but didn't. At the front door, he kissed me on my cheek. I caught the scent of Drakkar Noir, which I'd bought him for Christmas, and froze, lost in the moment. I wanted him to kiss me—which he did—and for seconds, my heart rose in a steady crescendo of desire for him. But the feeling faded quickly at his next words. "Maybe next year. We could go away then. France will always be there. We could be the next Victor Hugo and Adèle Foucher."

I laughed at his delusion. At least he didn't lack imagination. "Hugo was forced to leave his country and go into exile. He was gone for twenty years. You'd be fifty-something by the time you got back."

"You always think you know everything. You can't just let things go."

"I'm letting *you* go." I hadn't meant to be harsh.

"You know, *you're* the one who chased me. So now that you're done using me, you think you can just toss me aside? Is that it? That makes you nothing more than a little bitch." He might as well have slapped me.

I stared at him until he lost his composure and looked away, a wounded dog. My initial shock was replaced with disappointment, and a realization. I took a final look at the apartment. The old me would have said I was sorry, because that was my default response to everything, but now as I stood in the doorway, what came to me was a sweet relief.

I didn't need the last word.

Chapter 25

We had so many things to take care of since my mother passed away, but I put off cleaning out my mother's drawers and her half of the closet until last. Kate's mother had tried to prepare me. "I don't think it matters what age you are; you aren't ever prepared to lose your mother," she said. She offered to help me pack up the clothes, but I declined. This final act somehow felt too personal to share with anyone.

When I finally set my mind to the task, I was once again hit with the bitter reality of her death. The casual shirts and blouses she wore were easy enough to fold away into plastic bags. But seeing her one good suit, a beige Liz Claiborne jacket-and-skirt set she'd bought on sale to wear to our Canadian citizenship ceremony, blindsided me. The Canadian flag pin she'd placed on her lapel that day was still there when she wore the suit to my high school graduation. Next to the suit was the rose-coloured corduroy dress that she'd worn during our journey to Canada. She kept it even though it was now a couple of sizes too small for her. She'd looked so sad as we said goodbye to everyone at the airport. I ran my fingers down it and drew it close, hoping to catch a hint of her scent. We'd never hugged when she was alive. Why was I so desperate for her touch now?

When my tears had subsided, I put on the dress and stared at my reflection. I looked older, transformed somehow. The cut of the dress, with its short sleeves and a hemline that fell just above my knees, flattered my shape.

Feeling renewed, I continued exploring. A plain white box sat on the top shelf in the closet. I was expecting to find a shirt or sweater in it, and instead found a box of love letters my mother had received from my dad before they were married and he was off working in the mines somewhere in Germany. All his letters began with the words "My Lotus Flower" and signed off with "Your Humble Cactus." No wonder she'd kept so many cactus plants around the apartment! The letters were stored in their envelopes with the date stamped on each. They began in 1964 and stopped in 1967—two years before I was born. I remembered what my dad had once said about true love. Unlike an infatuation, which was about you and what you wanted, love was about the other person—thinking about his or her needs, desires. It was about giving freely and sharing an intimacy so profound only death could rob you of it. I remembered what I'd promised myself then.

There was also an old envelope with several newspaper clippings in it. Dated 1957, '58, and '59, they announced that my mother had won the district-wide writing competition. The town where the event was hosted was a three-day walk from her tiny village. When the reporter asked about her future aspirations, she stated, "I want to write and see the world. I want to climb Mount Kilimanjaro and hike through the Norwegian fjords."

I couldn't imagine my mother knowing about land formations in Norway let alone wanting to explore them. I'd learned about them in grade nine. Why was it so hard to imagine that she would have learned the same halfway around the world? I wondered what had happened in 1960. She must have lost the writing competition and been devastated. But then I realized that in 1960, she was sixteen—the age that she broke her leg falling into the well. That had happened in February. The competitions were held in the spring. She wouldn't have been able to make the three-day walk.

Everything in her dresser drawers was white—panties, bras, long underwear. "They used to force us to wear white," my mother had once told me. All peasant Koreans were required by law to wear white during the Japanese colonization. White, the colour of oppression and death for Koreans. The colour of snow and polar bears in Canada. Why had she continued to wear only white here? Out of habit? I would never know.

There were folders at the bottom of her drawers. One of them was labeled in her handwriting: *Piano*. It hadn't even dawned on me that my mother had been making monthly payments on the new piano I got years ago, replacing a used one with a broken middle C. It had irked me that my mother was so proud of it. She'd once told Mrs. Young, "Yes, it cost a fortune, not that it's improved her playing." The payments were spread over sixty months. Five years! All this time, I'd been annoyed that she paid five hundred for Josh's guitar, not knowing that she'd spent close to ten thousand on my Baldwin. How could I not have realized that? I leafed through the carbon copies of the monthly receipts. The last one had "Final Payment" and the date rubber-stamped on it: "September 1988"—the month after I'd quit piano lessons.

Why hadn't she said anything? Was it fair to get upset with me for quitting an instrument I hated? Was I being selfish? Ungrateful? What kind of daughter had I been to my mother? At my worst, I'd even wished her dead, although I'd had the comfort of naively believing that could never happen. The thought of her actually dying had occurred only in dreams. Some of them had been vivid enough for me to leave my bed in the middle of the night to check on her.

"If you dream of someone dying, they won't actually die," my mother had once reassured me when I was little. "If anything, it's good luck for the person who died in your dreams. They've been set free somehow."

That had never made sense to me, and I suspected she'd lied to make me feel better. I was never able to recall how my mother died in my dreams. It was the awful lingering feeling of losing her that stayed with me after I woke up. Now I feared that feeling would never go away.

"Death is merely a transition," I remembered my mother telling me at my *harmony*'s funeral in Korea. "From this life to the next. There is no need for sadness." But she'd cried then. And I too spent months crying for her. I also cried for Joon-Ho, knowing he'd suffered for the burdens he felt he carried. I hoped he had been "set free somehow." If that was a lie, I was happy to believe it now.

Just as we'd coped with everything else in our lives, we carried on quietly, each of us doing what we felt we needed to do. My dad and I tended to the required prayers, meeting Kate's mother, Mrs. Young, and a few of my mother's closest friends at Bur Kwon Sa

Temple, a plain brown brick building on St. Clair Avenue West, every seventh day after her passing. We did this until the forty-ninth day, which marked the end of our official mourning. We met in the main prayer room, where a bald monk always welcomed us with a warm smile. The pleasant smell of incense throughout the rest of the temple was replaced here with a stronger scent that hung heavily from the ceiling as several bundles of incense burned in brass censers next to a large gold Buddha statue at the front of the room. We prayed for about half an hour each week, then accepted the food neatly packed in Tupperware that my mothers' friends had prepared for us.

Kate's mother was the only non-Buddhist, but no one seemed to mind. She'd grown up in a Buddhist household and knew the rituals. Still, it was Mrs. Young who explained what we were doing. "We're here to guide your mother's spirit," she said, "so she can either go to the heavens and find permanent rest, or be reincarnated back here into a good family, in good health." We'd done the same when my *harmony* passed away.

Mrs. Young made us two white paper lotus lanterns to hang, one outside our home and one outside our battered store, signalling to the world that we were in mourning.

I was touched by the women and their commitment to my mother and her family. I knew each of them was busy with her own business and family. "Your mother was my best friend," Kate's mother said when I thanked her. "I know it's not the same as losing your mother, but losing your best friend is also very painful." She hugged me.

I hugged her back, imagining what it would have been like to hug my mother.

*   *   *

On the forty-ninth day, we closed the store so my dad, Josh, and I could all attend. An accident along the way delayed us. We arrived to find the temple parking lot full. My dad's eyes watered as he drove in, recognizing all the cars. We ended up having to park on a side street.

"So inconsiderate, all your *omma*'s friends not saving a single space for us!" my dad joked.

He made me smile when my heart was breaking. Love is always about giving.

Chapter 26

$\mathcal{W}$e reopened on a bright October Monday, but since I had classes all week I hadn't been around much. It was finally Saturday and, with both me and Josh available to work in the store, our dad was able to sleep in.

"I can't believe we're going on as if nothing happened," I said, staring up at the new pink lotus lantern that hung without my magic coin attached to it. Almost everything looked just as before, with all the merchandise placed in exactly the same places, right down to the white plastic bucket of individually wrapped Dubble Bubble gum next to the cash register. I tossed a piece to Josh, who was crouched on the floor sticking price tags on cans of dog food. When we were younger we used to have contests to see who could blow the biggest bubble. I was about to challenge him but then felt foolish. We weren't kids anymore.

The door opened and a customer came in. It wasn't until he walked down an aisle that we realized he was barefooted despite being dressed in a dark suit and tie. Even Josh tilted his head as we gazed at him. The man walked back with a bag of milk.

"Don't ask," he said with a quick smile and passed me a crisp ten-dollar bill.

I wasn't about to; we'd seen stranger things over the years.

"Truly nothing's changed," I repeated. "I can't believe we've put everything back together again." My mind drifted to the children's rhyme: Humpty Dumpty sat on a wall, Humpty Dumpty had a great fall. All the king's horses and all the king's men . . .

"It's what *Omma* would have wanted," Josh said.

I noticed that someone had left the latest edition of *People* magazine upside down. Annoyed, I walked over to fix it. How much time had I wasted over the years straightening the same magazines? Dusting the same shelves? Mopping the same floor?

"How could *Omma* and I want such different things?" I asked. "I could never live my life working so hard at doing so little."

The pricing gun stopped clicking. Josh shot me a disapproving look.

"What?" I said. It was true whether or not he was willing to accept it.

"So what is it that you want exactly?"

I shrugged.

"You want to write."

"I guess."

"Do you like to write? I just assumed."

I sighed. "It's the only thing I'm good at." If I'd never had a crush on Mr. Allen, I might not have discovered I could write. I felt foolish now realizing just how infatuated I'd been with him. Had our paths never crossed, I might be studying law, living my mother's dream. "It's fate," I said. "Blame it on the stars."

"You know what *Omma* would have said: 'Fate is determined by our ancestors and by our past lives—not the stars.'"

I thought of my mother and her mother and all the other mothers before them. It now seemed too easy, too convenient to blame them for our present circumstances. "I know. We could never agree on anything." Unlike my mother with her ideas of reincarnation, I regarded life as a one-way trip. I had one chance at an extraordinary life, a life where I could choose to become the person I wanted to be.

I said it out loud. "I want an extraordinary life."

"You're a dreamer. So was *Omma*."

"What?" I almost choked on the word. I'd always believed my need to be creative was quashed by my mother's need for order and control.

"How could she have built all this without dreaming?" Josh asked. "Dreaming big."

"What are you talking about?"

"She was a dreamer. What do you think brought her to Canada? To have the guts to buy this store and turn it around like she did."

"She was never happy, though—shouldn't that be part of the dream? She moved from problem to problem."

"She put our future happiness before her health." He remained calm.

"When were you elected her spokesperson?"

"And when did you get so blind and selfish? Look around. Why do you think we've rebuilt everything?"

"To keep *Omma*'s dream alive," I sarcastically threw at him.

"No—to keep *our* dream alive."

I didn't know what to say. The idea that the dreams I had for myself weren't any different from my mother's seemed absurd.

"Maybe you should talk to someone," Josh said gently.

I knew what he was thinking. Unlike him with his church and his prayers, I had nowhere to turn. But it was fine, I reasoned. It had always been our family way to deny anything truly uncomfortable, to not express our emotions. We didn't apologize, we didn't forgive. We just forgot and carried on.

The front door opened again and our dad walked in. "The sun's out," he said. "Good for business." He smiled and fixed himself a coffee to go. He and Josh were headed to a wholesaler.

Alone, I tried to dismiss everything Josh had suggested about my mother and me wanting the same things in life. If there was even a trace of truth in what he had said, how was I supposed to find any answers now? She was gone. How many people would bother finishing a puzzle if they knew there were missing pieces?

I was relieved when the door opened. It was Tico.

"Hey, it's not Tuesday," I said, smiling.

"Nope. I'm making me a special trip today. It seemed fitting." He placed a large Ziploc bag full of bread tags on the counter.

"Two hundred and thirty-three," he said. "One from each loaf of bread your momma gave me all these years. I kept 'em—each and every tag—to remind myself the world is a good place after all." He pushed the bag towards me. "I want you to have it. I thought about it, and it's the right thing to do. To remind you of what she taught me about the world."

I was moved. I'd often wondered why my mother had a soft spot for this man, of all people, but I understood now. There was something beautiful about him she'd been able to see beneath his torn rags, missing teeth, and crazy need to wear a horn around his neck.

"You should keep it," I said. "To remind you of her."

"I don't need anything to remind me of what your momma meant to me."

My eyes misted over. Because it wasn't his usual day to visit, I hadn't saved any day-old bread for him. I handed him a loaf of Wonder Bread from the bread rack.

"You're just like your momma."

"Thank you." It was then that I noticed Tico's shiny black leather shoes. They looked brand new.

"Nice, eh?" He saw me staring. "Some guy just gave them to me. Socks and all. Couldn't believe it. Said it was too cold to be out barefooted this time of year." He flashed a big smile. "I don't care what anyone says—there's a lot of good in the world, Mary." He waved, honked his horn once, and left.

What a great story, I realized. I thought about my SOC101 instructor, Rusaline Elliott, the person who'd had the biggest influence on my decision to choose sociology as my second major. I was still upset she hadn't been invited back after her first year at the university.

"I've learned not to waste time buried in other people's prejudices and ignorance," she'd said to me after some students launched a formal protest against her. She bravely stirred many fires by constantly challenging the thinking of her students.

"You've opened my eyes to so many new ideas," I told her. When I thanked her, she hugged me. It was irrelevant whether or not I agreed with everything she had to say. She'd taught me to think critically and not accept anything at face value. Whereas Will Allen had inspired romantic poems, Rusaline stirred a deep desire in me to write stories about everyday struggles. Poems about the homeless, inspired by Tico. Short stories about the plight of women, inspired by Delia and Rubina.

I looked out the window and was startled when I thought I saw my mother in my reflection. A fly bounced off the glass before settling on a leaf of one of the potted Chinese evergreens that sat on the sill. My father had replaced all the plants my mother had kept: evergreens, begonias, ferns, and cacti.

My thoughts returned to my mother and the heartache I hadn't been able to shake since the night of her death. We'd spent our lives together in a constant state of struggle, each trying to gain some sense of control. Could Josh be right? Could we have wanted the same thing all along?

PART III

Beginnings

Chapter 27

After peering at me and my aunt Mi-Ra through his viewfinder, then deciding the shot wasn't quite right, my dad pointed to the building in front of us and said in Korean, "Stand over there." He fidgeted with the settings on his camera, an imposing new Nikon.

"But *that's* the building I'm graduating in," I said, indicating the one behind me.

"No matter, this one looks better," he said.

As my aunt and I posed for the shot, she wrapped an arm around me. "I'm so sorry your mother isn't here with you today," she said. She looked as if she might start crying again.

This was her first visit with us since attending my mother's funeral three years earlier. Unlike my mother's friends or my *emoh*s in Korea, she'd prayed to her Christian God and was confident her sister's soul was resting peacefully in heaven.

Had she been at my graduation, my mother would have said in her usual weary way, "If you only knew just how many packs of cigarettes, bags of milk, and thousands of newspapers we had to sell to get you here today." Her eyes would have panned the campus grounds, and taken in the hundreds of graduates and their families assembled on the lawns outside Convocation Hall. She would have wondered how many other families were immigrants, and had worked as hard as she and my dad had to get their children to graduation day. She would have also been fiercely proud that Josh was here now, studying business at the university.

"We need to get inside," I told my dad. People were making their way into the hall.

"I bought this camera just for today."

"You sound just like *Omma*," I said, making him smile.

Inside, I found myself squeezed into a seat between two graduates I'd never seen before. I told myself to breathe deeply.

Every so often after my mother's death, a shadow would fall over everything. The first few times it happened, I panicked, an almost paralyzing despair overcoming me. I ended up turning to a therapist I'd found through the university's psych services. Her name was Priya and she was Indian. Her background helped her understand my own immigrant experiences. She helped me understand that everything I felt was related to my mother and Joon-Ho, and went as far back as the night of Leon's attack. She told me to be gentle with myself.

"Gentle?" I blurted out. "I practically killed my mother."

"What purpose is your guilt serving?" she asked. "Guilt, anger—they come in many forms. I'd be more worried if you didn't feel anything."

We even talked about Delia, and my inability to save her. "Is that why you tried so hard to save Joon-Ho?" she asked.

I didn't know. "I don't know if you can save me either," I said.

For months, I ventured into the dim, little-travelled trails of my mind, surprised at its vast and complex landscape. Time was suspended, and trying to see ahead felt like straining to see through a brick wall. I started to realize some things in life couldn't be reconciled regardless of the time that passed and the acknowledgements that were made. Every now and then the dark shadows would cast themselves. I rode them out and waited for the storm to pass.

I knew my father was suffering quietly and staying strong so I could focus on what he felt mattered—my studies. He woke up one night to find me sitting and rocking in my bed, the window open and the street light keeping me in semidarkness.

"You're shivering," he said in Korean, and shut the window. "You've been smoking again." He knew it was a habit I'd picked up from him after he'd started again. We were silent for some time, watching the shadows on the wall shift in shape and shade as headlights turned onto the one-way street outside. "It'll kill you. Such a bad habit to start at your age."

"I'd rather choose a long slow death if it gave me some pleasure over a sudden random one," I responded in English. "Besides, it's your fault." I knew it was childish reasoning but he'd lectured me about this before.

"I'm old," he said. He looked at the lotus lantern hanging from my ceiling. "You, on the other hand, have to get married. Have children if you want. Write your many novels."

My insides softened; how sweet it felt to have my dad believe in my dreams. I traced the blue swirls on my pillow case.

"I don't know the words in Korean," I said, "but I love you, *Appa*." I'd never said that before, in Korean or in English—not to him, my mother, Josh, or any of my past lovers.

Another car passed. More shadows. My dad drew the curtains. "Try to sleep," he said gently. The room was suddenly dark. "You'll be a graduate soon. I don't know anything about writing, but I think good writers write from the heart. Save yours—stop smoking."

I looked around for Erin, who was also graduating, but I couldn't see her from where I was sitting. How could I be surrounded by so many people and feel so alone? I thought about Linda. We'd lost touch during our final year of school. She would be graduating from York University—with top honours, I was sure. Of the four of us, she'd always worked the hardest. And Rubina? Where was she today? I imagined her both beautiful and broken, as she'd looked the day we said our final goodbyes. *She should be here with me,* I thought, as another wave of darkness passed through me. The July heat was unbearable. I used my program for a fan as the various greetings, speeches, and presentations blurred together.

I was graduating with a double major in sociology and English. I'd continued to write whenever possible about the lives of those around me, but it wasn't until my fourth year of studies that I found the strength to move my own stories of the past from my mind to paper. A robbery that took place during Halloween 1984, when our family had first taken over Kay's Lucky Coin Variety, inspired my first short story. A man wearing a creepy clown mask with a red-and-white-striped jester's hat came into the store. He grabbed a chocolate bar, AAA batteries, and toothpaste before he told us he had a gun. He took everything in the cash register. After he fled, my mother broke down and cried, angry with herself for not having emptied the register earlier. I eventually found the courage to submit the story, and it was published. After that, more stories, like butterflies, fluttered through the narrow passages of my memory, past the darkness, until they landed on white paper, ready to be shared.

As the first graduate crossed the stage, I felt nervous, then excited. Each of us had a small strip of paper with our name on it—the name the reader at the podium would call out as we crossed the stage. I looked at mine. I'd written "Mary," then crossed it out and wrote "Yu-Rhee" above it. As I headed onto the stage, I took a deep breath, crossed my fingers, and hoped they'd pronounce the name correctly. I looked into the audience at my dad and my aunt. I imagined my mother sitting with them in her beige suit, her little Canadian flag pinned on her lapel. I walked towards the presiding officer and kneeled before him. I closed my eyes as tears rolled down my cheeks. As I felt the graduation hood placed over my head, a peace fell over me, and when I stepped off the stage, that feeling stayed with me.

I took my seat again, remembering the envelope Josh had given me earlier, and took it out of my purse. As I was about to remove the card, something slipped out and clinked as it bounced on the floor. It was my magic coin! Or one that looked just like it. I smiled and read the card: *To luck and new beginnings.* The word *convocation* had been stroked out so the message read, *Congratulations on your emancipation.*

Freedom. The word rolled around in my mouth like bittersweet candy. The truth, as hard as it was initially to accept, was that my mother's dreams for me had actually helped and not hindered my dreams for myself. That realization had come to me slowly, the idea shifting like broken fragments of glass before they settled as a finished mosaic in my mind.

My mother had taught me that dreams didn't come true just by thinking about them. She'd chased after them, and in so doing had cleared a path for me to do the same.

Degree in hand, I stepped outside under a cloudless blue sky. The lush greenery of King's College Circle and University College, with its stately brick and stone building and tower, no longer intimidated me. Even Simcoe Hall next to Convocation Hall, the scene of Joon-Ho's expulsion hearing, had no effect on me. Now that I was finally a graduate, there was a promise in the air of things to come. I had always liked beginnings more than endings.

"We did it! Your mother would have been so proud," Erin said when I finally found her and her mother in the crowd. Seeing her with her beaming mother made my chest ache.

"And your father too," I said.

She squeezed my hand.

I wish you were here, my heart said to my mother. I had never thanked her for teaching me all the things I could never have learned in school. She had survived a war, immigrated to a new country, built a successful business, and stood up to anyone who challenged her. She had led an extraordinary life.

I watched as a little girl in a yellow dress blew bubbles at the graduates. They rose high in the air, and soon a small group of children, all dressed up to attend graduation, were chasing them across the lawn. Their laughter warmed me, and I wanted the moment to last.

My dad took a few more photos—evidence for relatives that I had indeed graduated.

"Today is a good day, Yu-Rhee-ah," he said, smiling.

I shielded my eyes from the sun to look up at two white gulls flying high above us. I smiled and patted his shoulder. "We'd better get back to the store," I said. "Josh will need a break."

Acknowledgements

$\mathscr{A}$ big thanks to the members of my writing circle, the 11th Floor Writers, who have seen this book from beginning to end. A special thanks to Maureen Lynch, Theo Kempe, Andrew Fruman, Saad Omar Khan, Ryan Dadoun, Thomas Allen, and Tina Dealwis.

I'm grateful to the many wonderful writer-mentors I worked with on this book, including Kellie Deeth, Dennis Bock, and Alexandra Leggat from the School of Continuing Studies at the University of Toronto, and David Adams Richards from the Humber School for Writers.

A huge hug and thanks to Lee Gowan for introducing me to my incredible editor, Phyllis Bruce, who saw potential in a story that was merely a whisper at the time. Many thanks to my agent, Jackie Kaiser, for her ongoing support and guidance.

Finally, to my parents, my brothers, John and Martin, my husband, Patrick, and daughter, Claire, thanks for your endless encouragement over the many years it took to complete this novel. You have my love always.